Felicity Pulman is the award-winning author of numerous novels for children and teenagers, including *A Ring Through Time*, the Shalott trilogy, and *Ghost Boy*, which is now in pre-production for a movie. *I, Morgana* was her first novel for adults, inspired by her early research into Arthurian legend and her journey to the UK and France to "walk in the footsteps of her characters" before writing the Shalott trilogy – something she loves to do. Her interest in crime and history inspired her medieval crime series, The Janna Mysteries, now repackaged as The Janna Chronicles.

Recently awarded the inaugural Di Yerbury writer's fellowship, Felicity will spend several months in the UK in 2015 researching and writing the sequel to *I, Morgana*. She has many years experience talking about researching and writing her novels both in schools and to adults, as well as conducting creative writing workshops in a wide variety of genres. Felicity is married, with two children and six grandchildren, all of whom help to keep her young and technosavvy – sort of! You can find out more about Felicity on her website and blog: www.felicitypulman.com.au or on Facebook.

Also by Felicity Pulman

I, Morgana
Blood Oath: The Janna Chronicles 1
Stolen Child: The Janna Chronicles 2
Unholy Murder: The Janna Chronicles 3
Pilgrim of Death: The Janna Chronicles 4
Devil's Brew: The Janna Chronicles 5

Day of Judgment

Felicity Pulman

First published by CreateSpace in 2011
This edition published in 2015 by Momentum
Pan Macmillan Australia Pty Ltd
1 Market Street, Sydney 2000

A CIP record for this book is available at the National Library of Australia

Day of Judgment: The Janna Chronicles 6

EPUB format: 9781760300272
Mobi format: 9781760300289
Print on Demand format: 9781760300562

Cover design by Raewyn Brack
Edited by Kylie Mason
Proofread by Keren Joseph

Macmillan Digital Australia: www.macmillandigital.com.au

To report a typographical error, please visit momentumbooks.com.au/contact/

Visit www.momentumbooks.com.au to read more about all our books and to buy books online. You will also find features, author interviews and news of any author events.

Prologue

"My lady, come quickly!"

Matilda, half dozing beside the fire, came to herself with a start at her tiring woman's urgent tone. "What is it, Margery?"

"A messenger's arrived with news that King Stephen has crossed the river along with his army. They're laying siege to the town!" The tiring woman was already unfastening and throwing open the shutters.

Alarmed, the empress sprang to her feet and rushed to the window. Just one look was enough. She rubbed her arms in an effort to bring warmth, but her gesture was absent-minded, reflecting not the evening air but the chill that had settled upon her heart. What lay beyond the castle walls spelled her doom, she had no doubt of that. She rubbed her eyes then looked more carefully at the scene outside, wondering if, despite appearances, escape might still be possible.

Oxeneford Castle had been her refuge throughout most of the year. She had thought herself safe after her ignominious defeat and narrow escape from the bishop's troops, and the queen's, following the siege of Winchestre. Not that she'd been idle; quite the contrary. Determined to shore up support among those barons who wavered in their allegiance, and with lands that were in her gift to bestow, she'd spent most of this year of our Lord, 1142, buying their loyalty in a last desperate effort to wrest the crown from her cousin. And where were those barons, now that their presence had become crucial to her survival? Gone! Her half-brother Robert, leader of her army and her most loyal supporter, had charged them to stay and protect her, but, one by one, they had melted away like snow in spring, intent on securing their new properties and poaching what they could elsewhere. Their defection had left the empress almost unguarded and extremely vulnerable.

She should have foreseen that Stephen would seize his chance and act to silence her once and for all. As now he had. The red glow in the sky testified that Oxeneford was under siege, the smoky air a manifestation that the town had been set alight, while the activity outside the castle walls and moat confirmed that the king's troops had converged on the castle and were already moving into position around it.

"What are we to do, my lady?" Margery's anxious query was echoed in Matilda's heart, which was heavy and full of foreboding. She had thought Oxeneford Castle impregnable – and so it was. But once the king's troops had finished besieging the city, they would make an attempt on the castle. And then what?

Matilda knew, well enough, that if an army couldn't get into a castle by force there were other tricks to try. All that was needed was cunning, and patience. She felt a faint flicker of hope. Stephen was not known for his patience, had more than once thrown away the promise of victory by leaving a siege too soon, lured away by a more promising conquest elsewhere.

But not this time – the prize was too great. Matilda gave a groan of despair, quickly stifled, for now was not the time for weakness. But she knew that the king would show no mercy once he had her in his grasp. She wished now that she'd been more kind to Stephen while she'd had him in captivity. Keeping him in irons was probably a great mistake, as was treating him like a common criminal. What revenge he would wreak on her, and on her supporters. Matilda knew it was only a matter of time before they ran out of supplies and starvation set in. It had happened once before, at Winchestre. Now it looked set to happen all over again.

"Earl Robert must surely come soon to your aid, my lady?" Margery asked hopefully. "And if your husband accompanies him, they'll bring troops from Normandy and Anjou to join your supporters here in England. Combined, our army will be more than a match for the king."

Matilda shook her head, bleakly dismissing the possibility. "I recently had word that the king has taken Wareham, and was busy laying siege to other ports. I sent word to my husband and half-brother, begging them not to delay, but the ports will be barred against them by now. They'll find it difficult to land anywhere in England."

It was Geoffrey's fault that Robert wasn't here to protect her, Matilda thought bitterly. Her fingers curled into fists at the memory of her husband's insistence that Robert must first join him in Normandy to secure the region before he would bring troops over to England to support her bid for the crown. For some months Matilda had expected Robert's return with Geoffrey, but every time her half-brother made plans to come home, her treacherous husband had found yet another pretext for keeping him in Normandy. And now it was too late, and she was trapped.

Damn Geoffrey! And damn her father too. She had raged against marrying the young Geoffrey of Anjou but her father had been implacable, seeing the joining of England with Normandy and Anjou as a mighty alliance against France. All very well for her father, but Matilda was the one who'd had to put up with Geoffrey's juvenile ways, and his womanising. Right from the start, her marriage had brought her nothing but heartache and trouble, for all that they'd made three sons together.

Matilda's mouth softened into a proud smile as she thought of her eldest son, named after his grandfather, Henry. So strong and fearless; so bright – and so used to getting his own way! Even though he was only nine, he already had the makings of a king. It was this promise she'd been using to buy the support of the barons: that she would take the reins only until Henry was old enough to rule in his own right. Matilda's hands clenched tighter as the reality of her situation became blindingly clear. Unless she could find a way out of this coil, her son would never be king. Like his mother, he would be denied the throne that was his by birthright. And if Stephen had anything to do with it, she'd never see Henry again. Not if she was kept imprisoned, sent into exile...Her heart cracked at the thought.

No use looking to Geoffrey for help, even though his son's future was also in jeopardy. No use holding out hope that Robert might save her either. Matilda closed the shutters with a decisive bang, blocking out the smoke and the sight of the burning town.

She sank back into her seat, fighting the anger and despair that threatened to engulf her. Unaccustomed tears came into her eyes but she dashed them away. She could not allow herself the luxury of tears – not now, not when there was so much at stake.

"Is there anyone else you could call on, my lady?"

There was the ever-faithful Brian fitz Count, but Matilda really needed someone with a connection to Normandy, someone able to take an urgent message to Robert. Someone she could trust not to betray her to Stephen.

A brief reckoning of those barons whom Robert had left with her but who had subsequently crept off home was enough to convince her that she could not look for help from any of them. In truth, they might already have turned to Stephen and be negotiating with him for land and favors. There was no-one with the authority to do what was necessary.

Matilda sat up straight, trying to recollect one of the rumors she had heard. Another of her half-brothers had recently arrived in England, one of her father's many bastards. John? John lived in Normandy, but apparently he had come to England to oversee the rebuilding of his house in Winchestre. She hadn't seen him since childhood. Would John support her against the king and his brother Henry, Bishop of Winchestre, given that the bishop's own firebrands had burned his property to the ground?

The brief lift in her spirits was quickly dashed as she recalled what else her informant had told her: that her half-brother was currently residing with the bishop at Wolvesey Palace, along with his wife and children. Matilda narrowed her eyes as she tried to recall some scandal attached to that. Something about an unknown daughter from a previous marriage who had appeared from nowhere, and announced herself to John.

She brushed the thought of it aside. Her life, and the safety of her retinue, was at stake. She had more to worry about than raking up old tittle-tattle that had nothing to do with the more important question: Would John help her? It was just possible that he was staying with his cousin, the bishop, simply because there was nowhere else for him to stay. Henry's firebrands had laid waste to much of the town, including the royal castle. How could she find out where John's loyalty lay, and whether he was willing to take her side? Having made his home in Normandy, he could be a great asset to her cause, for he would surely want to ally himself with her husband, who was gradually bringing all Normandy under his aegis, with Robert's help. More, John would know who might or might not be trusted there. He would also know the best and quickest way to get word to Robert and Geoffrey.

"It's possible there may be someone," she said slowly. "A slight chance, no more." She smiled at her tiring woman, hoping to bolster her own flagging spirits. "The problem is how to get a message out of the castle and through the king's lines."

"I know someone who might be able to do that, my lady." Margery hesitated. "I know how a message might be passed."

"Oh?" Matilda inclined her head.

Margery shifted nervously. "One of the grooms has a leman living outside the castle. He sometimes visits her at night. After curfew." She didn't have to say any more for Matilda to understand her. There were guards on duty night and day, both to authorize anyone leaving the castle and also to prevent any unwelcome intruders. After curfew there was no movement between castle and town, by order of the empress, to ensure her safety and that of her entourage.

"There is a need to act quickly, my lady, while most of the king's troops are still occupied with besieging the town. If you will but write a message, I will ask the groom if he can find a way past the king's guard. He is faithful to you, my lady, I know it. It is just that he...he..."

Matilda nodded. She understood the groom's dilemma, even while she seethed that he had disobeyed her orders so openly. Yet he might also be her salvation, if her gamble on a half-brother's loyalty paid off.

She had to take the chance, for she was trapped. She faced starvation or surrender. For herself, she would starve rather than give in to her cousin. But that meant all those held captive in the castle would also starve – and she could not have their deaths on her conscience. That left surrender. But not yet, Matilda thought bleakly, as she sent her tiring woman to find parchment, quill and ink. She stared into the fire, conjuring up old memories of her half-brother. She remembered that she had liked John all those years ago; he had been kind to her. And she'd admired his courage when, on one occasion, Stephen had challenged him to a race and he had fallen from his horse during the course of it. He'd hurt his arm – she seemed to recall that he might even have broken it – but he'd got back on his horse and finished the race, albeit well behind his older cousin. And now she was about to put her safety into his hands.

Matilda knew she had no other choice but to trust him to get word to Robert and to carry out Robert's instructions. If a miracle was possible, then she would pray for it, pray with all her heart and soul.

Chapter 1

"We should return to the palace, my lady. It's almost time for dinner."
The young groom's tentative suggestion was born out by the sound
of bells from the cathedral. With a regretful sigh, Janna turned her
mount in the direction of the town and her new, if temporary home:
Wolvesey Palace, residence of Henry of Blois, Bishop of Winchestre
and brother of King Stephen.

Riding was only one of the new skills Janna was trying to master.
As her fear of horses had subsided, she'd come to enjoy the freedom
of riding out with the bishop's new groom and her two half-sisters
and half-brother. Her father's gift of a beautiful bay palfrey had
helped her to gain confidence, as had the careful tuition of Thomas,
the groom. But, more than anything, Janna cherished her time out on
the downs as a chance to escape the close and hostile scrutiny of her
new stepmother.

As they began the journey homeward, Janna watched Richildis,
Rosy and Giles riding ahead of her. As usual, they were ignoring her
presence, though they seemed to have little liking for the company
of each other either. Giles, the second born, was always intent on
proving his superior skills and speed. Of course, it helped that he'd

been in the saddle since he was old enough to learn how to ride, whereas Janna still had the uncomfortable notion that if her horse went too fast she would slide right off its back. It also helped that Giles was fearless. His latest game was to use his skill to unnerve and unsettle her, his tactic being to speed on ahead, whirl abruptly, and then thunder back to the riding party, frightening everyone as he sped straight at them. The fact that he tried to unseat Janna by brushing too close as he swept past hadn't escaped Janna's notice, or the groom's either. But neither said anything, for it was already well established that, in his mother's eyes, Giles could do no wrong, and that any attempt to curb his behavior would result in trouble – although never for him. Even his sisters had learned not to say anything against him, perhaps in relief that he now left them alone and tormented Janna instead.

Janna's gaze rested thoughtfully on Richildis, eldest of her father's children with her stepmother, Blanche. Even though Richildis treated her with cold disdain, she found it in her heart to feel pity for the girl who was thirteen summers and growing out of childishness into maturity, growing up beautiful, much to her mother's dismay. Janna wondered if part of Blanche's hostility toward her daughter was because she resembled her father's side of the family, just as Janna herself did. True, Richildis had the dark hair of the Normans, while Janna had inherited her mother's fair tresses, but in fact Richildis was closer in looks to Janna than to her own younger sister, Rosy.

Blanche's acid tongue wagged constantly about Janna's lack of a suitable husband, comparing her dismal prospects with those awaiting her own daughters. "Eat your food like a lady, don't gorge like a peasant, Richildis," she'd sneer, with a meaningful look in Janna's direction. "You don't want to end up unloved and unwed like your half-sister."

Janna kept her own thoughts on the matter to herself. She had no desire to take a husband of her father's choosing, but she knew it would be folly even to mention the name of the man she loved. So she kept quiet in the face of Blanche's taunts, letting them pass over her head while trying not to let them ruffle her heart. Meanwhile, she watched Richildis at mealtimes, and saw how the girl had begun to pick at her food, or push her plate away, all the while watching her mother in hope of praise for her dainty appetite. But Blanche's attention was usually focused on the little whippet that was her constant companion, tempting him with morsels from her trencher or, alternatively, offering her son the choicest portions from the serving platter, "so that you might grow up big and strong, like your father." If she noticed her unfortunate daughter at all, it was only to purse her mouth and tut her disapproval. And yet Richildis followed her everywhere, doing whatever she could to win her mother's praise and trying to mimic her in every regard. Only when out riding was she free from her mother's influence.

But the fresh air and exercise weren't doing her much good, Janna reflected, as she noted how pale the girl was, and how listlessly she sat upon her mount. Partly as an effort to befriend Richildis, and partly because she was worried about her, Janna had tried to compliment her on her looks, and for her accomplishments, but Richildis had made it clear she set no value on Janna's opinion, so after a while Janna had stopped trying.

Her frown of concern relaxed into a smile as her gaze rested on Rosy, who was riding slightly ahead of her sister on her fat little pony. Her real name was Rohesia. She was the only one of her father's children to show any friendliness toward Janna, and then only if the other members of the family weren't around to witness it. She was a chubby, merry child, full of enthusiasm and high spirits. Janna wondered how long it would be before Blanche managed to squash the life out of her youngest child as well. At the thought, Janna sat straighter in the saddle and made a silent vow. Blanche could do what she would, try whatever tricks she could, but Janna would not allow herself to be intimidated by her stepmother. She knew Blanche wouldn't relent. Her hatred and fear of this cuckoo in her nest was manifest in her every word and deed, even if she kept it well hidden when Janna's father was around.

Notwithstanding her spite, Janna felt some pity for the woman. The sham of her marriage to John had been exposed once Janna had introduced herself into the family. Not only did Blanche have to live with the knowledge that he'd married her out of duty rather than love, she also had to come to terms with the fact that her marriage to John was bigamous and their children illegitimate. Janna acknowledged, with a rueful smile, that Blanche had a lot for which to forgive her, even though she'd made it plain she had no intention of trying.

"Good posture, my lady. But may I suggest that you loosen the reins a little, and hold them just so." The groom's voice cut through Janna's preoccupation and she turned to heed his instructions. As she tried to follow his advice, she heard the pounding of a horse's hooves and saw Giles flying toward her, whip raised, seemingly intent on a collision. With a quick step, the groom positioned his horse sideways in front of Janna to protect her, thus presenting a much greater obstacle for the racing horse to circumvent. With a high whinny it skidded and reared, almost throwing Giles from the saddle.

He clung on, screaming curses at Thomas and pulling viciously on the reins as his horse danced perilously close to the groom. Once his mount came finally to rest, he began to whip it savagely, earning at last a rebuke from Thomas.

"You did well to control Thunder, Master Giles, but you should not have put him in that position in the first place. Nor should you be punishing Thunder for having the good sense to pull up in time, before anyone got hurt."

"Don't you dare tell me what to do, Thomas! Take care, lest I tell my father that you forget yourself in criticizing *me*."

11

Thomas bowed his head and said no more, but Janna was seething on his behalf, and her own. Shock had set her pulse racing, but now that the danger had passed, disgust and fury had taken its place. "You say anything about Thomas to our father and I will tell him how badly you ride and how you put us all in danger with your antics," she hissed.

Giles glared at her. As his father's only son and would-be heir, Janna knew his hatred of her was equal to his mother's, but she was beyond caring now. She glared right back at him, meaning every word she'd said. Little beast! Spoilt brat! What a monster her half-brother was. It was time someone took him in hand and her father was the one to do it. It was time he found out what his only son got up to in his absence.

It seemed that she'd called his bluff, for he said no more. Instead, he dug his heels into Thunder's side and trotted off, ignoring them all. The two girls glanced at Janna and looked away again. But Thomas came closer and quietly thanked her for supporting him.

"It would be the end of me if I was dismissed from my lord's employ, my lady," he added, in a low mutter meant for her ears alone. "I have a new wife, and we're expecting our first child soon. I've seen that the young master means you harm, but it's more than my life is worth to say so."

"I know, Thomas," Janna reassured him. "Thank you for saying as much as you did." She wondered if Giles would carry out his threat, and was fully determined that she would carry out her own, if so. Nevertheless, she kept close to the groom as they completed their journey back to Wolvesey Palace.

*

Janna was surprised when their father joined them for dinner in their private rooms. Usually he was to be found at the opposite end of

Winchestre where his manor house was being rebuilt, the house that had been destroyed by the bishop's fireballs during the siege the year before. It made for some discomfort, given that they were now the bishop's guests, although everyone was careful to skirt around the topic. Nor did the bishop ever question where his guests' loyalties lay in this fight for the crown: with his brother Stephen, or with John's half-sister, the empress.

It was just as well, Janna thought, for she'd been extremely nervous when she'd first realized that she was expected to stay at Wolvesey with her family. She could only pray that no-one would divulge her role in unmasking the bishop's spy and bringing the truth of the bishop's treachery to Robert of Gloucestre, half-brother of both the empress and her own father. Her actions had caused great grief at the time, not least to Janna herself. And it had resulted in the siege of Winchestre, the siege that had led to the destruction of her father's house. And because of that, her father had come to Winchestre to oversee the rebuilding of his estate, and thus had met his unknown daughter for the first time.

How strange it is that so many seemingly unconnected happenings have a common thread, Janna mused as she sat at the table, waiting for her father to say the blessing. She looked without much interest at the dishes presented for the family's inspection. Fish, and some meat stew in sauce by the look of it. The bishop's cook apparently didn't believe in seasoning his dishes with herbs and spices; consequently, Janna found the food bland and tasteless. Small wonder that Richildis picked and poked when there was nothing delicious to tempt her appetite. Perhaps she could make a few suggestions.

Janna nodded to herself and spooned up a portion of trout. Her mind was busy planning what she might plunder from the bishop's kitchen garden and the uses to which she could put the herbs when she became aware that her father was speaking.

"…would like you all to stay on in the solar after dinner," he was saying. "There is something on my mind that I must discuss with you. Johanna, this affects you in particular."

Conscious that all eyes were now on her, Janna gulped and nodded, and even managed a smile for her father's benefit. Inside she was quaking, for her father's approval was crucial to her plans for the future and the outcome of her quest. What now? Had Giles given their father some glossed-up account of the morning's ride? Had Blanche found something else to complain about? Mentally, she did a swift review of her activities over the past few days, but could find no wrongdoing among them. She always did her best to fit in with the family, although her efforts to be friendly had met with either hostility or indifference. But she would continue to try, Janna resolved. It was in her interests to do so, at least until she could hold her father to the promise she'd made on her mother's death: that she would avenge Eadgyth's murder and bring the man responsible to justice.

After that, whether or not she stayed would depend on the love and comfort she found within this family and, more importantly, if they would support her own choice of husband. If not, she would leave, just run away; the thought cheered Janna slightly, making her realize how low her spirits had sunk since she'd moved into the bishop's palace.

"We had an enjoyable ride today, sire," she said, deciding to draw Giles into the open – if he dared. He scowled at her, but kept silent.

"Really?" Her father's quizzical smile lifted Janna's confidence. After a difficult beginning, she and her father had started to get along quite well. John was always interested to hear about Janna's childhood with his beloved Emanuelle, as he called her, although Janna took care never to mention her mother's name in Blanche's presence. But she appreciated that her father was making an effort to know her, and also to introduce her into his own world and instruct her in its ways.

They'd spent time together over the past few months, talking not only about Janna's childhood but also about his interests in England and where his estates were located. Occasionally he summoned his steward to tell her what produce came from which locale and where it was marketed, whether at home or abroad. Janna listened, and learned, and marveled that her father had proved so unexpectedly well connected, when her mother had given no hint of her birthright whatsoever.

Once, when they were sitting privately, she ventured a question as to where his loyalty lay, for she was greatly worried by recent reports of the empress's entrapment at Oxeneford Castle. But her father had shaken his head and said, rather severely, "It does not do to talk of this, not while we are guests of the king's own brother."

Fortunately for Janna, the bishop was hardly at the palace, for he seemed far more interested in following his brother's fortunes than attending to Episcopal affairs. It was widely said that it was through the bishop's machinations that his brother had come to England to claim the throne before Matilda had any inkling that her crown was in danger. It was also said that the bishop was one of the few whose advice King Stephen respected. Janna suspected that the bishop might be in Oxeneford even now, although she wasn't sure. All she knew was that she was glad he wasn't often in Winchestre, watching and observing her family. That he was clever as well as devious she knew beyond doubt. She wouldn't be able to keep her secret for long, should he get any hint of her role in his spy's undoing. All the same, she wished passionately that, in this latest conflict, the king and his brother would not prevail, for she had long been a supporter of the empress and she hoped, with all her heart, that the lady might find some means of escaping her present predicament.

The lengthy meal came at last to an end, and with some trepidation, Janna waited for the servants to clear the dishes and stack the trestle table and benches before leaving the family to their discussion. She could tell from the glances coming her way that John's family also had misgivings about the coming announcement.

Once they were left alone, John beamed at Janna before turning his attention to his wife. "My dear," he said, and took her hand. "I know you have had some concerns regarding our marriage and your security since Johanna has come to live with us. I have given the matter a great deal of thought, and it seems fitting that I should share with you what provisions I intend to make for you and for Johanna in my will, so that there are no false expectations and we all know where we stand." His gaze rested thoughtfully on Giles, who wriggled uncomfortably under his father's cool assessment. "In particular," John resumed, "by bringing this issue out into the open, you will understand, once and for all, the high esteem in which I hold my long-lost daughter." Now it was Janna's turn to shift uncomfortably under the family's baleful glares.

"While Johanna had an unfortunate start in life, I have been watching her carefully and I am more than pleased with her progress," John continued. Janna blinked, wanting to protest against her father's assumption that she'd had an unfortunate start in life. Every day she felt more and more grateful that she'd been reared by Eadgyth rather than by the cold-hearted, self-centered Blanche. Yet she was too intrigued by the inherent promise in her father's speech to correct him.

"I am conscious of the need to divide my wealth and property fairly, so that there will be no dispute after I am gone." Again, John's gaze fixed on his son. "To that end, I intend to travel to the king at Oxeneford so that he may formally witness my intentions to have my children legitimized. So you need have no fear, my dear." He patted his wife's hand, while his gaze remained on Giles. "Should I die, Giles will be my heir and you'll all be well provided for.

There'll be more than enough to keep you in the luxury to which you are accustomed."

Janna smothered a grin as she understood the barb beneath her father's reassurance.

"While Giles is my heir, you and our children will all have a share in my property in Normandy, Blanche. That is, our home and our estates, all the manor farms that come under my aegis."

Giles visibly exhaled. A smile crept over his face, but his mother remained tense and watchful.

"But I wish to make provision for you too, Johanna. To that end, I have decided to bequeath to you my manor house here in Winchestre, for you were born and raised in England, and I suspect this is where you would prefer to remain." John's smile slipped into a frown as he added, "Part of this decision is because I have watched your efforts to fit in with my family and to become a dutiful daughter. I have observed how difficult a task it is when my family has been so unwelcoming. No!" He raised a hand as Blanche uttered a strangled protest. "I know how things stand between you and Johanna." John glowered at his son. "I have also been speaking to young Thomas. It seems he expressed his concerns over your behavior to the head groom, who was sufficiently concerned to bring the matter to my attention. Once we are back in Normandy, Giles, I intend to send you into the care of my half-sister's husband, Geoffrey of Anjou, to learn the duties of a squire. You have been indulged for long enough. In fact, it's long past time you left your mother's fond clutches and learned how to behave like a gentleman."

"But John – "

Blanche's protest was stilled as he again raised his hand. "I shall speak more of your behavior in private," he told his son. "You will remain here after the family disperses."

Giles shrank into his seat. Blanche hastily rearranged her face into a strained smile. "We have done our best to make

Johanna feel welcome," she said sweetly. "I hope she has not told you otherwise?"

John ignored her. "I have sent out a summons to the bailiffs of my various properties and I shall be introducing them to Johanna over the next few days. That will give her time to question them, and look at the accounts they bring. I have discovered that Johanna – unlike you, Giles – is well able to read, write and reckon. It's something you should turn your own attention to, my son, if you wish to inherit the bulk of my property after I am gone, and manage it in a manner befitting your station in life."

Janna wondered if only she understood the threat underlying John's words.

"I'm good at my studies! My tutor says so himself," the boy protested sulkily. Having sat with Giles and his sisters as they struggled unwillingly through the rudiments of reading and writing, Janna knew that Giles's tutor, like the groom, was reluctant to cross the obnoxious brat to his face. Behind his back was obviously a different matter altogether.

John spoke over his son's protest. "While my steward will continue to have the responsibility of managing my estates here in England, he will set aside some part of that income for Johanna's use."

"Pity she doesn't already have a husband, no matter how lowborn." Blanche cast a smug smile toward her own daughters. "She's more than past the age to be wed. Besides, it's not seemly for a single woman like Johanna to be left here on her own."

"That, too, has been exercising my mind," John said, with a smile in Janna's direction. "I know of several possible suitors in Normandy, but Johanna may well prefer to take someone from this country if she is to live here."

"Yes, indeed, sire!" Janna spoke up quickly, her heart leaping at the chance to tell him about Godric. "There's a…" Her courage failed her as she realized the impossibility of explaining the man she truly loved to her father and his family.

"Don't trouble yourself, my dear. I shall make enquiries while I am in Oxeneford," her father promised. "The king may well know of some suitable prospects among his noblemen."

Janna bit hard on her lip to stop her cry of dismay.

"You need to marry, Johanna, and produce heirs. And, as my wife says, you will need the protection of a husband if you are to stay here in England on your own." John rose from the table. "I think that's all we need to discuss for the moment." He flapped his hand at them, shooing them away. "You. Stay," he told Giles, much as he would order a dog to obey him.

"I'll stay too," said Blanche, determined to protect her precious son.

But John shook his head. "What I have to say to him, I shall say in private."

Blanche gave an angry sniff and flounced out, followed by her daughters. Janna walked behind them, relieved that, at last, the boy was going to be pulled into line without the benefit of his mother's interference.

Once out of the solar, Blanche sailed off to the small sitting room she had commandeered for her own use and where she liked to sit sewing with her own serving woman. Richildis trailed after her, but Rosy stopped by a window to look at the hill of St Giles and the world beyond. Janna paused beside her, wanting time to think. Her mind was spinning after her father's announcement. She would become a wealthy woman in her own right! That alone would take some getting used to, quite apart from the thought that she would soon have her own home in the heart of Winchestre, a home she could share with Godric, if only she could bring her father around to her way of thinking.

Hard on that thought came another: once the family was back in Normandy, she and Godric could be wed without interference from anyone. Unless her father made good his promise to find her a husband and forced her into a marriage before he left for Normandy.

Janna's elation died as quickly as it had arisen. An unwanted husband was too high a price to pay for a life lived in a golden cage. She looked outside, seeking distraction from her dark thoughts.

Autumn was giving way to winter. The last of the leaves had fallen, revealing the skeletons of trees that thrust knotted grey arms out to the sky. The dismal scene was relieved by small splotches of evergreens and the red berries of holly. They were coming to the time of Christ's birth and the earth was sleeping, waiting for the warmth of spring to generate new life. Nevertheless, the day still promised fair, a silvery sun brightening the pale blue sky before the early dark set in. Tempted to escape into the fresh air, and remembering the flash of inspiration that would give her good reason to go outside, Janna turned to her half-sister.

"Rosy, you've been here longer than I have. Would you like to show me where the bishop's kitchen garden lies?" she said.

At once Rosy looked around, searching for her mother or sister. Finding neither, she beamed up at Janna and held out a trusting hand. "I don't know where it is, but I'll help you find it," she said.

They collected their cloaks and together traversed the great hall, where servants were still tidying up the remains of the dinner partaken by others in the bishop's employ. Janna led the way downstairs and out into the courtyard. Everywhere was a great hustle and bustle as workmen rushed about, burdened with barrows of cut stone and other building materials. These, in turn, were overseen by master craftsmen, who alternately shouted directions or swore at the laborers, earning the disapproval of resident clerics and the bishop's justiciar, who had emerged from his own rooms to inspect the builders' progress. With the dismantling of the old palace in the center of town, the bishop had commanded that the rubble be brought to Wolvesey, to repair the damage caused during the siege, and to construct a great new public hall and suite of apartments across the courtyard from the west wing.

Janna looked around for any sign of a garden, but Rosy was more practical. "The kitchen's over there," she said, tugging on Janna's hand. "Let's ask the cook where the garden is."

"We may need to go beyond the moat," Janna said.

But Rosy shook her head. "He'll have his vegetables close at hand."

Janna acknowledged the sense of Rosy's observation and said no more until they entered the large kitchen. It was hot and stuffy, the air carrying the rich scent of roasting meats and fish. Janna looked about for the cook, determined to question him before she went out on a quest that she knew might well prove futile at this time of the year. At the sight of the two girls, the bustle stopped and the noise ceased. Everyone turned to stare and Janna wondered if, yet again, she'd broken some unknown rule by coming in here. Too late to worry about that now, she thought, as her gaze flitted over the boy turning the spit in one of the huge fireplaces, past a man plucking a goose and a young boy dicing vegetables, searching for someone who looked to be overseeing this frenzy of activity.

The decision was taken out of her hands when an older man waddled forward, wiping his hands down an apron to clean them and bobbing his head in obeisance as he came. "May I be of some assistance, my lady?" he asked.

Janna hesitated, wondering how to phrase her question. "We very much enjoy the fare you provide for us," she began. "But I wondered if there was some shortage of herbs and spices, for the food is so very...bland." She could think of no way of phrasing her description other than "tasteless," which sounded even worse.

The man drew himself up, deeply offended. "I have express orders from Bishop Henry himself that the food must not be spiced. He has a weak stomach and is used to plain fare."

"But Bishop Henry is not presently in residence," Janna pointed out. "Surely you can be a little more...adventurous with your seasoning in his absence?"

The cook considered her request. "I suppose I might," he said grudgingly, "if there were herbs and spices available to do so. But there are not. I'm afraid I cannot help you, my lady." He gave her a triumphant smile and turned away, obviously pleased to have bested her.

"You dismiss me too quickly," Janna said sharply, unwilling to give up her quest just yet. "Show me where your kitchen garden is, if you please."

The cook's eyes widened, but he did not dare to refuse her request. As Rosy had predicted, he led them to a garden close by. There was little growing there at this time of the year. Janna knew that just about everything, including herbs, vegetables and fruit, would have been picked and carefully dried or preserved with salt, vinegar or honey, depending on what sort of foodstuff it was. Nevertheless, she traversed the garden, looking for signs of any living thing that might add zest to their daily fare. Her sharp eyes noted a small patch set to one side. A cursory inspection revealed the wintry appearance of herbs, no doubt of use in medicaments if not to enhance the bishop's meals.

She leaned over for a more careful examination, followed by the obedient and now deeply curious Rosy.

"What are you looking for, Johanna?"

"Some herbs for the cook to use in the kitchen. That food is so tasteless I'm not surprised your sister won't eat it."

"She won't eat because Maman doesn't like her to stuff herself," Rosy said matter-of-factly. Janna was surprised how sharp she was, and felt some relief that the younger girl might not be so easily squashed as her elder sister.

"If she doesn't eat, she'll become ill," Janna said carefully. "Ah!" She pounced on a creeping plant with little leaves. With the small knife she carried in her purse, she carefully snipped off a few sprigs.

"What's that?" Rosy dropped to her knees to have a closer look.

"It's called thyme. I see we're having goose tonight and this will help to flavor the sauce." Janna kept searching along the length of the garden bed, seeking any plants that still survived the cold. "And some winter savory," she said, nipping off several leaves. Rosy picked a leaf of her own, crushed it between her fingers and gave a tentative sniff. With a nervous glance at Janna, she put it in her mouth. Janna laughed as she quickly spat it out again. "It's peppery," she agreed. "Only a little is needed for a sauce. It'll do nicely for the fish."

"How do you know about all these plants?"

"My mother was a healer. She taught me all about different plants and herbs and how they could make people well again. She also knew what to use to flavor food and ale, and other helpful things like that."

"She used to heal people and make them well?" Rosy's eyes grew round with wonder.

"Yes." Janna felt proud of her mother and of the skills that had been passed on to her. "She knew the different properties of plants and how each might be used to heal the sick people who came to her for help. But we were very poor; sometimes we didn't have much to eat, so we'd gather food in the wild. She knew which plants were edible, and what herbs we should add to make the pottage more tasty."

"Why were you poor? Why didn't you have enough to eat?" Rosy's questions served to illustrate the huge gulf between their circumstances, a gulf Janna was reluctant to explain. But the child was waiting for an answer.

"I didn't live in a big house like the bishop's palace," Janna said quietly. "My mother and I lived alone in a small cot close to a forest. We had no money, and very little land. We survived as best we could, and the villagers gave us food and – and other things in return for the help my mother gave them, and the medicaments she made to ease their ills." To forestall any further questions, for so many painful memories already besieged her, Janna said quickly, "My mother told me a lot of other things about herbs too. Do you know that you can put thyme in your pillow so that you don't have nightmares?"

"I never have nightmares."

Rosy was lucky, Janna thought. "It's also said that there's always a scent of thyme wherever a murder has been committed. But it's also an emblem of courage and it's supposed to cure shyness." Rosy wouldn't need it for that purpose either! She smiled. "Something even more important," she said solemnly, "it's the favorite flower of the fairies. If you give them flowers of thyme they might show themselves to you."

Rosy held out her hand to take a sprig from Janna. "I'm going to try even if it doesn't have any flowers," she said. Clutching the stem with its small leaves close to her chest, she asked, "Will you teach me about herbs and healing things, Johanna?"

Janna smiled down at her. "Of course I will," she said, pleased that she seemed to have a new ally. She moved on slowly, pointing out what she could to Rosy. "If we're still here next spring, I'll be able to show you a lot more," she promised. "There'll be all sorts of new things growing by then, but now they're sleeping under the earth."

Rosy cocked her head to one side to consider this, and nodded. "They're alive, like us, and we need to sleep too," she said. "But Janna, we won't be here in the spring. Papa has promised that we shall celebrate the Christ mass in our new home, for he hopes it will be ready for us to move in by then."

"Our new home here? Or over the sea?" Janna asked, instantly alarmed.

"Here, silly!" Rosy laughed at her expression. "Maman wishes we could return to Normandy now. I heard her ask Papa, but he won't leave until he is sure the new house is finished properly, and the new steward knows enough to look after his affairs. He said he'd been burned by his last steward, but I think he meant to say his house was burned down, don't you?"

Janna nodded, although privately she understood exactly what her father meant. She knew his previous steward had been lazy and had probably also been careless in his administration of her father's affairs, even if he hadn't been actively corrupt. Certainly he was a coward, for all members of the household had fled Winchestre even before the troubles started, leaving her father's property unprotected throughout the siege. She suspected part of her father's promise of the manor was to ensure that she would be here to keep an eye on the new steward.

"Come with me, Rosy," she said at last, after she rose to her feet and brushed herself down. "Come and help me tell the cook how to make a tasty sauce for the goose!"

*

"Aah!" Blanche's shrill scream broke the silence that had prevailed around the dining table as the family savored the fare set in front of them. "Poison!" She clasped her chest in a dramatic fashion. "We've all been poisoned!" She snatched up a goblet of wine and drained it, set it down on the linen tablecloth, and sank back into her chair with a deep groan.

Janna looked at her stepmother for explanation, for it seemed that Blanche's accusation had been aimed directly at her. Until then, they'd all been enjoying the goose. Even Richildis, Janna was pleased to see, had been persuaded to have a few slices of breast meat with some sauce, while Blanche's whippet, Fleur, had been gorging itself on helpings dropped from her trencher.

"Poison, my dear?" John paused in the act of cutting another portion of goose. "But this is delicious."

"It's poisoned," Blanche said hoarsely. "Rohesia told me you've been searching out plants in the kitchen garden, and now I know why." She pointed an accusing finger at Janna. "You're not content

25

with inheriting the manor here in Winchestre, are you? You want all of your father's estates in Normandy too. And with us out of the way, that's what you'll get!"

"That's enough, Blanche!" John said sharply.

"What's this, then?" Blanche pointed at the flecks of thyme in the sauce.

"It's a sauce with herbs in it," Janna said calmly. "I gave the cook instructions on how to make it, but there's nothing in it of concern, my lady. It's just a regular sauce, but with the addition of thyme and a few other herbs to add flavor."

"Thyme?" Blanche's mouth pulled down in distaste. "Is that poisonous?"

"Johanna says you can smell thyme at the scene of a murder," Rosy said, proudly showing off her new knowledge.

Blanche drew in a sharp breath. "I can smell it now," she said, with a loud sniff.

"And it'll help you to see fairies," Rosy added in the silence that followed Blanche's pronouncement. But her mother paid no attention. She was glaring at Janna.

"It's a herb used to savor a dish, that's all," Janna said, thinking it was probably useless to try to defend herself when Blanche had already made up her mind.

"Johanna's mother was very skilled in the use of herbs," John said mildly. "She has passed on her knowledge to her daughter, it seems. However, Johanna, I would prefer it if you did not confer with the servants or meddle with domestic affairs in the bishop's kitchen. It's not seemly."

Stung, but unable to defend herself further, Janna said nothing.

Blanche shot her a triumphant glance. "I'll be watching you very carefully in the future," she promised, and with exaggerated care she scraped the sauce off her goose. She turned to her daughter. "Don't eat any more, Richildis, you've had quite enough."

Seething, but giving every appearance of enjoyment, Janna smothered a piece of goose with sauce and ate it. If she'd had her way, she thought sullenly, the family might actually have relished their food for a change. She cheered up slightly as she recalled the other herbs she'd given the cook, with instructions for their use. Unless someone told him different – which was unlikely, given that no-one knew about it – further meals might also taste better. Hopefully the cook himself might be inspired to extend his culinary arts.

"May I have some more goose?" she asked, determined to prove to the family that there was nothing wrong with the sauce which she then poured over it. To her dismay she noted that Richildis had obeyed her mother and pushed her trencher to one side, the goose barely touched, although the girl had seemed to be enjoying the meal before Blanche's intervention. While her father had noticed some of what was happening within his family, he remained blind to other, equally pressing problems. Perhaps she should try to open his eyes even wider? She drew a breath and prayed for courage, for she knew how deeply her stepmother would resent her interference in this.

"You haven't eaten properly for days, Richildis," she said. "Please, don't heed your mother's warning. The goose really is delicious, and it's quite sound, I promise you."

"She eats more than enough for a young lady in her position," Blanche said sharply. "It's only peasants who gorge themselves," she added, with a meaningful stare at Janna's heaped trencher.

Janna thought back to the great hardship and terrible hunger people had suffered after the destruction of Winchestre during the siege. She was about to retaliate, but her father got in first.

"Why are you not eating your meal, Richildis?"

"She's already had quite enough!" Blanche's tone was higher than usual, strident in her effort to put Janna in the wrong. "You have mistaken my concern for my daughter, Johanna."

Janna, in the act of taking a sip of wine from her goblet, almost choked. "I know you have your daughter's best interests at heart, my lady," she said, carefully replacing the goblet. "As who would not? Richildis is beautiful, but she is far too thin and she's also lacking in strength."

"What nonsense is this?" John seized his daughter's hand and looked searchingly into her face. "It's true," he said worriedly. "What ails you, daughter, that you will not eat?"

"I...I..." Tears came into Richildis's eyes as she glanced in appeal at her mother. "Maman says I will not find a husband if I am greedy."

"Your marriage is already arranged, and it will take place," John assured her. "You will be wed just as soon as we return to Normandy." He scooped up some goose and held it to Richildis's mouth as if she was still a child. "Eat," he urged softly. "It is true that you are far too pale and thin. I want to see some roses back in your cheeks, my dear."

With a worried glance at her mother, Richildis obediently opened her mouth to the spoonful. She chewed, and swallowed. John immediately offered her another mouthful and, like a little bird, she took it. Janna watched, noting with delight the dark flush of fury on Blanche's face as John put down the spoon and Richildis picked it up and refilled it. Under her father's watchful eye, Richildis finished what was on her trencher and he nodded with satisfaction.

"Let us have no more of this silliness," he said severely, and looked directly at his wife. "Richildis will be in your care while I am in Oxeneford, my dear, and I charge you to make sure our daughter continues to take proper nourishment."

There were so many ways to say "my dear." Janna was convinced that if her father had ever addressed her mother in such a fashion he would have sounded as if he actually meant it. She glanced around the dining table, and sighed. Her interference had not helped her mission to be welcome in this family. John's announcement had served to harden their prejudice against her, while Blanche would never forgive her for drawing his attention to Richildis. Even Giles had made his hostility plain, bumping against her and giving her ankle a hard kick under the table in revenge for the lecture he'd obviously received from his irate father. They hated her, that much was clear. And given the depths of their hatred, perhaps she should be on her guard in case there was retribution to follow.

Chapter 2

Janna found there was little time to brood, for the days were taken up with visits from John's bailiffs, whose reports both impressed and alarmed her. Her father had more properties and greater wealth than she could have imagined. To her surprise, she found herself feeling some sympathy for John's family, cut off so unexpectedly from a goodly portion of what they had expected to inherit. Nevertheless, she was touched by her father's generosity and determined to keep a careful watch, even though he'd made it clear that the steward would be in charge. "I want you to know everything about my affairs in England," he told her. "You have sharp eyes and a keen mind, and I know that you will bring any irregularities to my attention."

As she could not speak of what was in her heart, Janna had decided to put the prospect of a husband behind her for the moment and concentrate instead on impressing her father both with her knowledge and her willingness to put it to good use. And so, together, they read the bailiffs' accounts and discussed what else might be put in place for the future. John told her of the markets at home and over the sea, with interjections from the new steward, who was eager to learn and anxious to prove his worth.

The man was a marked improvement on the previous steward, although Janna would withhold judgment until she had seen how he managed affairs once the new manor was rebuilt and her father returned to Normandy. Meanwhile, she welcomed the opportunities her father gave her to consult on the design of the house and, at her insistence, on the garden that would be established there. Thanks to her father's unexpected announcement, a plan had begun to form in her mind. She had long thought of putting the knowledge she had learned from her mother and Sister Anne to good use. Her father's manor house would be the ideal premises for a hospitium where anyone might seek treatment. The prospect gave her great delight. But it was a plan for the future, for Janna was ever conscious that, first, she had a promise to fulfill: her promise to avenge her mother's death. As she and her father drew ever closer, she decided she would raise the matter on his return from Oxeneford. By then it would be almost time to celebrate the Christ mass, but after that surely he would agree to go with her to Wiltune, to clear her mother's name and bring her mother's killer to justice. And, if the nuns at Ambresberie had been unable to carry out their promise to have her mother reburied in consecrated ground, or had been thwarted by the abbess, then she would ask her father to arrange that too. She was in her father's favor now, and she hoped he would trust her enough to take her word for all that had happened. Of course, it would also help if she could persuade Cecily to tell the truth. That would decide the matter beyond any doubt. But Cecily had never spoken of her fall from grace, and it was unlikely now that she ever would, not if she hoped to find a good husband. Nor would she want to jeopardize her position in Hugh's employ.

Janna thrust her anxiety aside and tried to join in the conversation around the dining table, for the family was at dinner once more, and again her father had joined them. In his presence, Blanche and her children smiled at Janna until their faces must have ached. All the same,

Janna appreciated their efforts, although she was more than surprised when Blanche suddenly cleared her throat and made an announcement.

"Today, we have special fruit pastries to finish our repast," she said, beckoning a serving lad bearing a tray of sweetmeats. "I ordered them myself, for I wanted to demonstrate to you how much we welcome and value your presence, my dear daughter."

Janna swallowed hard, forcing down a gurgle of disbelief. John beamed his approval at his wife, who turned a sweet smile on Janna. "This is for you, my dear." She indicated one of the honey-glazed pastries, which was slightly larger than the others and had a baked pastry heart on top as a decoration. "Please give that one to Mistress Johanna," she instructed the servant, who obediently slid the sticky confection in front of Janna.

Janna's mouth watered. She loved the taste of honey, relished its sweetness. At this time of the year it was in short supply. She wondered that Blanche would squander both honey and the dry fruits that had been marinated to make the filling, but felt unduly grateful that her stepmother was putting on a brave face and making a show of affection. "I thank you, my lady," she said.

"Surely, Johanna, you may call your stepmother 'Maman' now that she has gone to such lengths to welcome you as our daughter?" her father said.

Janna almost choked. She noticed that Blanche looked as horrified as she felt. She could not deliberately flout her father's wishes, but made a silent vow that never, while she still had the ability to draw breath, would she ever think of Blanche in the same terms as her own mother. True, she wanted her father to love her as if she'd always been his daughter, as if he and her mother had made a life together and she had come along to complete it. But Blanche would never be a part of that, nor could she ever take the place of Eadgyth.

"As you wish, sire," she said demurely, without committing herself to anything.

"And you should call me 'Papa.' I am your father, after all," John added.

"Yes, Papa." Janna was delighted. For the first time since she'd approached her father, she felt not only acknowledged, but also loved.

Blanche was eating her pastry with gusto, and even Richildis, Janna was pleased to note, had taken a dainty bite of the sweetmeat. Suddenly impatient to taste it, she raised it to her lips and quickly licked away a few droplets of the honey glaze that threatened to spill onto her gown. She was about to bite into the confection itself when she caught the faint whiff of an unpleasant odor. It seemed familiar, but for the moment she couldn't place it. Buying time, she lowered the pastry and tested the taste of the honey on her tongue. Beneath its sweetness lay something else – something that Janna did not quite trust. And now that she was looking at it, the honey glaze on her pastry looked somewhat different from the others; it seemed thicker and darker.

Blanche was watching her carefully. Janna didn't have the courage to question her openly, so she took a bite, held it in her mouth, and raised her napkin to her lips to dab the stickiness. Under cover of the napkin, she spat out the mouthful and lowered the cloth to her lap while pretending still to chew and swallow. "Delicious," she lied, smiling at Blanche. "Thank you for this lovely surprise."

Blanche's little whippet was snuffling under the table, scavenging for scraps as usual. Instead of offering a taste of her sweetmeat to her dog, as she usually did, Blanche held out the pastry to her son, who'd already demolished his own treat in two swift bites. "Giles, dearest," she cooed, "would you like some of Maman's fruit pastry?"

With Blanche's attention elsewhere, Janna quickly scooped the remaining pastry shell into her napkin and dropped it on the floor. It was an instinctive reaction to danger; she hadn't considered the consequences until a smacking noise revealed that the dog had found the pastry and was wasting no time devouring this unexpected treat. Janna's conscience pricked, slightly assuaged by the thought that she wasn't sure there was anything wrong with it. In fact, she rather regretted her hasty action. Blanche certainly seemed happy enough to share her portion with her beloved son. She would never do that if the pastry had been tampered with.

But perhaps it's just my portion. Janna remembered the heart that had marked her pastry from the others – the heart that was meant to show love but might mean just the opposite. She peered surreptitiously under the table, relieved to find that the little dog had curled up at its mistress's feet, seemingly replete. She gave a wry smile, happy to admit she'd been wrong. It really had been a gesture of good will and she had been stupid to be so suspicious.

And then it came to her. The smell! There'd been an old woman in their village who had suffered dreadfully from crippled, twisted joints. Her mother had made up a rubbing lotion of hemlock to give the woman relief from pain, giving her also a solemn warning never, ever to taste the lotion, for it would kill her. Which wasn't quite true, Eadgyth had told Janna later, for the tiniest amount of hemlock taken internally might relieve pain, but it was too great a risk when even a small amount could prove fatal.

Janna peeped under the table again at the dog. Was it asleep? Or dead? Hemlock, Eadgyth had told her, caused paralysis before death. Janna knew of no antidote and could only hope that she herself had not consumed a fatal dose. She flexed her fingers and toes, testing their mobility. All seemed to be in working order, although she wondered if she felt a little giddy. She looked around the table at the watchful Blanche, and at the girls, who were sharing a joke with their brother and father. Blanche would expect some reaction, Janna realized, and would also take great care to stay away from her so as to maintain an air of innocence. The thought spurred her to action.

"May I be excused from the table, Father?" she asked. Not waiting for an answer, she ran from the solar. She wasted no time in going to the sleeping quarters that Blanche shared with John. Fortunately the servants were all in the hall having their own dinner, and there was no-one to witness her actions as she commenced a thorough search of their room. She knew exactly what she was looking for: a phial of rubbing oil designed to ease aching joints – and at the same time rid oneself of an unwanted heir to the family fortune.

The knowledge of just how much she was hated seared her heart; she felt panicky as she understood that Blanche would not give up trying once she realized her first attempt had failed. All that could save Janna was evidence, and truth. She wondered what her chances were of finding either.

There was no trace of a phial in the room, and Janna was wondering where else to look when she became aware of the hullabaloo outside. The door burst open and a weeping Blanche was escorted in by John. She jerked to a stop when she saw Janna.

"What are you doing in here?" she demanded. "Haven't you done enough damage already?"

"I don't know what you mean, my lady," Janna said steadily, although she could guess only too well.

"My little dog. My Fleur. She is dead! You have poisoned her!" Blanche burst into hysterical tears once more.

"Come, my dear." John patted his wife's hand. "You mustn't throw such accusations around, not without proof. And I am willing to vouch for Janna's innocence in what has just transpired."

"Innocence?" Blanche's voice rose to a shriek. "How can you say that girl is innocent? Didn't she try to poison us all with that sauce! And when that failed, she poisoned my little Fleur in revenge. You yourself said she has a knowledge of herbs from her mother, a knowledge that must include those that are harmful as well as those that heal. And she has put that special knowledge to use, husband, for none of us know of such things. Oh!" Blanche gave a deep shudder and clung tighter to John. "You must send her away, and quickly, before she tries once more to poison us all!"

"Sire – Papa, I am innocent of this, I swear it!" And yet Janna knew full well that she was not. She could have stopped the dog from eating the dropped pastry – if she'd been sure enough of her suspicions. But she was not, and consequently the dog was dead. And wasn't she glad, after all, that it was the dog who had died and not herself? She drew a breath, summoning all her courage to speak out.

"I didn't eat the pastry because I thought it had been tampered with," she said, keeping a careful eye on Blanche to gauge her reaction.

"I saw you eat the pastry!" Blanche retaliated. "And you enjoyed it, as did we all!"

"That was pretence. In truth, I spat out the mouthful and dropped it and the rest of the pastry under the table – and your little dog found it and ate it instead."

"What lies are these! See, husband, how she insults me, how she turns my welcoming gesture against me to her own purpose."

Janna waited, hoping desperately that her father would give her his support, or at least defend her against Blanche's accusations. But he did not. Instead, he gave a deep sigh and said, "Lie down, my dear, and I will order a tisane to help you compose yourself."

"Make sure you keep her away from its preparation," Blanche instructed, with a venomous glare at Janna.

John nodded. "What you have said has given me much to think about, and we shall talk again when you are calmer." He did not look at Janna as he added, "Come, daughter, come away with me now."

"You must send her away from us forever," Blanche's voice hissed across the room. "I shall never feel safe unless you do!"

Close to tears, Janna followed her father out of the room. All the love, the trust that had been slowly building between them, had been destroyed by Blanche's accusation. If only she could have found the preparation and shown it to her father. Any apothecary would confirm what Janna herself knew: that the concoction was beneficial for aches and pains, but poisonous if swallowed. On an impulse, she asked, "Do you or Dame Blanche suffer from aching joints at all, Papa?"

"No, I don't, and neither does my wife. What are you suggesting, Johanna?"

Janna knew a moment of blind panic as her theory crumbled to ash. "A rubbing oil containing hemlock may be used to relieve aches and pains. It may also be used in a lotion to treat tumors and ulcers," she added hopefully.

"I believe my wife recently sought advice from an apothecary here in Winchestre for a sore that wasn't healing as it should."

"And would you know where she kept the preparation for it?"

"There was a phial. I believe it came with a warning of some sort." John's eyes sharpened as he scrutinized his daughter more carefully. "Is that what you were looking for in our room?"

Janna hesitated, not having courage enough to openly accuse Blanche. Finally, she said, "I thought I could smell hemlock on the pastry. It has quite a distinctive scent. And it is very, very poisonous."

"Are you accusing my wife of deliberately trying to poison you?" John's voice rose in disbelief. "Jesu, Johanna!"

"Hemlock gives great relief when applied to sore limbs, and to ulcers and swellings," Janna said steadily. "I know not how it found its way onto the pastry I was given, but I do know that it causes paralysis and then death if ingested – and the dog died after eating my pastry." She looked up at her father, trying to mask her distress. "I swear on my life I didn't mean for the dog to die. I just thought the pastry was tainted in some way and I didn't want to eat it."

"Come with me." Abruptly, John whirled toward the stairs, taking Janna down and across the courtyard and into the kitchen. All activity stilled in his presence and, after a quick look around, he beckoned the cook forward with an imperious finger.

"Those fruit pastries," he began.

The nervous cook immediately interrupted him. "I hope they were to your liking, sire? Dame Blanche was very particular as to their making, and stood over us to watch that we did everything just so."

"Did you see my daughter here during their preparation?" John pointed a finger at Janna so there could be no mistaking his meaning.

The cook hesitated, perhaps trying to work out an answer that wouldn't get him into trouble. "No, sire. That is to say, I have seen her here before – but not today."

"And once the pastries were ready?" Janna asked quickly. "What happened to them?"

"They stayed on a tray right here until the servant took them in to you."

John nodded thoughtfully. Janna felt a great relief that the cook's testimony must surely clear her from suspicion – while calling the actions of Dame Blanche into question. But it seemed that John was not prepared to lay any blame on his wife.

"So anyone could have tampered with them between the time of their preparation and their serving," he mused. "Thank you." He removed a coin from his purse and, after leaving instructions for a tisane to be made up for Blanche, he pressed it into the willing hand of the cook and shepherded Janna from the kitchen.

As they crossed the courtyard once more, they were hailed by one of the bishop's guards, who hurried forward and dropped to his knee in front of John.

"Pardon my interruption, sire, but a messenger has arrived, and he wishes to speak to you. He appears lowborn, but he would not tell me even his name, nor would he state his business. He says only that he must speak to you in private, and that the message is urgent. Do you wish to see him?"

"No, indeed. Tell him I can't see him now." John waved an impatient hand, unwilling to be distracted from the problem of the little dog's death and his wife's hysterical accusations. He strode on, but Janna paused and looked toward the gateway in the hope of glimpsing the servant.

"Did the messenger say where he was from?" she asked the guard, curious as to the contents of the message he brought.

"No, my lady. He would tell me nothing at all."

A sudden suspicion prompted Janna to probe further. "Did he ask to speak to Bishop Henry before he asked for my father?"

"No, my lady. He asked only for your father."

"Tell him my father will not speak to him. Ask him if he will speak to me instead." She was taking a huge risk and knew it might well rebound against her; she would have to proceed carefully. She watched the guard return to the gate, while her mind raced through the questions she might ask in order to protect herself.

She'd become increasingly worried by the reports coming from Oxeneford of the empress's misfortunes. The bishop was still away from Wolvesey, said to be with the king, his brother, at Oxeneford. Stephen's troops had blockaded the castle, preventing any supplies from getting through. Everyone knew that the empress was trapped inside with her entourage. It was a matter of speculation how long they could hold out before they were starved into surrender. What intrigued Janna was why a lowly servant should demand to see her father. If the message was from her father's steward, he would have come in person to speak with him. If the message was from the bishop or the king, the messenger would have traveled in style to deliver it. But what if the message was actually from the beleaguered empress? That was what Janna intended to find out, if she could.

She watched thoughtfully as the guard approached, dragging the man along with him. Persuading him to divulge the message to her was only the first hurdle she must overcome. Because, if the message was from the empress, she would not allow it to be delivered to her father until she had first ascertained where his loyalty lay. Not for anything would she deliver this man to his enemy, and with the same stroke destroy all the empress's hopes of escape.

If that was what the message was all about. But what miracle could the empress hope for from her half brother? Janna was tempted to change her mind and dismiss the man after all. Yet she remained in the courtyard, waiting for him. She admired the empress and had always supported her bid for the crown, even when that loyalty had brought her great personal grief and anxiety. She could not give up now, not if there was something she might do to persuade her father to give the empress the help she so desperately needed.

The man was travel stained and looked exhausted. A deep wound, seeping with a yellow matter that indicated it was not healing properly, marred the side of his forehead. Janna could see no sign of a mount. Doubt crept in, for surely the man would have been given a horse – or might even have stolen one – if the message was as urgent as she supposed.

"Have you traveled here on foot?" she asked as he approached her.

The man hesitated. "I was ambushed on the road and my mount and pack were taken, my lady," he said at last, perhaps believing there was nothing incriminating in admitting this much at least. He touched his forehead and winced.

"Is that when you suffered your wound?"

"Yes, my lady." He hesitated. "I was lucky that I was found by a traveling packman, for I was out of my senses and incapable of walking. He took me to the nearest village and there I was looked after until I was well enough to make my way here."

"And where have you traveled from?"

The man shook his head, wincing again at the movement. "I have orders to speak only to Sire John."

"And my father will not speak to you, for he is busy at present," Janna said impatiently. "So you have a choice: either you speak to me, his daughter, or your message goes undelivered." She did not say straight out that she was prepared to help the empress if he would only answer her questions. She waited for him to say something, but he stayed obstinately silent. Maybe there was some other way to make him speak? As a first step she dismissed the guard. If her suspicions were correct, the messenger would not want someone in Bishop Henry's employ to overhear anything he might have to say.

"I shall give you a lotion to cleanse your wound, and also a healing salve for it. If it is left untreated it will continue to fester. It may even prove fatal," she told him, not hesitating to stretch the truth if it would serve her cause.

He blinked, and touched his forehead once more, then scrutinized fingers that now bore a trace of the yellow pus. "I would be grateful, my lady," he muttered.

"These are dangerous times to be on the road," she prompted. "Who was responsible for the trouble you encountered? Outlaws? Or supporters of the king? Or the empress?"

He shot her a swift glance.

"Who stole from you and left you wounded almost to death?" Still the man didn't speak. "My father is in a position to help you if you can give a description of the culprits and where you encountered them." Janna didn't know if this was true, but hoped her promise would prompt him into speech. "Did you get in the way of the king's barons?"

He made a growling noise in the back of his throat. Encouraged, Janna questioned him further. "Or is it the empress's supporters who are preying on innocent travelers?"

"She would never permit such a thing!"

Janna wasn't so sure about that, but was not about to cast doubt on his statement. "Outlaws, then? Where are you from?"

"Oxeneford." The man hesitated, perhaps understanding the significance of what he'd just admitted. "I was attacked soon after I left the town," he added quickly. "Thereafter I traveled only at night, and took care not to attract attention."

Janna nodded thoughtfully. "Wolvesey Palace is the Bishop of Winchestre's residence. Will you speak to him instead of my father?" she asked, deliberately omitting to mention that the bishop wasn't home.

"No, my lady," the man answered quickly.

Janna took a deep breath. She was already at odds with her father, and risked widening the rift if she couldn't convince him of the justice of the empress's cause. So now she must make a choice: she could stay safe or once again risk everything for the sake of the empress. If she miscalculated, she would face her father's wrath and a possible charge of treason. But she'd come this far; she could not give up now. "You must tell me the truth about your message for my father. Will it help if I tell you that I have ever been a supporter of the empress?" She watched the man's reaction to her words. Had he relaxed slightly? Did he look a little less anxious? She couldn't be sure.

"If the empress has sent a message to my father, you would do well to give it to me first," she urged. "I don't know where my father's loyalty lies, and it would be best to find that out before giving him your message. I would not jeopardize the empress's safety by letting it fall into the wrong hands."

The man stared down at his feet as if he could read there the answer to the quandary in which he found himself.

"Is the message written, or will you tell it to me?" Janna hoped that the outlaws had not robbed him also of the letter, for if so, the empress was doomed. But, after what seemed like an eternity, he reached into the neck of his tunic and untied a leather thong. Silently, he passed the thong, and the small pouch attached to it, to Janna.

At once she undid the drawstring, found the parchment enclosed within and quickly unfolded it. With an exclamation of annoyance, she realized that the message was written in the language of the church. "I shall have to show this to my father, for I cannot read it," she told him, "but first, can you give me any sense of what it might say?"

The man threw up his hands. "The empress is trapped in the castle, my lady, and looks set to stay there until she surrenders to the king, for there is no escaping the guards he has posted around the castle walls. I am one of the empress's grooms, and I was only able to escape because I – " He paused, and his face turned a dusky shade of red, making him look suddenly much younger and very ill at ease. "I have a young woman in the town and I sometimes broke curfew to visit her at night. So I was able to creep away in the first early confusion of the king's siege of Oxeneford. I waited quite some time before departing the town, hoping that the empress and her entourage might follow in my footsteps. I'd told her tiring woman the route to take, you see, but I finally realized that all ways had been barred to them and they were trapped within the castle. And so I came to deliver the message, as instructed. But the ambush has delayed me, and so has my need to travel at night and stay hidden. I fear what may have happened to the empress in my absence."

"What does the message say?"

"I know not. All I know is that when I left Oxeneford, the empress's most loyal supporter, Robert of Gloucestre, was out of the country helping the empress's husband secure Normandy, while most of those barons the earl left to protect her in his absence had fled to their own demesnes. The empress had no-one on the outside she could trust. Her tiring woman told me as much. This message may be to ask your father to send word to the earl to let him know of her plight, or to muster troops to come to her defense before they all starve or are forced into submission. I believe the empress hopes for your father's help, my lady, but I cannot know for certain. All I know is that the message has been made far more urgent because of the delay."

Janna nodded thoughtfully. Her father had property in Normandy, he was known there. It made sense for the empress to call on him – so long as her father could be trusted to support her cause.

"I will talk to my father and see what we may do to aid the empress," she said, and pointed in the direction of the kitchen. "Go there and ask for food and drink. Tell no-one what you have told me, but you can tell them Mistress Johanna sent you. Have a rest while you may, for this will take some time. I shall call for you when I have prepared the medicaments to treat your wound. What is your name?"

"Osbern, my lady. And my thanks to you."

Janna turned away. She quickly folded the parchment and replaced it in the small pouch, clutching it tightly in her fist to hide it from prying eyes, and hurried off in search of her father. She hoped that this recent calamity would not prejudice him against her. She also prayed that he would prove sympathetic to the empress's cause and be able to come up with some plan to help Matilda escape.

Escape. A smile twitched the corners of Janna's mouth as a memory came back to her – and with it the beginnings of an idea. It was a mad idea, but was yet so daring that it might even succeed. Her thoughts raced ahead. She would not confide all that was in her mind to her father, but if she could get him to agree to just the first part of her plan, not only might she help the empress to escape the king's cordon, she would be able to protect herself from harm at the same time.

*

She found her father, grave-faced and alone, in the solar. Blanche must still be having hysterics over her pet dog in their bedchamber. To Janna's relief, there was no sign of her siblings either.

"I have a question for you, Papa," Janna said, going straight to the heart of the matter, while keeping the small pouch carefully hidden in her fist.

"And I have a question for you, Johanna," he said sternly in return. "Blanche is right about one thing. I cannot have this continuing conflict between you and my family. If this cannot be resolved I shall be forced to send you away and make other arrangements for your welfare."

A flash of rage swept through Janna that he was so quick to judge her. "I've already sworn a solemn oath that I had nothing to do with poisoning the pastries," she said hotly. "Why do you take your wife's side against me, when all the evidence points to her, not me?"

"I'm trying to get to the truth of the matter," John defended himself, "but I also have your safety – and my family's safety – to consider. I have asked Blanche where the lotion is, and she tells me she stopped using it some days ago. She believes the phial was thrown away. She says she knows nothing of it."

"Have you asked the servants to look for it?"

"Are you asking me to doubt the word of my wife?"

Janna didn't answer, but made a private resolution to look for the phial herself. She would know the contents instantly by the smell. And she also had a very good idea where to start looking.

"I apologize, Papa," she said icily, making an effort to calm herself. "I seek only to find out the truth so that I can clear my name in your eyes." She knew she would get nowhere if she was at odds with her father; she must do all in her power to keep his good opinion. Yet it seemed her father no longer trusted her. How, then, could she trust him with the groom's message? But the situation was serious and time was running out for the empress.

"I have spoken to the man who brought you the message," she ventured.

John made a dismissive gesture. "I have more important things on my mind at present, Johanna. I will deal with him later."

"This is important," Janna insisted. "Much more important even than what is happening within our own family. But I need to ask you a question first."

John raised his eyebrows, clearly annoyed by her persistence.

"The empress and the king. Who do you support in this war for the crown?"

"I support the king, of course. After all, he is still the king, and anointed as such by the Pope. Plus, we are staying at the home of his brother, the bishop."

"But the empress is your own half-sister," Janna said desperately. "Just as you want me to become part of your family and befriend my half-brother and half-sisters, don't you feel any loyalty to the Empress Matilda? Or to your half-brother, the Earl of Gloucestre? Or to the empress's husband who, even now, is bringing Normandy – and your estates – under his control? You've talked of sending Giles to serve under him. Forgive me for speaking so plainly, Papa, but surely you have some loyalty to your own family?"

John's eyebrows rose higher. "You are remarkably well-informed on affairs of state. Have you been listening to the servants' prattle?"

Janna kept silent. She had, but only out of a desire to keep abreast of the changing fortunes of the empress.

"Why are you so interested in the plight of my half-sister?"

"Because…" Janna's mouth went dry. By confessing to her father, she was taking an even bigger risk than in speaking freely to the groom. Yet it seemed she had no choice. "Because I have always supported the empress, ever since I met her while living as a lay sister at Wiltune Abbey."

She waited to gauge her father's reaction, but he made no comment.

Janna drew a breath and ploughed on. "I was the one who alerted the Earl of Gloucestre to the bishop's treachery after I found and read a letter from the bishop to his brother. The letter bid the king be of good cheer in his imprisonment and stated that he and the queen were working to secure the imprisonment of the empress – and this at a time when the bishop had sworn his support for the empress in her bid for the crown."

"Jesu, Johanna, was that you? But..." John blinked as he tried to come to terms with Janna's revelation. "Your friend in the tavern said something about your bringing my half-brother a message, but I'm afraid I didn't believe him at the time," he said slowly. "But I remember now that Robert told me the girl bore a marked resemblance to our sister. He couldn't understand it, for the girl claimed to be a poor peasant of no consequence."

"And so I was, at that time," Janna said. Nevertheless, she felt encouraged by her father's admission that he knew what had happened over the business with the letter. It meant that he and the earl, and possibly the empress too, had communicated with one another. It must mean that they were close and that they trusted him, for otherwise her father would never have known so much.

Her father stared at her intently. Unexpectedly, he gave a short laugh. "You are your mother's daughter, even if you do resemble our side of the family," he said then. "She was a brave one, my Emanuelle. And clever. She would try anything, do anything. Nothing daunted her spirits, even when it meant defying the abbess of Ambresberie in order to come away with me."

Janna was always happy to hear his reminiscences of her mother. But there was a more pressing question to be dealt with right now. "I have confessed where my loyalty lies, Papa, but you say you are on side with the king. Can that really be true?"

"My wife and family support the king," John prevaricated. "It doesn't do for a family to have divided loyalties."

Janna gave a sigh of frustration. Surely her father was not so weak that he would allow his wife to form his opinions for him? She was about to say as much, but John forestalled her.

"Nevertheless," he said, "and for your ears only, Johanna, I am fond of Matilda. We were friends as children, and I thought it wrong of Stephen to usurp her throne, especially when he had been among the first to swear allegiance to her in front of our father, the old King Henry – as we all did at the time."

Hearing his words, Janna felt a huge wave of relief. Her way was open after all; a way that might solve her own problems as well as those of the empress. "I think you should read this," she said, and handed over the pouch with its precious contents.

John quickly scanned the letter and then held it out to Johanna. "Have you read this letter?"

"No, Papa. I cannot understand the language of the church. But I do know that the message comes from the empress. It was brought by a groom in her employ."

"It says…" John quickly translated the contents, which were much in line with what the groom had told Janna. "In fact, Robert has already been informed of Matilda's captivity and is trying to reach her," he added.

"But I understood all ports are barred to him now."

"So they are, but I'm told that Robert was able to recapture Wareham. He is now in England, along with his supporters from Normandy, and is busy gathering together all those who still remain loyal to the empress – and all without the aid of Geoffrey of Anjou who, in the end, has let him down once again." John's expression hardened for a moment. "But Robert will have a fight on his hands to reach Oxeneford, for the king is determined to prevent any attempts to rescue her. I only pray he'll reach the empress before they are forced to surrender." John gave a deep sigh. "If I only knew more about the English barons, I could try to rally them myself," he mused. "But Matilda warns me that they are not to be trusted, and I dare not take the risk. So in truth, my hands are tied."

"Not quite." Janna was tempted to tell her father of the plan forming in her mind, but suspected that he would forbid it if he knew of the part she intended to play. "You said that you planned to go to Oxeneford to see the king about legitimizing your family," she said, thinking to lead her father to her way of thinking one step at a time. "While you are there, surely you can talk to him, appeal to his better nature, for it is said that he let the empress go free when first she landed in England. Could you perhaps persuade him to let her go free once again?"

She could tell from John's skeptical expression that he knew he'd have no chance of success. Janna agreed, but at least she'd put that thought into his head. It might encourage him to agree to a further plan – once she'd had the chance to think it through properly. But first she needed to ask for a favor, for without her father's consent she could do nothing to help the empress. "If you go to Oxeneford, Papa, please will you take me with you?" She waited in some trepidation for her father's reply.

He frowned as he considered her request. "Why do you want to accompany me?"

"Because..." Janna swallowed against the sudden constriction in her throat. "Because it's my future you wish to discuss with the king." She could tell from John's expression that he was not convinced by her argument. It seemed she would have to trust him with a little more of the truth. "And because your wife and children hate me," she added huskily. "Because I fear how they will treat me if you are not here to protect me." It hurt Janna to admit how fearful she felt.

"Dame Blanche wants me to leave, she's already asked you to send me away," she continued. "Surely it would be for the best if I'm no longer here to upset your family. And it would be safer for me to be away from them." She waited a moment, giving her father time to ponder her words. "That pastry was meant for me," she reminded him. "Whoever was responsible for its contamination may well try again to harm me, not having succeeded the first time." She wondered if she'd gone too far as she noticed John's face darken into a scowl.

There was silence between them. Janna longed for some acknowledgment, some gesture of affection from her father. But it didn't come. The silence continued.

"Please take me with you to Oxeneford," she begged, knowing that her plan would fail unless she could convince her father. Unless he'd changed his mind about her after what had just happened? Perhaps her father was no longer planning to bequeath anything to her? In which case, he should inform his family so that the threat to her safety would no longer exist. She waited for him to speak. But he remained silent, frowning down at the letter in his hand.

"Very well," he said at last. "We shall both go to Oxeneford, although I shall not tell my family about this message or my intention to intercede on behalf of the empress while I am there. Nor shall I tell them of your accusations, for that would only provoke another scene. I shall merely explain that you'll accompany me because I wish to consult the king about your marriage."

Janna felt a slight easing of tension. It seemed he'd not given up on her quite yet.

But John hadn't finished. "Remember that we'll be traveling into a highly dangerous situation," he warned. "You are to keep out of sight, and obey my instructions for your safety. Any hint of trouble and I shall have to send you back to Winchestre."

"Yes, Papa," she said meekly, pleased that he valued her enough to want to protect her. All the same, she kept her fingers crossed behind her back. What she had in mind was far more dangerous than her father knew or could possibly guess.

"Just between the two us, I want to see for myself how the situation lies in Oxeneford and if there is something – anything at all – that I might do to help free Matilda."

Janna was greatly relieved by her father's words, both on the empress's behalf and even more so on her own. She was desperate to escape her stepmother, for she knew exactly where the threat to her safety had come from, and knew also that she could not always be on her guard against whatever plan Blanche might devise next. The woman might have fooled her husband, but she could not fool her husband's daughter. Putting distance between them was the only way Janna could think of that would help her stay alive.

Chapter 3

Traveling with her father reminded Janna of her days on the road with the pilgrims and the jongleurs as she'd followed the trail of information that had helped her unravel her mother's past, and finally led her to her father. There were certain differences, of course. Winter had now seized the land in its icy grip, and they journeyed through freezing winds and flurries of snow, which made their passage difficult and unpleasant. But Janna was clad in an expensive woolen gown and a fur-lined cloak, she was traveling on horseback rather than on foot, and she was staying in lodgings rather than taking shelter in a barn or under a hedge. Not that anyone knew who they were, for John had taken the precaution of dressing as a merchant, not wanting to draw undue attention to their party in these troubled times. The empress's messenger traveled with them, his wound now healing fast thanks to Janna's ministrations. There were also several armed guards who were passing themselves off as servants. Janna herself was introduced as the merchant's daughter, a role with which she felt entirely comfortable.

To her relief, her relationship with her father had eased considerably after she, in company with Rosy to act as her witness, had searched the kitchen garden for healing herbs to make up medicaments to heal the groom's wound, but also – and more important so far as Janna was concerned – for the phial that once had contained the lotion made of hemlock. As she'd hoped, they found it lying beneath a window which opened from the kitchen, thrown out by a careless hand. Janna had bid Rosy find their father and ask him to come immediately, while she waited beside the phial to bear testimony both to its location and its contents.

John had made no comment but, under Janna's urging, he had smelled the dregs inside it. He'd taken the phial from her and returned to their quarters. Janna didn't know what he'd said to Blanche, or even if he'd said anything at all, but they had left the bishop's palace soon after that, much to her relief.

They were some days on the road, their destination being Godstow Abbey, where John intended to leave Janna while he went on into Oxeneford to negotiate with the king. The abbey was close to the town, and the groom had told them that the sisters there were known to sympathize with the empress's cause. It was there that Janna intended to put her plan in train, although she fervently hoped she wouldn't have to go through with it. Meanwhile she wrestled with her conscience about telling her father what she planned. She couldn't bear to sit by and do nothing, not while the empress and her entourage were being starved into submission by Stephen, yet she feared that her father would never agree to her voluntarily placing herself in danger. Finally she decided to keep her plan a secret. Part of her decision hung on the fact that she was used to acting independently and hated the idea of having to ask permission to do what her heart decreed she must. Following from that was the belief that her father would forbid her request, and then she would be obliged either to abide by his ruling or risk her own future by disobeying him.

They came at last to the small abbey, and were welcomed by the nuns and housed in the guest quarters, which at this time of the year were otherwise unoccupied. Once her father had left the abbey, with the warning that he could be gone for several days, Janna was again assailed by doubts. Her plan seemed foolhardy in the extreme; she wondered if it might be prudent to wait until her father's return in case he managed to secure the empress's release. Finally she decided to act, justifying her decision with the realization that later would be too late, for then she'd have the added difficulty of needing to slip out of the abbey without her father's knowledge. Either that, or take him into her confidence, with the probability that he would forbid her to do anything at all.

Now that the time had come, she knew a deep and all-encompassing fear. What had seemed rather heroic when seen at a distance now seemed risky beyond belief. What drove Janna on was the knowledge that this might be the empress's best and only hope of escape. Her plan was daring enough that it just might work. She could only hope that, if the ploy was successful, Stephen would show mercy to those of the empress's entourage who were left behind.

Committed to action, Janna's first step was to rinse her fair hair in the dark dye she'd prepared and brought along with her. Once her hair had dried, she dressed herself in the elaborate gown that her father had ordered for her audience with the king, warning that she might well be summoned for Stephen's inspection if his business with the king bore fruit. It was dark green and embroidered at the neck with gold thread and small pearls. It was finer, more costly and far more beautiful than anything she had ever worn in her life. She was glad to have such a thing in her possession, although not for the reason her father intended. She wished now that she had a mirror to check her reflection, but apparently the good sisters of the abbey had no time for vanity and did not encourage it, for she could find no signs of one.

She carefully draped a gauzy veil over her newly darkened hair, and secured it with the gold band that completed her ensemble.

So might an empress appear, she hoped, as she ran her fingers lightly over the fine woolen fabric. Would it be enough to convince Osbern? She went down into the guest hall to test her new appearance.

The groom's response was all that she'd hoped and more. At sight of her, he leaped up from his stool and fell down on his knees. "My lady! You have escaped! This is surely a sign from God, a miracle!"

"I have not escaped, Osbern. I have always been free. But alas, the empress is still in captivity."

The groom gawked at her, then shook his head as if to clear it of phantoms. Janna laughed, elated that her ruse had worked.

"But...I don't understand. Why do you impersonate the empress, my lady? And why has your father gone to Oxeneford to see the king?" The groom's expression had changed from shock to suspicion. Janna wondered if he was having second thoughts about divulging the empress's message to them, and for a moment she shared his doubts. Had she been too ready to trust her father's word? If so, it was even more important that she act, and quickly.

"My father told me he wanted to ask the king if he could see his half-sister, the empress," she said, trying to allay the groom's doubts as well as her own. "He also plans to plead with the king to set her free, as the king did once before when first she came to England. But I suspect the king won't agree, so I have a plan of my own, Osbern, and that's why I look the way I do. And I need your help. Can you go into Oxeneford and look around, find out what you can about where the king's soldiers are deployed, and if there are any blind spots where the empress might be able to slip through the enemy's lines if the king's troops are occupied elsewhere?"

The groom nodded, still looking somewhat bemused. Janna knew she would have to tell him everything sooner or later, and now was as good a time as any. She thought she could trust him, for he had shown his loyalty by almost forfeiting his life to bring the empress's warning to her father. If he did as she asked, he would be risking his life once more in the empress's service. She needed to have his agreement to her plan; otherwise, she would have to think again.

"My father doesn't know this, but my intention is to go into Oxeneford dressed as I am now. You thought I was the empress, and I hope others will too. If I can show myself to the king's troops, if I can make them believe that the empress has somehow managed to escape, and tempt them to come in pursuit of me, that will leave the castle unguarded for a time, hopefully long enough for the empress to slip away to safety. But I need your help. First, you must find out whether or not the king has agreed to my father's request to release the empress. If he has, then there's no more to be done and you may return. But if my father's mission has failed, then I shall take matters into my own hands. And I'll need you to play your part. Do you think you can find a way back into the castle so that you can tell your mistress of my plan, and set a time for her escape?"

"Yes, my lady. They'll be looking to stop anyone coming out rather than going in," Osbern said eagerly. "I'm sure I can find a way."

"But you must first reconnoiter the surrounds of the castle, because I need to know what route I should take and where I should show myself." Putting her plan into words sent chills of fear through Janna. She would be lucky to escape with her life if the guards were overzealous, or if she wasn't quick enough. "You must take Gervase with you. He's the strongest and most trustworthy of my father's men, and he can bring word back to me if the plan is to go ahead. Show him where you think I should walk, and also the best route to escape any pursuers, for I shall need to draw them away from the castle. Tell him when I should come to Oxeneford to rescue the empress, so that he can serve as my guide and my guard. But tell no-one else of this plan. Do I have your word on that?"

"Yes, my lady." The groom looked at her with new respect. "But..." Suddenly flustered, he stopped abruptly.

"But?" Janna prompted.

"Forgive me for saying this, my lady, but although you look something like the empress, you do not walk or behave as she does."

Janna cast her mind back to her meeting with the empress at Wiltune Abbey, and smiled at the truth of the groom's words. She threw back her shoulders and tilted her head in an imperious fashion. She strode closer and looked down her nose at him. "Go about the task I have given you, and make haste," she said coldly.

The groom gave a delighted smile, lightly clapped his hands, and bowed before bidding her farewell and wishing her a safe journey and success in her quest.

"Good luck, and may God go with you," Janna called after him.

After he'd gone, Janna was filled with misgiving. She'd been told often enough that she bore a resemblance to the empress, but that likeness had never been more crucial than now. Would it be enough to fool the king's troops, to lead them away from the castle? If her father couldn't secure the empress's release, then the groom's role became just as vital as her own. But what most exercised Janna's mind was the weather. Winter had begun unusually harsh and looked set to continue that way in the foreseeable future. They had suffered its icy grip on their journey to Oxeneford, had passed through blizzards and even traversed small streams that had frozen so hard they were able to step across the ice in safety. Yet she needed the day, or night, of the empress's escape to be calm and clear enough for people to be abroad to witness her passage and sound the alarm.

Waiting was hardest of all, Janna decided, as first one day passed and then another. She was filled with foreboding, her imagination conjuring up frightening scenes of pursuit and death, scenes which spilled over into her dreams. Just when she thought she was likely to go mad with the phantoms that tormented her, Gervase returned to the abbey and was shown into her presence.

"Well?" she demanded, as soon as they were left alone.

He swallowed nervously. "Your father is still with the king, my lady."

"Has he seen the empress? Has he managed to secure her release?" Janna held her breath, hoping for a last-minute reprieve.

"No, my lady. He was allowed a brief meeting with the empress, but that is all. He asked me to tell you that he will return once he's discussed some family matters with the king. And I – I am told by Osbern to let you know that – that you should be outside the castle walls tomorrow night, before the rise of the moon."

So Osbern had set their plan in motion! Part of Janna was relieved that there would be action at last, even while her heart thundered with dread. "You know you are to come with me?"

"Yes, my lady." Gervase glanced at her and quickly looked away. "But I beg you to reconsider. Your father will not approve your actions, I am sure of it."

Nor would he approve of Gervase's part in the escapade. Janna knew that was the man's real worry, and she sought to allay his fears. "With luck, my father need never know. We shall ride there tomorrow afternoon, and we'll be back before daybreak."

He pursed his lips, looking dubious.

"I am going, Gervase, and I bid you come with me," Janna said sharply, borrowing the empress's own imperious manner.

"Yes, my lady. But could you not ask a few more of your father's guards to come with us? You face great danger, and I would feel more comfortable with some extra men at my back to protect you from the king's soldiers."

Janna considered Gervase's request. While it was reasonable on the face of it, there was far too great a risk that someone would talk, that word would get out, either to the king or to her father. Janna wasn't sure which of the two she feared most. "No," she said. "I'm sorry, Gervase, but this must remain a secret between the two of us."

He nodded, his face smoothed into resignation. "Osbern has shown me the streets and laneways close to the castle so I'll be able to take you to safety once you've attracted the attention of the soldiers and drawn them away from the castle walls, my lady. The empress will make her move just as soon as the alarm is sounded."

"The empress's life is at stake – and mine too – if you betray our plans," Janna warned.

"Yes, my lady." His hand went to his side, but found no weapon. Janna knew he would have been told to leave his arms at the abbey's gatehouse. "I shall be armed when I escort you," he reassured her, cheering slightly at the thought. "And the weather works in our favor too. The river has frozen hard, hard enough to bear the empress's weight. If Osbern's secret way out of the castle is still barred, then he will advise the empress to escape out the window facing the river and walk across the ice to safety. There is a groom known to Osbern, he's in the employ of a baron who is still faithful to the empress. Osbern plans to accompany the empress when she escapes. He's asked the groom to make arrangements for men and horses to wait for him at Abingdon, without telling the groom the reason for it. Once the empress has left the castle, they will need to move quickly to escape pursuit."

"Are you sure it's safe for her to walk across the river?"

"Yes, my lady. I've seen people with animal bones tied to their boots, skating across the ice." Gervase's voice reflected his wonder at such a sight. "If the empress can only escape from the castle, cross the river and walk to Abingdon, she will find men and horses waiting to take her to safety.

"Some of the magnates who deserted earlier have been shamed into returning to Oxeneford in the hope of taking the city from the king," Gervase continued. "I have been listening to the talk in the taverns. There have been several skirmishes, but the magnates and their men are not enough in number to defeat the king and drive him away. Their plan is to wait for the Earl of Gloucestre. He's defeated the king's troops at Wareham and made a safe landing, and is now fighting his way toward Oxeneford."

"How close have they come?" Janna felt a surge of hope that she wouldn't have to risk her neck after all.

"Not close enough. We've heard that the situation in the castle is dire. They are almost out of food and water. I doubt they can hold out long enough for the earl and his troops to save them, my lady, but the empress's supporters who are here now may come to your aid if you need them – if only you can tell for sure who they are."

Janna knew there was no hope of that. Nevertheless, she forced a smile for his benefit and dismissed him. She'd made the plan, and it was too late now to change her mind. Although she was impatient to leave at once, for she was frightened and wanted to get the ordeal over and done with, she knew she must delay to give Osbern enough time to breach the castle, to reach the empress and prepare for their escape.

Waiting had frayed Janna's nerves almost to breaking point, particularly as she was forced to stay in seclusion in the guests' quarters so that no-one could see the new color of her hair and start tattling about it. She fretted under the strain, while her sleep was broken by nightmares. On the day she was to put her plan into action, she woke with a pounding heart and soaked with the sweat of fear. She ran to the window, anxiously looking for any signs of a change in the weather, or her father's return. But the snowfall continued, while her father remained safely in Oxeneford.

It was still snowing when, at noon and dressed in all her finery but with a hood covering her face and hair and a rough blanket thrown over to shield her from the weather and from prying eyes, Janna set out with Gervase. She huddled into her fur mantle, relishing its warmth against the freezing air but not begrudging the cold, for it meant that the ice would hold fast for the empress's flight. On Gervase's advice, they circled the town's earthen ramparts and entered through the North Gate. Janna let Gervase talk to the guard. She kept some distance away, making sure that her face and hair were well shrouded. Once they were safely through, Gervase called a halt close beside the church of St Michael. "We should delay here a little longer, my lady," he said, drawing Janna into the shelter of a wall, and preparing to dismount.

Janna hardly heard him; her eyes were fixed on the high motte and stone tower of the castle that dominated the skyline. There were thin slits in the tower, for firing arrows at the enemy but also, perhaps, for looking out onto the town. She wondered if the empress had noticed their arrival. A sudden fear set her heart jumping in her breast: what if Osbern had been intercepted? What if the empress didn't even know that help was at hand? What if all of this was for nothing?

Gervase was waiting beside her, arms held out to catch her as she slid down from her mount. She shivered, conscious that she was committed now and that there was no turning back.

"The castle is surrounded by a moat, which to the west gives on to the millstream and the River Thames itself." Gervase passed on his new-found knowledge in a whisper. "The empress will wait until she hears the horn sounding the alarm, but failing such a signal, she will leave just before the moon rises. Osbern will accompany her to Abingdon, and from there they'll be able to ride under guard to Wallingford. She'll stay there under Brian fitz Count's protection until it is safe for her to move on to the Earl of Gloucestre's castle at Devizes."

Janna nodded her understanding, while she turned to survey the ruined town. The snow gave a look of innocence and purity to the shattered buildings, but the forlorn air of abandonment reminded her of Winchestre after the siege. How cruelly this fight for the crown affected innocent townsfolk. They were the ones who suffered the most when their homes and their livelihood were destroyed. For a few treacherous moments, Janna wondered if all this ambition was really worth the hardship it caused. The seasons would change and life would go on no matter who sat on the throne. But she brushed the thought aside, for she had already endured so much to aid the empress's cause that she could not give up on it now.

"You must stay close to me at all times, my lady, so that I can protect you." Gervase was looking more troubled by the moment. "Until the moon rises, our own passage will be difficult."

"But the darkness will aid the empress's escape," Janna said cheerfully, hoping to lighten Gervase's spirits as well as her own. Even as she spoke, she was busy tethering her horse to a gate post. "We must leave our mounts here, Gervase. The guards will expect the empress to escape on foot. I don't want to alert them to the possibility of a trick. And if, by some mischance, I should lose you in the dark, this will be our meeting place for later."

"No, my lady!" Gervase sounded panic-stricken as he continued. "The king's men may well be mounted. There's a danger they'll run you down if you're on foot! It's more than my life's worth to risk your safety."

"I believe I'll be able to evade the king's troops more easily on foot than on a mount." Janna examined the higgledy-piggledy remains of shops and houses, assessing her chances. She shuddered, not only with cold, but she wouldn't let Gervase know that she shared his fears. "There's no need for concern, Gervase. We'll be back at Godstow Abbey late tonight, and no-one any the wiser as to the true purpose of our absence."

"But what if someone steals our mounts, my lady?"

It was a good point. "We'll have to take that chance." She looked around, and after some thought she untethered her horse and led it over to a huge yew tree that cast a deeper shadow on the pale snow. Grudgingly, Gervase followed her. He took the reins from Janna and knotted them fast to a branch at the back of the yew, out of sight, then tethered his own mount beside hers. Shivering in the bitter cold, Janna shrugged off the rough blanket that had disguised her, and left it draped across the horse's saddle.

"Come, it is time." She couldn't bear to delay any longer. She was also aware that they must not stay still, for she would surely freeze to death if they did.

Muttering dire warnings coupled with instructions for her safety, Gervase led her back to the main street connecting the North Gate through the town to the South Gate. Janna kept her shoulders slumped and her face shrouded as they zigzagged streets and laneways, until finally they approached the southern ramparts of the castle. Once there, she cast off her hood, intent now on starting a chase that she hoped would drag the guards away from the castle to hunt the empress out in the streets. Although her heart was hammering with fright, she tilted her chin and assumed a haughty expression worthy of the empress herself.

There were few people about in the intense cold, but she earned some startled glances as she hurried along. One man barred her way; Janna gave him a freezing stare down an imperially tilted nose before he turned aside and hastened away. She glanced after him, and saw him speeding off in the direction of the castle, shouting the alarm as he ran. She shivered and moved closer to Gervase, taking some comfort from his solid presence.

As planned, they began to circle the castle, hoping to entice the guards from the western and southern ramparts and lead them north, thus leaving the way clear for the empress's escape. All Janna's senses were alert, for she knew that at any moment the king's troops would come after them. Her back prickled as she anticipated the clutch of a heavy hand or the stinging point of a dagger. She resisted the urge to keep looking over her shoulder for signs of pursuit. "We should go a little slower," she warned, as Gervase quickened his pace. "We want it to appear that we are in haste but trying not to attract attention. And I also need to be recognized."

"We should not be on foot," Gervase fretted. "Please, my lady, let me sound the alarm myself so we can hurry on to the North Gate to reclaim our mounts."

"No, not yet. While we're on foot we can twist and dodge through laneways and streets and lead the pursuit well away from the castle.

We must draw the guards away and give the empress enough time to escape, Gervase." Not giving him a chance to say more, she moved on with determined steps, pausing only to give a passerby the chance to look at her for a few moments before drawing her hood around her face in what she hoped seemed a furtive gesture.

"You must not linger!" Gervase said, his voice too loud in the quiet night. In his panic he grasped her arm, trying to hurry her along. "Please, my lady, give them only one quick glance, just long enough to establish who they think you are so that they will sound the alarm. Then we must flee, just as they would expect."

Janna nodded. By now she felt sick with fright, but still she kept her head up and her chin tilted, determined to carry this through with the courage the empress herself would have shown under the circumstances. She walked beside Gervase, fighting the urge to run. This, she thought, was far worse even than her nightmares.

A strident blast on a trumpet was followed by a cry that was taken up by a multitude of voices. The chase was on! Even as Janna thought it, she heard the thunder of a horse's hooves coming up fast behind her. Acting on instinct, she ducked out of the way, separating from Gervase as she did so.

"My lady!"

The horseman had come between them now, and was bending from his saddle to catch her up into his arms. Not waiting to see if Gervase followed, Janna flung herself sideways and dodged down a narrow alleyway. One frantic glance behind her showed the horseman vaulting out of his saddle to follow her. She took to her heels, stumbling blindly in the dark, hampered by her long skirt. She snatched it up with both hands and, holding it high, continued to sprint down the narrow laneway, tripping over unseen objects in the dark and keeping her balance only with difficulty. The cries of pursuit followed her, men summoning their comrades to the chase. The footsteps following her were getting louder, coming closer.

"Stop!" her pursuer shouted, but Janna kept on running. She had no way of knowing who was behind her, friend or foe, but as he hadn't called out to the empress, or even to her, she thought it best to treat him as the enemy. Her guess paid off when she heard the blare of a trumpet from behind, telling others of their whereabouts.

Terror-stricken, she put on a burst of speed, not stopping to reason that it was not her but the empress whom her pursuers were really after. Nor did she stop to think that they would be careful to take the empress alive for the huge ransom she would be worth to her captors. Janna's mind was wholly occupied with imagining the sting of cold steel piercing her skin and slicing through her body. She dared not look around, but knew from the sound of pounding boots behind her that her pursuer had been joined by others and that they were gaining on her.

The narrow lane came to an abrupt end. She shot out onto a wider street that was lined with an uneven cluster of small workshops. They were mantled in snow, but with collapsed roofs and gaping holes that gave them the appearance of a row of rotten teeth. A quick glance as she sped past told Janna that none of them held the promise of shelter. But a sharp pain in her side was almost crippling her; she knew she could not evade her pursuers for too much longer. She swerved closer to the buildings and ran into a burnt-out shop front, burrowing quickly through the ruins to the back where once had been a merchant's home. Like everywhere else, what hadn't been burned had been looted. There was nowhere to hide. After a brief moment to reconnoiter, Janna turned to run in the direction from which she'd come, keeping to the back lanes while hoping that the king's soldiers would continue to ride on down the street in pursuit of her.

Her body was on fire; her breath came in great gasping sobs. She had to find somewhere to rest, if only for a few moments. Desperately, she looked about for cover as she ran. One small workshop and dwelling stood isolated at the end of the row. It seemed to have escaped the worst of the firestorm that had razed everything else, and she dived into its shadows. She crouched, trying to quieten her panting breaths so that she could listen for sounds of pursuit. A loud cry close by and another trumpet blast told her that her ruse had been discovered. She could not stay where she was. It would take only moments before the king's soldiers tracked her down. She searched frantically for a possible hiding place, but the small work space was bare, stripped and looted. Nor was there any way out of the ruins that would not result in her capture. She was trapped. Had the empress escaped yet? Would it be safe, now, to show herself and tell them her true identity?

No! Although it felt as if she'd been on the run for hours, Janna knew it was not so long since the cry had gone out. Somehow, she must evade the search for a while longer. The dim outline of an abandoned smock hanging from a hook caught her eye. A smile of relief spread over her face. Here was her means of escape. Here was her salvation, if only she had the nerve to carry it off! With shaking fingers, she threw off her fur mantle and veil, untied her girdle, and quickly eased herself out of her gown. What a surprise the trader would have if he ever came back! Of course, the garments would be no use to him, but a wife or a daughter would be thrilled to own such costly apparel. She gave a huge sigh of regret. These were the most beautiful things she had ever owned and it hurt her to discard them, but if she was to escape from this coil she had no choice.

She pulled the smock over her head. It was burnt in places, and stank of mold and damp. It was also far too large and far too long, but at least it would go some way toward hiding her bare legs. After a moment's thought, she snatched up her discarded gown and stuffed it inside the smock, both to keep it safe and to alter her appearance even further. Disappointed that she had no room to save the fur mantle as well, she bundled it up with her veil and cast them into the darkness. Shivering with fear, she hurriedly tied her own girdle firmly around her waist and hitched up the smock so that it bulged over the cord. Attached to her girdle was her purse; not for anything would she leave *that* behind, not when it contained everything she most valued, including coins that she might need to bribe her way to safety. Regretfully, she slipped out of her dainty shoes, wishing there was a pair of boots to complete her ensemble. As she realized that the alternative was to walk barefoot through the snow, she hastily slipped the shoes back on, praying that no-one would notice them.

She glanced about for something to hide her hair, but could find nothing. Glad she'd changed the color of it to match the dark night, she rapidly braided it into a long plait and tucked it out of sight inside the tunic. As a last touch, she scooped up some sooty, damp earth and smeared it over her face and hands and, after some thought, her shoes.

She was about to creep out when she discerned the dark outline of a man coming toward her. At once she dropped to the ground, hoping that he had not seen her in the dark. But he had noticed the movement, and he strode in and stood over her. "Get up!"

Janna yawned and stretched and rubbed her eyes to spread the dirt further, then stood up and hung her head. "What?" she snarled, in as low a voice as she could muster, speaking in the language of the Saxons.

The soldier held up a flaming torch, the better to examine her. Janna shielded her eyes against the sudden flare of light, hiding much of her face at the same time. Terror struck her heart at the thought that he might search the ruins and find her fur mantle. She took a few steps toward him, forcing him to retreat. "What do you want?" she growled.

"The empress has escaped and is hiding nearby." He was back at the door now, his torch lighting the street rather than the ruined interior of the shop.

"I haven't seen her." Janna cleared her throat and spat on the ground. "Rousing honest Christian folk from their beds, keeping them from their sleep," she grumbled. "Our life is already hard enough, thanks to you." She wondered if she'd gone too far when the soldier held up a threatening fist. But, caught up in the urgency of the chase, he turned away then and hurried off to the next shop along the row. She watched him, praying he would not return.

Soldiers roamed everywhere, flaming torches held high as they prowled around the small shops and the ruined dwellings behind them, poking and prying, and no doubt pocketing anything of value they might chance upon along the way. After quickly bundling some burnt and broken remains of the shop's fittings on top of her abandoned garments, Janna walked outside. She peered about for Gervase but couldn't see him in the crowd. With shoulders hunched, and already missing the warmth of her fur cloak, she began to move along the street, eager to put as much distance between her and her hiding place as possible.

To her relief, the soldiers paid her no heed, being more intent on interrogating any women they could find. Although numerous townsfolk had come out into the streets to see what the fuss was about, most of the single women were there for one purpose only: to ply their trade. They flirted with the soldiers and some of the men lingered, although most stayed focused on the task in hand. Janna eyed them cautiously as she strolled along, keeping a keen lookout for Gervase, or even her father or one of his men. But all were strangers to her.

She had no idea, now, where she was, and wished she'd thought to disguise herself and go out earlier with Osbern and Gervase to learn the layout of the town. She dared not ask the way lest she arouse suspicion, yet she did not want to linger on the streets either, in case her disguise was penetrated. She grew colder and wetter, for it was still snowing, and her tunic was thin and ragged, and she had no leggings for protection. Finally, driven to desperation, she approached a couple of monks who were gazing at the scene about them with lively curiosity.

"I ask your pardon for troubling you," she said breathlessly, once more lapsing into the speech of her childhood, as befitted her apparel. "Can you tell me where to find the North Gate?"

The two brothers looked at her. One of them shrugged. "I've no idea what he is saying," he commented to his companion in Norman French. The other brother smiled at Janna. "Go here," he said, his words so halting that Janna had difficulty understanding him. But his pointing finger was direction enough, and she caught the gist of what he was trying to say when he added, "There is cross of roads." He crossed his hands to show what he meant, then raised his left hand to point as he said, "Turn that way to church. St Michael. There is town wall and North Gate."

Janna was shaking with cold by the time she came to the churchyard where they'd tethered their horses. She hammered on the door of the church, planning to throw herself on the mercy of the priest or anyone else who might hear her, but no-one came in answer to her summons. At last, shivering violently, she crept under the thick branches of the yew tree to find the old blanket she'd left lying on the horse's saddle, hoping it, and the horses, would provide some measure of warmth, for her tunic was wet from melting snowflakes and her blood was colder than ice. There was no sign of Gervase; she assumed he was still out searching for her, probably half out of his mind with worry. There was little she could do about it, though, other than cower close to the horses and wait for him.

Minutes passed as slowly as hours. Janna wiggled and jigged to try to keep warm, but was chilled through by the time she heard a slithering footstep followed by a dull thump and a loud curse. She peered through the prickly yew and saw Gervase struggling to right himself in the slippery snow.

"I'm here," she said, and crawled out from her hiding place.

"Thank God you're safe! Jesu! What has happened to you?" He gaped at her blackened face and bare legs in horror.

"Shh. I'm safe and everything is all right." Janna smiled at him.

"But my lady – your clothes! Your face!" His voice quavered with alarm.

"Later, Gervase. We must make haste to reach the abbey before daylight. There's no time to lose." Janna fumbled with the tethered reins, her hands numb and clumsy with cold.

"Allow me, my lady." As he spoke, Gervase removed his cloak and handed it over.

"No," Janna protested, holding up her hands to fend him off. "You need it yourself, Gervase."

"I am more warmly dressed than you, my lady." He cast an eye over the old blanket and Janna's exposed limbs, and glanced quickly away.

Conscious of propriety, she took his cloak with heartfelt thanks and wrapped it around her, grateful for its warmth. But they still had a further hurdle to pass before they could gallop to safety.

"The North Gate, my lady? It will be barred against us by now."

"Then we must bribe the gatekeeper." Janna patted the fat purse that hung from her waist. A thought stopped her: How would she explain her riches when her appearance was that of a beggar? After a moment's thought she untied the purse and handed it over to Gervase. Together, they approached the gate.

"Who goes there?"

Gervase moved forward to answer the guard. To Janna's surprise, for he'd shown no capacity for flights of fancy in the past, he launched into an explanation of an unexpected delay and a cruel master who would skin them alive if they did not make it home before daybreak. Janna kept her head meekly bowed as the gatekeeper subjected her to a careful inspection before waving them through. It was clear that he had been alerted to the empress's escape and was bidden to watch out for her. It cheered Janna's spirits greatly to realize that the empress must have managed to escape, while his caution meant she must still be free.

Once they were through the gate, Gervase handed the purse back to Janna. Murmuring her thanks, she extracted several coins and dropped them into his palm before securing the purse to her belt once more. Cutting off his protestations and thanks, she spurred her horse to a gallop, anxious to reach Godstow Abbey before dawn.

It had finally stopped snowing. Clouds were lifting to reveal moonlight through their ragged edges, giving them some light along their way. Shivers still racked Janna's body, from cold but also from the aftermath of fear and shock. She wanted to shout in triumph that she'd managed to overcome all obstacles and had survived, yet underlying her elation was concern that, after all, the empress might yet be captured and her ordeal have been in vain.

But her problems were by no means over, Janna realized, as they came at last to Godstow Abbey and were shown, with some reluctance on the part of the gatekeeper, who didn't recognize her in her new guise, into the guest quarters. There, she was confronted by her father. Not immediately recognizing her, and being too anxious to pay any attention to a shivering wretch, he immediately turned his wrath on the unfortunate Gervase.

"Where have you been?" he thundered. "I left you here and charged you to look after my daughter, but I suppose you've been sneaking off to visit the town's whores. And in your absence my daughter has disappeared! I am in fear of her very life, for no-one seems to know what's become of her."

There was a brief and awkward silence. Janna did not dare look at Gervase as she stepped forward and said meekly, "I am here, Father."

John took an audible breath of relief as he swung around. His face darkened as he studied her. Disbelief turned into anger. He turned on Gervase, his hands knotted into fists. "So this is how well you undertake your duties." Janna rushed forward and grabbed hold of her father just in time to prevent him taking a swipe at her anxious escort.

"You are not to blame Gervase for any of this for I ordered him to come with me," she said breathlessly. "But I alone am responsible for my absence from the abbey, and I can explain everything." A shudder shook her body; her teeth chattered from the cold. "But may I first exchange my clothes for something warmer?"

"Yes, and clean yourself up at the same time." John surveyed Janna's mud-smeared face and tattered clothing with a scowl. "And your explanation, when it comes, had better be good, for I swear to you that if you were any younger I wouldn't hesitate to…" His threats died away as he realized they were not alone. "Get to your quarters," he told Gervase. "I will speak to you later, after I have heard what my daughter has to say for herself." He stalked over to a stool beside the fire, sat down, and held out his hands to the warmth.

Janna fled, relieved that she was to escape the beating her father had been too circumspect to mention, yet knowing that any other punishment would also hurt, even if not in quite the same way.

As she changed out of her clothes and sponged herself clean from a basin of hot water brought from the kitchen by a young lay sister, she tried to rehearse what she might say in her own defense. To her dismay, every argument seemed to reinforce her own folly. How could she have thought to place not only herself but also Osbern and Gervase – and yes, even the empress – in such danger, when, if she'd only taken her father into her confidence, there might well have been a simpler and more effective solution to the problem?

But every time Janna argued herself to that point, she could go no further, for it seemed to her that there was no solution, simple or otherwise, other than taking the risk. Nevertheless, she was feeling greatly chastened by the time she reappeared. Once faced with the irate John, all words deserted her. Instead, she ran into his arms, pressed her face against his chest, and began to weep as fright and its aftermath took their toll.

He stood stiff and unmoving at the start, but then Janna felt his fingers move across her hair, petting and soothing her as he might a stray kitten. The tender gesture utterly unnerved her and she wept harder, all the while struggling to regain control of her emotions.

"Hush now. Shh...shh." John held her close. This, then, was what it felt like to have a father, Janna thought, and her throat constricted in sorrow for all the years she'd felt his absence. She also knew a deep sense of shame that she hadn't trusted him enough to tell him of her idea, and ask for his help. Now, though, she would tell him the truth. The thought that it was too late for him to stop her helped in some small measure to dry her tears. Wanting a father, but not wanting to be controlled by him, was something she needed to ponder for the future. But for now she must explain her actions to him, and in such a way that no blame at all could attach to Gervase. She owed her loyal guard that much, at the very least.

Once she had composed herself enough to talk, she broke away from her father's embrace and sat down beside the fire. It had been newly tended, and she took comfort from the roaring flames and their cheerful warmth. In her absence, John had called for mulled wine and now he thrust a goblet into her hands. Janna took a long swallow, relishing its heat as the liquid slipped down her throat and into her belly. She took a last sip and began to speak of the night's escapade, including her close brush with the king's men and the measures she'd been forced to take to evade capture.

"I...I'm so sorry, Papa, that I had to leave behind my fur mantle and veil," she stammered, feeling her heart beat faster as she noticed how furious he looked. "But you must not blame Gervase for my actions. I commanded him to accompany me, even though he first argued against it and then urged me to take more men to guard me, once he saw I was committed to my plan."

She stole a glance at her father. His expression had changed to a sort of grim amusement that went a great way toward cheering

Janna's spirits. "Young woman you might be, but you still deserve a thrashing for this night's escapade," he growled.

"Yes, Father." Janna was hopeful now that he wouldn't carry out his threat.

"But my sister will likely want to honor you for your efforts on her behalf."

"Have you heard anything?" Janna asked eagerly. "Has she managed to escape?"

"I know not, but I shall try to find out. And, Johanna, next time you're tempted to risk your neck on such folly, will you please talk to me first?" From the angry glint in her father's eyes, Janna knew this was a command, not a request. And yet she felt some sympathy with his viewpoint. Her capture and unmasking would have caused an irretrievable rip in the relationship between her father and the king. And if it had come to the worst, she was hopeful enough to believe her father would honestly mourn her death. His shock and anger surely bore witness to the fact that he cared about her.

"As for the king…" John surveyed his daughter thoughtfully and shook his head. "I cannot call on him again. Although he has asked to meet you, I dare not introduce you to him now, for he will have heard of the chase after the empress and may well suspect your part in her escape – if escaped she has." He gave a regretful sigh. "He must not see you, at least until your hair has returned to its rightful color. And until the memory of this night has faded somewhat in his mind. The problem is – " He stared into the fire. Janna waited, wondering what was to follow.

"The problem is, I spoke to Stephen about finding an eligible husband for you, and he is waiting to introduce you to someone whom he believes will be a good match. I have agreed to it, because I am determined to see you safely wed before I go back to Normandy."

Janna listened with a sinking heart, not quite sure what to say. Her every instinct was to flatly refuse to marry anyone of her father's choice. But she knew full well that now was not the time to say so, although she was still determined to win him around to her way of thinking. "I hope he's young, handsome and rich," she said, trying to make a jest instead.

"I hope so too. The king did not say – perhaps because I did not ask. But he must meet you before we can take this any further."

Janna was pricked with curiosity. But her desire to follow her heart came well before her desire to meet the empress's captor. "Is my prospective husband someone with whom I can fall in love?" she asked, desperate for any shred of information, no matter how slight.

"Love?" John raised an eyebrow.

"You married my mother for love!" It was the best weapon she had, and Janna prayed that it would be powerful enough to change her father's mind when the time came.

"That was different."

"But you would not want me, the child of your love, to settle for anything less, surely?"

Her father gave a small huff of disagreement. "We shall see, when you become presentable once more. And a further thing. I mentioned my intentions regarding my family, and also my property here in England. The king has promised to honor my wishes if I draw up a document to that effect. I shall just have to make up some excuse about being called away before I could present you to him. Bear in mind, Johanna, that this night must never be spoken of again, for if word of it reaches Stephen…" John picked up the goblet of wine and stared gloomily into its depths. He took a long draft and set it down carefully. "I shall visit a notary to draw up a testament, but I'm afraid that's all I can accomplish on this visit to Oxeneford."

"Yes, Father. I understand." Although Janna was sorry the matter of her inheritance could not be dealt with just yet, it was canceled out by her enormous relief that the matter of her marriage could not be dealt with either.

Chapter 4

When Janna and her father returned to Winchestre, bad news awaited them. A winter storm had sunk the boat carrying a load of stone needed for the rebuilding of the new house. It seemed they would have to spend the holy days of Christ's birth with the bishop at Wolvesey after all.

Perhaps because of John's conscience over the defeat of the king's plans for the empress – or more likely, because he feared the wily bishop would take one look at his daughter and suspect the truth if he came home – he immediately looked for lodgings close to where his manor was being rebuilt. The family was removed there without delay, on the excuse that closer supervision was needed.

With all the fuss and bother that the move entailed, Janna escaped too much attention. She was grateful not to have to answer questions as she washed and washed her hair, until it gradually lightened to its true color. She and her father had pretended innocence when a report came of the king's fury over the empress's escape, seemingly from under the noses of his soldiers who, despite Matilda being spied by several bystanders out in the streets, had been unable to capture her. A later report, from someone claiming to be an eyewitness, said that the empress and her small party had escaped through a window in the tower. They'd let themselves down on a rope and, clad in white cloaks, had walked across the frozen river. It seemed that the empress had found men and horses waiting at Abingdon to speed her way to safety. The latest report, passed on by one of John's stewards, was that the empress was now safe with her brother at his castle in Devizes, and overjoyed to be reunited with her oldest son, Henry, who had accompanied the Earl of Gloucestre on his passage back to England.

This news John shared with Janna, but not the rest of his family, while once again issuing a warning. "You must tell *no-one*," he said. "It is impossible to be sure where anyone's loyalty lies in these difficult days, and I will not put you in further danger – or jeopardize my own position – if news of your recent activities leaks out. Say nothing even to my wife, or Giles and the girls."

Mention of Blanche dampened Janna's joy at the confirmation of the empress's safe escape from Stephen's blockade. Perhaps her father read this in her expression, for he sought to reassure her.

"You need have no fear, Johanna. I have given much thought to what has occurred, and I have now charged my wife to keep you safe or else find her own inheritance forfeit. I hope you'll find my family more welcoming as a result. Indeed, I hope that in time you will think of my family as your own."

While she believed that there was more chance of hell freezing over, Janna took some comfort from her father's words. Nevertheless, she recognized that there were other, more subtle, tricks that Blanche might play; she must not allow herself to be lulled into a false sense of security.

As they gradually settled into their new quarters, and joyfully celebrated the birth of the Christ child and the gift giving of the new year, Janna's fears began to subside. Blanche kept her and her half-sisters busy with spinning and stitching when it was too bitter to venture out. A study of Latin also kept her occupied, her father having decided that it might benefit all of his children to have some knowledge of the language of the church. But there were also numerous festivities to enjoy, parties and games, although Janna was forced to acknowledge that her siblings' ability to play music and their skill at board games far outstripped her own. Nevertheless, she was learning the duties, manners and skills of a noblewoman – and learning them fast.

On several occasions, Janna accompanied her father on visits to the stone manor that was being constructed over the ruins of the old house. Further building would not be possible until the new shipload of stone arrived, but there was still much other work to be done and many decisions to be made. To Janna's delight, her father consulted her on everything, for, as he reminded her, this would be her home in time to come.

She cherished this time alone with him, but even more, she delighted in the chance to escape from the close confines of his family. She'd quickly learned that it was not considered desirable for a young woman to walk out on her own, so the time spent outside the house with her father was her only relief. And she used it well to order things as she wished, most particularly in the garden, for in that rested her hopes for the future. There was little to do during the winter months, but Janna approved the design of the raised beds where, in spring and on her instructions, medicinal and kitchen herbs as well as flowers, vegetables and fruit trees would be planted.

Godric was constantly in Janna's thoughts, but she knew she must be patient and wait until the manor house was completed and furnished before she spoke to her father regarding her mother's death and the manner of her dying, and requested him to act on it. It would mean a journey back to her old home, and to Godric, but there was no telling how long they would be gone and Janna was sure her father would want everything to be in place here in Winchestre before he undertook such a mission. More than anything, she hoped that Blanche would grow tired of waiting and return to Normandy, as she'd threatened to do on more than one occasion.

But it seemed the woman preferred to stay in order to keep an eye both on her husband and her newly acquired stepdaughter. As the weather warmed into spring and John encouraged his wife to return to their family home, Blanche found any number of excuses to delay. Worse, so far as Janna was concerned, she spent her time casting doubts on the steward's management of the estates in England, while in the same breath extolling Giles's superior expertise and his greater authority as his father's only son. Janna wondered if Blanche's words would erode John's resolve, just as drops of water could wear a hole in stone, yet she could find nothing to say in her own defense that her father did not already know.

This was only one of the concerns that kept her occupied, as green shoots began to poke through the dark earth and bare branches drew on soft mantles of spring green. Her plan for the future was taking shape along with the new garden, a plan that she had no intention of sharing with anyone, least of all a husband chosen for her by her father. Somehow she must convince him she had no need of a husband, at least not yet. After all, she could read, write and reckon more skillfully than Giles, and she was well able to ensure that the steward handled her father's affairs with honesty. Nor did she need anyone's help to put her future plan into action. She already had the knowledge of herbs and the healing skills she'd learned from her mother and from others she had met along her quest to find her father, and soon she would have the premises to fulfill her dream of establishing a hospitium for those in need of her knowledge.

Her unfinished quest also nagged at Janna. She needed to convince her father to return to her old home in order to prosecute the man responsible for her mother's death. And, if her mother's body had not been taken to Ambresberie, she and her father must also persuade the abbess of Wiltune to rebury her mother in consecrated ground, and give her the full rites of a funeral mass.

Even more important to Janna was the need to bring her father and Godric together and convince her father of Godric's true worth. Her father had married for love – how could he deny his daughter the same chance of happiness? But here Janna's imagination always faltered, for her future was so precarious; seemingly bright but potentially terrifying. She could not face the prospect of what she most desired being snatched from her grasp, but knew that if her father insisted she marry another she would have no choice but to obey his command – or run away to be with Godric. And if she did, she would take Godric to ruin with her.

With her mind preoccupied with the future, Janna forgot to take precautions in the present. So the accusation, when it came, took her completely by surprise. The family was assembling for dinner when Blanche strode in and stood, arms akimbo, facing them.

"My brooch has been taken," she shrilled, piercing Janna with an accusing eye before turning to her husband. "You gave it to me when we were wed, do you remember? Gold and pearls in a-a love knot." She choked up, genuinely upset by the loss.

"You must have mislaid it, Blanche. Have your maid look for it more closely."

"We have already hunted everywhere, both of us, but it has gone!" Blanche turned to face Janna once more. "Where is it?" she demanded. "What have you done with it?"

"I don't know where it is!" Caught unawares, it took Janna a few moments to realize how unconvincing she sounded. By then her father had already jumped to her defense.

"That's a monstrous accusation, wife. I am sure Johanna has no knowledge of the whereabouts of your brooch."

"Then ask her to show us the contents of her purse. Let us see just how innocent she is."

Janna looked to her father for direction. To her dismay, he gave a curt nod. With unwilling fingers she untied the drawstring of the small purse dangling from her waist. She withdrew a small lacy kerchief, several silver coins, and Godric's letter, now crumpled and tattered after being read and reread so many times. Finally, reluctantly, she withdrew a brooch.

"Aha!" Blanche pounced on it. She held it up for a closer inspection and then dropped it as quickly as if it had seared her hand. Janna could understand why: its inscription, *amor vincit omnia*, which Janna knew meant "love conquers all", signified her father's devotion to her mother. While Blanche could not have known its provenance, she must have guessed it easily enough. Looking at her pale face and shaking hands, Janna found it in her heart to pity this woman who had always been second best in her father's affections.

But finding the love token served only to inflame Blanche's anger. "If my brooch is not on her person, then it must be among her belongings," she insisted. "We must go straight away to search them before she has time to remove anything. I insist you come with me, husband."

Janna wanted to tell Blanche she was wasting her time, that she was showing herself as a vindictive fool, but she knew very well that the woman would not rest until a search had been made. She was already dragging John out of the room. Their children followed after them and Janna hurried behind, sickened at the thought of Blanche prying into her private possessions. But she wanted to be there, to witness Blanche's face when her search proved futile and she was forced to apologize.

Blanche flung open the lid of the small coffer that held Janna's possessions and began to throw them out onto the straw-covered floor, one by one, with little regard for cleanliness or care. Janna watched, seething with a fury that turned instantly to alarm when, with a cry, Blanche's fingers closed over something at the very bottom.

She held it aloft, brandishing it just inches from her husband's nose. "See! I told you that little she-wolf had stolen my brooch!"

"But…" Janna could find nothing to say, nothing to explain how the brooch had got into her chest. Unless Blanche had put it there herself? She had seemed genuinely upset by its loss, but her insistence on looking first in Janna's purse might only have been a ruse to show her own innocence.

By now Blanche was on her feet again. She thrust her face into Janna's, so close Janna could smell her clove-scented breath. "You're nothing but a common thief," she sneered, and turned to her husband. "She has to go, John. We are not safe while she stays here with us. First she tried to poison us, and now it seems that our possessions are hers for the taking."

"You're making a mistake!" Janna's voice shook with the effort of hiding how upset she was. "I know nothing about this, Papa, on my life I swear it!"

"Then how did the brooch come to be among your possessions?" John's voice was as hard and cold as iron.

"I don't know! I certainly didn't put it there." Janna looked from one face to another, desperate for some signs of belief and support. Richildis and Giles both wore spiteful smiles, although Rosy seemed merely perplexed. Blanche's face was red and swollen with anger. And her father? Janna's heart sank as she read his stern, unforgiving countenance. Even if she had the courage to accuse the true culprit, Janna knew he would not believe her, not without proof. To be branded a thief stung worse than a hive full of bees, yet Janna knew she was powerless to change John's mind. He had seen the evidence. He was convinced. And her future now hung in the balance.

Janna could think of no way out of this coil, none at all. Worse, with this misunderstanding between them, she realized she had very little hope of persuading her father to accompany her back to her old home. Which meant her mother's murder would go unavenged, for even if she made her own way there, her situation now would be no different from how it was before. She was powerless to act without her father behind her. Despair overwhelmed her.

Unless she could find something to prove to her father that she was innocent of this charge? Once she was alone, Janna resolved to look more carefully at the contents of her chest, which were now scattered over the rushes. Maybe the thief had dropped something, left some telltale trace of her passing, something Janna could use as evidence of her own innocence.

She became aware of their silence. They stood around her like a circle of crows, waiting for...what? A confession? It would be a black day in hell before they got one, Janna thought grimly. "I am innocent," she said firmly, even while knowing it was useless to say so.

"A poor girl, brought up with nothing. It's not hard to see why you might be tempted by a precious object," Blanche said. Janna noticed that she no longer seemed quite so pleased to have found her brooch. Instead of pinning it to her gown, she had dropped it into her purse and tightened the string with a vicious tug. What had been treasured had now been shown for what it truly was: a token gesture denoting a loveless marriage. Even though she hadn't examined Blanche's brooch, Janna would have staked her life on there being no loving message inscribed on it. Another wave of pity for Blanche swept over her, surprising her, even while she warned herself to guard against it. The woman was a formidable adversary, with just one thought in her mind: to get rid of Janna and the threat she posed to her own and her family's inheritance.

"I have a precious object of my own. I don't need yours." Even as she said the words, Janna understood how spiteful and vindictive she sounded.

"Enough of this." John sounded weary to death. "Johanna, we shall leave you to repack your belongings and contemplate your –

your actions. The rest of you, come away with me." He put a firm hand on his wife's arm and drew her out of the room. To Janna's relief, the two girls and Giles went with him.

Once she was sure she was alone, she dropped down onto her knees in front of her box, but she could not hold back her tears. It seemed that no matter how hard she tried to become a part of this family, they rejected her, and worse, took steps to drive her away. She was tired of trying to fit in, tired of leading a life where she was no longer free to make her own decisions and control her own destiny. A picture of Hugh's manor farm flashed into her mind, and she was seized with an urgent desire to go back there; go back to a time when he had offered her sanctuary, and even his love. But he was wed now, and besides, her heart belonged to another. It was cold comfort to know that, even if she traveled back to her home on her own and saw Godric again, there could be no future for them unless he had his liege lord's permission to marry her – and that would not come without the blessing of her own father.

Missing Godric, longing for his love and support at this darkest of times, made Janna's tears fall faster. She ached with loneliness and despair; the futility of her situation, and even of her existence, almost overwhelmed her. She wept for all that might have been, when she was younger and all things seemed possible. And she wept for the family that might have been hers had they not turned so resolutely against her.

Finally she became aware that she was cold and hungry, and as her tears ceased and the reality of the present intruded once more, she rose to her feet. With a tired sigh, and mindful of her idea that the real thief might have dropped something, might have betrayed her presence in the room without realizing it, she began to gather up her possessions.

Blanche. She had tried to poison her stepdaughter with a fruit pastry, but that had failed. She would not dare try again in the face of John's warning, for fear of endangering the family's inheritance, but Janna was sure that she would not stop trying to discredit her. She'd already succeeded only too well, Janna thought drearily, as she carefully restored her possessions to the chest, finishing with the beautiful gown that she had managed to save from the ruins in Oxeneford, and the fur mantle and veil that Gervase had been dispatched to recover. Without much hope, she began to search the room she shared with Richildis and Rosy. Traces of them were everywhere: a discarded comb carved from ivory; Rosy's rag baby that she loved and cherished; a crumpled kerchief. There was nothing to mark Blanche's presence in the room.

Suddenly desperate to escape the close confines of the house, Janna hurried outside and into the small garden behind their lodgings. Uncoiling tendrils of green thrust toward the light of a pale sun; primroses poked gilded faces through the grass; the heady scent of spring was in the air. On the thought that she might find plants that would be of use in her own garden, Janna crouched to inspect them more carefully. Absorbed in her task, and grateful for the distraction, she finally became aware that she was not alone. Her father stood behind her. She wasn't sure how long he'd been there, watching her, but as he saw that he was noticed, he cleared his throat and held out his hand to help her rise.

"Daughter, we need to talk," he said.

It seemed to Janna that there was little left for her to say. She'd already told her father, and his family, that she knew nothing about the theft of the brooch. Now it was up to her father to tell her whether or not he believed in her. She waited for him to continue, but he stayed silent. So did she. This was the second time she'd been accused of something she hadn't done, and she would not argue her innocence all over again.

Her father was the first to give in. "Perhaps we should go inside where it's warmer."

"I would rather stay outside, Papa." At least here their conversation couldn't be overheard.

Her father cupped his hand under her elbow and propelled her forward to walk with him. "We cannot go on like this," he began. "Do you have anything to say about what's happened?"

"Only that you must look for someone else, someone wanting to cause trouble for me, for it was not I who took that brooch. Nor did I hide it among my belongings." Janna lengthened her stride to match her father's, glad to have the chance to walk, for her stomach was fluttery with nerves. "If I had taken it, I certainly would not have been so stupid as to hide it in such an obvious place." She glanced at her father, praying to find in his expression the love and trust she craved.

He sighed. "I would like to believe you, for I have seen with my own eyes your courage and your generosity of spirit." He paused. "And your intelligence. If you were given to a life of crime, I suspect you would be far more successful at it than appears to be the case in this regard."

It was a backhanded compliment, and Janna wasn't quite sure how to react, other than to point her father's suspicions in a different direction.

"I have seen how much your family resents me. If they cannot get rid of me in one way, there are other ways to discredit me in your eyes."

"No, Johanna, you must not think that. My wife is very upset by what's happened. So is Richildis. She feels things so deeply. As for Giles..." John sighed. "I cannot believe the boy would steal something from his mother or that he would interfere with your possessions in that manner. No, I think we must look to one of the servants for the answer, and that is what I intend to do next. I shall interrogate them to see if any can shed light on what's happened."

Janna didn't like to tell him how very unlikely it was that a servant had stolen Blanche's brooch and then stashed it in a place to which there was no ready access in the future. But there was a small hope that someone among the servants might have seen something untoward, something pointing to the real culprit, and would speak of it.

"I don't know what else I can do if we can't resolve this affair."

"You could send your family back to Normandy." Janna didn't see why she should be either the problem or its solution.

"I shall suggest it again to Blanche. The weather is more clement now." John released his hold on Janna, and studied her intently. She suspected that, while he was reluctant to believe she'd taken Blanche's brooch, he was also not entirely convinced of her innocence. The thought brought a deep sadness, but there was nothing left to say on her own behalf. After what had happened they could not continue as before, she understood that well enough. But pride, and the fact that she had nowhere else to go, kept her from offering to move out of their lodgings.

"Can you keep out of my wife's way in the meantime? Can you keep peace between you?"

Janna wanted to protest that he would do better to extract the promise from the rest of his family, for they were the ones causing the problems – but perhaps he would do that even without her prompting. "I shall do my best," she agreed, knowing she could promise no more than that.

Seemingly satisfied, her father nodded. "I shall speak to the servants," he said abruptly, and strode off toward the house.

Left alone in the garden, Janna realized she was shaking with nerves. Her eyes burned with tears; angrily, she dashed them away. A gate in the wall caught her eye and desperation drove her to it. She didn't have to put up with this. She could just run away, go back to the tavern and live an independent life once more.

She was at the gate, testing to see if it was unlocked, before common sense overcame desire. She was not in the wrong, but if she left it would confirm everyone's suspicions about her. Everyone but the real thief, who would know then that she had succeeded in discrediting Janna.

No! She would not give up, nor would she give in. She must stay until, somehow, she could clear her name. But there was no one around to see her, and the urge to escape was strong. Tempted, Janna tried the latch; the gate swung open. The laneway spread before her, enticing her to freedom. It was a siren song Janna could not resist. Quickly, before anyone came out to stop her, she slipped through the gate and hurried on down the lane. She had no clear idea of where she was headed, she just knew she had to get out for a while, get away from everyone until she could calm down and think more carefully about her future.

She walked on, relishing being alone, although the laneway was crowded with people making the most of the spring sunshine. The crowd thickened as she approached the high street. Without making a conscious decision, she found her steps taking her to the Bell and Bush and to Sybil Taverner, who had taken her in when she most needed a home and employment, and who had no illusions about the world and the people who inhabited it. She could do with a dash of Sybil's common sense right now. Her steps quickened with the anticipated pleasure of seeing Sybil again.

She was pleased to note how crowded the tavern was when she arrived. While she'd been employed there, a series of problems had seen Sybil deserted by her customers, and it had taken strategy and hard work to entice them back. As she looked around for Sybil, Mary rushed past, balancing several laden trenchers in her arms. Janna was delighted to see her; it seemed her replacement had worked out well. There was no sign of the taverner, and Janna debated going through into the yard to find her. Giving in to a sudden whim, she sat down instead and waited for Mary to serve her. Was Sybil still brewing ale to Janna's mother's recipe? Her mouth watered at the thought of it;

she remembered how thirsty and hungry she was, as well as being in great need of reassurance.

"My lady?" It was clear Mary didn't recognize her. She stood waiting to hear Janna's order, but then, as Janna began to speak, her face split in a delighted grin. "Is it really you?"

Smiling, Janna nodded. Mary clapped her hands in delight. "Let me fetch Sybil Taverner," she cried. "I know she'll want to see you. And my lady...I thank you every day for finding me a place here! I swear to you, you saved my life!" And she hurried off before Janna had a chance to place her order.

Soon enough Sybil emerged, and after exchanging all their news, Janna found herself pouring out her woes in between mouthfuls of ale and stew that Sybil had insisted on providing free of charge.

"They sound like a real nest of vipers," Sybil commented, when Janna finally came to the end of her recital. Janna shrugged and took a swallow of ale, relishing its taste and the memories of her mother it evoked. How she wished her mother was still alive to advise her now. Yet how differently her life would have turned out if her mother hadn't died in the way she did.

"Can you find out who is behind this trouble and expose the culprit?" Sybil glanced sideways at Janna. "You were clever enough to work out who was behind my problems here at the tavern. I'm sure you can do the same to save your own skin!"

"I know who it is," Janna said fiercely. "My stepmother! But proving it is something else again, for my father will hear nothing against her. And I fear what that she-devil will think of next to set my father against me."

Sybil reached for her own mug of ale, frowning as she mulled over Janna's words. Then she brightened and snapped her fingers to summon the potboy, who was busy clearing trenchers and mugs from a nearby table. "There's an old friend of yours back in town," she told Janna, after she'd quickly muttered directions to the lad and bid him make haste. "He's been looking for you, but he told me your father's new home is not yet finished, while his contact at the bishop's palace thinks that the family might have returned to Normandy."

"Who is he?" Janna's heart leaped with joy at the thought that Godric might have come to town.

But Sybil just smiled. "You'll see soon enough," she said. "Maybe he can advise us. But in the meantime, tell me how it is to live like a lady!"

Janna laughed. It had taken a little while to persuade Sybil not to call her "my lady." She was pleased that the taverner had reverted to their old friendly footing. She was in the middle of bewailing the fact that her father found it necessary to find a husband for her when a huge dog pounced on her, almost pushing her off the stool.

"Brutus!" She put her arms around the animal and gave him a big hug, smothering a smile in his rough fur as she recalled how frightening he could be to anyone he regarded as a foe. But she had long ago won his affection, and he gave her a great slobbering lick to confirm it. "Ugh!" She pushed him away and wiped her face on her sleeve, then turned her attention to the dog's owner.

"Ulf!" She jumped up to give him a hug, but he took a step away from her. He began to bow, noticed her frown, and opened his arms wide instead. "I am so glad to see you!" She walked into his embrace. If not Godric, Ulf was the person she most wanted beside her now. They had been through so much together, and he had proved himself a loyal and entertaining companion on more than one occasion.

After the flurry of greetings and exchange of news, at Sybil's urging, Janna once more recited the problems she was having with her family, being careful to omit any mention of her visit to Oxeneford and what had transpired there.

Ulf was thoughtful when she finally fell silent. He scratched his chin, stubbly with grey whiskers, and raised the brimming mug that Mary had set down in front of him. "It's all of them against you, lass," he mused. "It seems even your father is not wholly on your side. So I ask myself: if we can't appeal to their better natures – "

"That won't work, they don't have any," Janna interposed.

Ulf nodded and continued, "How can we scare them into treating you with proper courtesy and consideration?"

"Scare them?" Janna laughed at the very notion.

"There's more than one way to call their bluff." Ulf bent down and grabbed his heavy pack. He heaved it up onto the table in front of him and began to root around inside. Janna watched, still amused, as first a roll of parchment was dropped on the table, followed by several fat parcels wrapped in linen and then a couple of small boxes. Ulf was a relic seller, and judging by the girth of his pack, he had a bumper haul of bits and pieces to sell to those who wanted the comfort of knowing that a saint was on their side. She waited to find out what was on Ulf's mind.

Sybil watched in some bemusement. She'd not come across Ulf's treasures before, but Janna was willing to wager that she would not be conned into making an offer for any of them either.

"Aha!" Ulf withdrew a shiny gold box, far grander than anything else that had already landed on the table.

"What's that?" Sybil asked, before Janna had a chance to open her mouth.

"The small toe from the right foot of St Swithun, Winchestre's very own patron saint," Ulf said proudly.

Janna wondered if she could believe in this relic at least. Certainly it was housed in far grander style than anything she'd ever seen before.

"And you want it for…?" Sybil asked cautiously.

"Janna's stepmother." Ulf turned to her. "What do you think? If you can make sure she sees me, I guarantee she'll part with many coins for this. And once she has – "

"Made a donation?" Janna interrupted. Ulf grinned at her. This was a long-standing jest between them.

"Once she has expressed her gratitude in a material way, then – and only then – will I tell her the story of how I came by this sacred relic."

"What story?"

Ulf settled himself more comfortably on his stool and stretched out his legs. "The relic once belonged to a poor merchant who lived a good life but who had encountered much misfortune along the way," he began. "His wife died giving birth to their first child, and the child died too, much to the merchant's grief. His troubles were made worse when he was ambushed and robbed, and then his stall caught fire and all his goods were burned to ash. Indeed, he was at his wits' end. All he had to show for his life's work was a precious gem set on a chain that once had belonged to his wife. It was of no practical use to him, but it was a reminder of her, and of happier days, and so he kept it until the time came when he knew that he must either sell it or starve."

Ulf paused to take a deep draught of ale. Janna knew that he delighted in spinning out his stories and so she waited, wondering where all this was leading and if there was any point to it.

Sybil was not quite so kind. "What's this to do with Janna and her problems?" she snapped impatiently.

Ulf set down his mug and wiped his mouth. "The merchant didn't want to sell the necklace," he said, ignoring Sybil's protest. "But then he met a relic seller, who offered him the toe of St Swithun in return for it. He was so sure his luck would change with the saint on his side that he happily agreed to the swap. And so it went. His luck did change. He found employment with an elderly jeweler and became so invaluable to him that he inherited the business on the jeweler's death, the man having no close kin to lay claim to it. And the merchant prospered. He opened a larger shop, and began to travel overseas to all the big fairs in Europe. In fact, he was on his way home from one such when the ship foundered and sank, taking all of the merchant's goods down with it. But the merchant managed to survive.

He grabbed a floating plank and clung to it, until eventually he found his way to safety. He was ruined, but he still had the saint's toe in his purse, along with a few coins."

"Get on with it," Sybil muttered.

Ulf grinned, took another long swallow of ale, and carefully replaced his mug. "Although the merchant was ruined he was not dismayed, for he still had the blessing of the saint. But by now he had a high position in the town and a reputation to maintain, and so he began to take short cuts, ordering goods and promising payment when he knew that his coffers were empty. He hoped to trade his way out of trouble, but word got around that he wasn't paying his bills, and even that he was selling stolen goods, although he swore on the saint's relic that it was not so. But he lost those customers who previously had given him a good income and guaranteed his reputation. Finally he was arrested and sent to trial for his misdeeds. So far as I know, he still rots in prison somewhere."

Janna shuddered, but Sybil had reached the end of her patience. "What's the point of this? It's Janna's problems we're interested in now."

"I watched his arrest. As the guards came for him, he reached into his purse, pulled out this sacred object, and flung it at me. 'Take it,' he shouted. 'It will bring you good luck, but only if you are an honest man.'"

Janna smothered a smile. Ulf, honest? She didn't believe a word of it, but was sure Ulf was leading somewhere with his story. Sybil had no such illusions. She leaned forward, clicking her tongue in angry frustration. "What has this gibble-gabble to do with Janna?"

"Everything. I went to visit the merchant where he was being held captive. I was curious to find out what he meant, although I was a little nervous that he might ask for the relic's return. But he seemed to think it was cursed, that he had cursed his luck when he had used it to do wrong. He told me the whole story, just as I have told you –

and just as I shall tell your stepmother, but only after she's given me a donation for it."

"That the relic is cursed?"

"That the relic is cursed if she does wrong while it's in her possession." Ulf sat back with a satisfied smile, and drank down the rest of his ale.

"Brilliant!" Janna clapped her hands in admiration.

"Brilliant." Ulf bobbed his head in mock humility.

Sybil laughed. "Brilliant," she agreed, and beckoned Mary over to refill their mugs.

After much discussion, their plan was decided. "You must not know me," Ulf reminded Janna. "It'll make your stepmother suspicious if she sees you hab-nabbing with the likes of me. Just bring her down the high street tomorrow after dinner, and express an interest in seeing what I have in my pack, should she insist on moving on. You can leave the rest to me."

"I shall," Janna promised, adding with a twinkle, "and I hope her donation is a large one, Ulf."

"The larger it is, the more anxious she will be to heed my warning. Fear not, Janna. I trust you'll lead a trouble-free life after this."

"It seems you are always coming to my rescue. How can I ever thank you enough?" Janna reached out and gave the relic seller a hug.

"No thanks are necessary. Just have your stepmother out on the street tomorrow after dinner – or failing that, on the following day."

Getting back into the family's lodgings without detection exercised all Janna's ingenuity, but getting her stepmother to agree to go out into the town proved even more difficult. "If I need anything, I summon traders to come to me," Blanche said haughtily.

"But it's exciting to be out in the street, seeing the sights," Janna urged, with a quick glance at Rosy. She'd ensured the child was present, knowing Rosy's curiosity would make her add her voice to Janna's plea. "There are street stalls and peddlers selling everything from spring vegetables and spices to gloves and candles, and even wares from across the sea."

"How do you know?"

"I remember it from before," Janna said, without thinking.

"I believe you were a common serving wench in a tavern?" Blanche looked down her nose.

"Did you work in a tavern, Johanna?" Rosy's eyes were round with wonder.

"Yes, I did. I needed to earn my keep." Janna kept her voice carefully neutral as she continued. "I need a new gown. I thought to visit the cloth makers to choose something I like." As she glimpsed Blanche's frown of disapproval, she added hastily, "If you prefer, I can make it up myself."

There was a long silence. Then Blanche said frostily, "We do not go out into the town like beggars. Cloth makers bring a selection of their wares for us to choose, and the garment is made up to specification. That's how we do things in this household, Johanna."

Fortunately, Janna's words had worked their magic on Rosy. "Please can't we go out, Maman?" she begged. "It would be so exciting just to go for a walk down the high street. I'm tired of staying here day after day doing the same old things."

"Rosy can come with me if you don't wish to go," Janna said quickly, sure that Blanche would consider her far too disreputable an influence on her daughter. She held her breath until, at last, and with bad grace, Blanche agreed to accompany them, along with Richildis and Giles.

*

The one thing the conspirators hadn't planned for was Brutus. As soon as he saw Janna in the street, he raced forward and jumped up, putting his paws on her shoulders and licking her face.

"Down, Br – bad dog!" Janna pushed him away, hating having to use such a scolding voice. "You have a very boisterous hound," she said grandly, giving Brutus a surreptitious pat to make up for scolding him.

"I do beg your pardon, my lady." Ulf swept them all an elaborate bow. "'Tis astonishing! I have never seen him so friendly before. You must have a winning way with animals, my lady."

Janna hid a smile. "He is a handsome hound, I grant you. And a good watchdog, I warrant."

"Not if he greets everyone like that," Blanche muttered.

At once, Ulf switched his attention to her, and bowed again. "I see you have a keen eye and discerning judgment, my lady." As he spoke, he held out a hand to Rosy, with a coin nestled in his palm.

She hesitated, not quite sure what she was supposed to do. Giles shoved forward, about to snatch the coin, but with a smile, Ulf rubbed his hands together and displayed them again. The coin had disappeared. As Rosy stared at him, he reached forward and produced the coin from behind her ear. She laughed with pleasure and clapped her hands. "Show me how you do that!" she squealed.

But Ulf was now busy unfastening his pack, once more facing Blanche. "I can see that you're not wanting in good fortune, my lady, but – " he produced a small square box and held it up, " – you may well wish for a saint's protection to guard you from harm and illness."

Alarmed, Janna wondered what had happened to the gold box and its contents. This wasn't what they'd discussed at all.

Blanche pushed Ulf out of her way with an impatient hand. She was about to stride on when Rosy tugged on her mother's sleeve, stopping her progress. "Please, Maman, let us see what's in the box," she pleaded. Janna sent up a silent prayer of thanks for Rosy's intervention.

But Ulf had put the box away. He stared intently at Blanche and then, in a low voice, muttered, "Not for you the comforts of the common folk, not for someone of your status, my lady, I see that now. But I do have in my possession something I never thought to see in my lifetime, the most costly relic I have ever possessed."

Blanche leaned closer, intrigued in spite of herself.

Ulf shook his head. "No," he said. "What was I thinking? It has brought me so much good fortune I cannot bear to part with it."

Aghast, Janna watched as he began to tie up his pack.

"Maman!" Rosy wailed.

Blanche hesitated. "Show me what you have in there, peddler," she commanded, while beside her, Rosy jigged up and down with excitement.

It all went just as Janna had hoped, and by the end of it Blanche was the proud – if somewhat chastened – owner of the toe of St Swithun, while Ulf had scored coins enough to keep him in comfort for quite some time to come. Janna lingered to whisper her thanks, and he gave her a wink and sauntered on, summoning Brutus to his side with a whistle.

Rosy was still staring after them when Janna caught up with the party. "I wish I had a dog like that," she said wistfully. "You liked him too, didn't you, Johanna?"

Blanche sniffed. "Nasty, dirty brute."

"Well, I liked him," Rosy said firmly, and took hold of Janna's hand as they continued to walk along.

Chapter 5

Thanks to Ulf and the toe of St Swithun, the next months did indeed pass without incident. In fact, Janna was almost inclined to believe that the saint's influence extended to all areas of their lives, for with the arrival of a new load of building stone, the house was soon almost ready for them to move in, while the garden bloomed and burgeoned in a most satisfactory way. Her father's family, if not exactly taking her to their bosom, now appeared to tolerate her, and the days passed happily enough, and uneventfully. Janna hoped that Blanche would soon remove her family to Normandy, but it seemed she preferred to keep an eye both on her husband and her family's inheritance, for she continued to find excuses to delay their departure. Meanwhile, the poisoned pastry and the missing brooch were never referred to; it was almost as if they'd never happened. What pleased Janna most was her growing closeness and ease with her father. It was almost time to trust him with the secret of her mother's death and ask for his help in bringing the murderer to justice.

It was her father who, innocently and with all good intentions, brought the influence of St Swithun to an end. Once more he bade them wait on after dinner, for there was something he wished to say to all of them.

"The time has come for me to settle my daughter's future," he told them, when the servants had cleared the table and they were alone.

"Which daughter?" Blanche asked, while Richildis sat straighter and patted her hair into place.

"Johanna." John turned to Richildis. "Your future is already secure, my dear." He frowned as his gaze moved from her pale face to her slim body and fragile wrists. "She's still not eating enough," he told his wife, before switching his attention back to Janna.

"I've been watching you these past months," he told her, "and I've been impressed by what I've seen. I have decided to let my steward continue to manage my estates here in England until such time as you are married and have a husband's protection, after which the responsibility for my affairs will devolve upon you, my dear. No!" He held up a hand to silence Giles, who'd uttered a loud squawk of protest. "Johanna is more educated and therefore more capable than any of you to take on this task. And I shall watch how she goes, for I intend to bequeath to her all my estates here in England, along with their income, when I die."

A shocked silence greeted John's announcement. Even Janna had difficulty taking in what she'd just heard. All her father's estates! She would be wealthy beyond her wildest dreams. More, this showed how highly her father esteemed and loved her. The thought warmed her heart.

"To this end, I shall need to see the king, to secure his agreement that he will honor my intentions at the time of my death. I understand he has moved to Wiltune, so that is where we shall go, Johanna. It is more important than ever that you meet the king, for I need to find a suitable husband for you, someone befitting the granddaughter of the old king and a wealthy heiress in her own right."

Janna watched Richildis's shoulders slump and understood the cause. Her father intended to find someone more noble for Janna than the man to whom Richildis was betrothed. Once again, the cuckoo in their nest would triumph at the family's expense. Her elation ebbed lower as it became clear that her father's intention to elevate her would put Godric even further out of her reach.

And then the full import of her father's words struck home with the force of a thunderbolt: He intended to take her to Wiltune to see the king! And only a mile or two from Wiltune was her family home, and the manor belonging to her mother's murderer. Hugh was there, and Godric. God must have sent her this chance to see her quest through to a successful conclusion. Janna bowed her head in a brief prayer of thanks, even while she was seized with an equal mix of fear and elation at the thought of going back to her old home. But she resolved to say nothing to her father of this, not until they had arrived there, when it would be too late for him to find reason to prevaricate.

She became aware that her father was looking disappointed at her lack of response. "I thank you, Papa, with all my heart." She jumped up and kissed his cheek, hoping that he understood how much she valued his faith in her. She could not say as much in front of his family, for she knew it would look as though she was glorying in her triumph at their expense. "I shall do all in my power to carry out your wishes and make you proud of me," she said, and retreated to her seat.

Blanche was the first to recover from the shock. "No-one will want to wed a deceitful nobody like her."

"She is not a nobody. She is my daughter!" John corrected sharply.

"And before that she was a nobody," Blanche retorted, adding, "and she's a thief! You can't possibly entrust your estates to her, husband. She will beggar us all!"

"We will talk of this in private." John took hold of his wife's arm and marched her out of the solar, leaving Janna to face the rest of his family.

"Maman is right. No-one will want to marry you. You know nothing of what it takes to be a lady of the manor." Richildis smoothed her gown and hair, imitating her mother's gestures. But her face was set in a disconsolate scowl that twisted her pretty features into ugliness. Janna wondered why Richildis disliked her quite so much, but a moment's consideration made her realize that the young girl worshipped her mother and was probably only reflecting the hatred and spite she'd found there. The girl looked pale and ill, and was still far too thin. Her expression bore a marked resemblance to her mother's as she added, "No matter what my father has promised you, you'll never be happy."

How could Richildis say such things? Janna wondered if it was only wishful thinking on her part, or whether she knew something she wasn't telling. A shiver of fear turned her cold as she remembered the poisoned pastry and the stolen brooch. How much further might Blanche go to protect her family now that so much more of their inheritance was under threat? Janna drew a quick breath as another possibility struck her: How far might Richildis herself go in her search for love and approval?

Chilled by the unwelcome thought, Janna warned herself to be on guard until such time as she and her father could leave for Wiltune. Although she feared what she might find there, she hoped they could depart soon, before anything else could happen to endanger either her life or her future.

*

It seemed to Janna that, having announced his intentions, her father now found endless reasons to delay their departure. It was time to move into the new house and her father wanted to oversee their move. Then a farmhouse on one of the estates was burned to the ground following a dispute. Despite her entreaties to accompany him, John went to sort matters out, taking only his steward with him. This mission kept him away for several days, leaving Janna feeling abandoned and frightened.

She could almost feel the hate emanating from the family in her father's absence. Several other things went missing, for which she was blamed. Each time she heard the accusation, she was the first to search her belongings. But the thief, whoever it was, had become more cunning. This time the stolen property was not found, leading Janna to wonder if her father had been right all along and that a servant was responsible.

But it was not only things that went missing. Other tricks were played too: Giles found a spider in his shoe, which led to hysterical shrieks and tantrums. If Blanche hadn't been so vicious in her condemnation of Janna, the occasion would have caused her great amusement. She'd had no idea that the lordly Giles was so frightened of spiders!

The next trick was more malicious: Rosy's favorite rag baby, Marie, was found lying out in the garden, headless and muddy and beyond repair. Rosy had been looking everywhere for Marie, and her desolate howls brought all the family running outside. Janna's inspections of the garden were well known, and Blanche was the first to accuse her of destroying Rosy's baby.

"But you know I wouldn't do such a thing, Rosy," Janna protested. She tried to put an arm around the child, who was sobbing bitterly, but with an extra-loud howl Rosy pulled away. "You were with me all the time I was in the garden yesterday. We went indoors together," Janna tried again. "Don't you remember? We walked all around while I told you about the plants I'm growing and what uses they have, and you helped me pick some herbs."

"Rosy should not busy herself with kitchen affairs," Blanche retorted sourly, seemingly unaware or perhaps not caring that she was trampling some of Janna's precious plants underfoot as she paced. "'Tis not seemly for a young lady of her station in life."

Janna sighed. She was tired of defending herself against the family's spite, so she stayed silent.

Blanche stared at her with cold eyes. "You can be sure I'm making a note of everything that's happened in my husband's absence. He will hear all about it on his return."

Janna shrugged and turned away.

"Manners!" Blanche hissed. "You will not turn your back on me, miss."

Even in her despair, Janna felt a quirk of amusement that someone like Blanche could lecture her on manners. Briefly, desperately, she once more contemplated running away. She could leave word for her father that she'd already left for Wiltune and that he would find her there. The realization that he might not come, and instead believe Blanche's accusations and decide to cut her adrift, stayed her footsteps.

"I beg your pardon, my lady," she muttered, keeping her eyes downcast so she would not have to look at that hated, sneering face, or the smug smiles of Richildis and Giles. Only Rosy was worth anything, Janna thought, and even she was being turned against her. She wondered at the sort of spite that could wreck a young girl's treasured possession, and what motivated it.

She stayed out in the garden, pondering the question after the rest of the family moved indoors. That Blanche would poison a pastry in order to remove the threat to her family's inheritance – yes, that was feasible. That Blanche would hide her own brooch in order to accuse Janna of theft – yes, she was prepared to believe that too. That Blanche would risk the wrath of St Swithun by putting a spider in Giles's shoe, knowing how much the insects terrified her beloved son?

Janna shook her head slowly. That was a child's trick. And so was spoiling Rosy's beloved baby Marie. Surely no mother would do such a thing, especially a mother who was so averse to being in a kitchen garden!

Rosy had suffered, and so had Giles. But not Richildis! Janna stayed perfectly still as she contemplated the possibility. The young girl worshipped her mother and trailed her everywhere. Even, perhaps, to the kitchen to supervise the making of the fruit pastries? She remembered now that her father had asked if his daughter had been in the kitchen during their preparation, and the cook's slight confusion until John had indicated which daughter he meant.

Janna would have to visit the bishop's palace to interrogate the cook herself. She was willing to wager every possession she had that Richildis had accompanied her mother to the kitchen, and that she'd also been with her mother when Blanche had visited the apothecary. She would have heard for herself the warning that would have accompanied the lotion: that it was poisonous and for external use only. But suspicion was one thing – what she needed was proof.

Janna's first challenge was to get Blanche's permission to leave the house without raising her suspicions. She could not go alone, for she wanted a witness to her conversation with the cook. Finally, and in front of Blanche, she asked Rosy to accompany her. "I don't want you to think that I was responsible for spoiling Marie, Rosy, so I thought I'd take you into the town to see if we can find you a new rag baby." It was a good excuse for a walk, even though Janna felt uncomfortable not telling Rosy the real reason for it.

"You may not leave the house unaccompanied," Blanche objected. "And I am certainly not coming with you again. I did not enjoy tramping about the streets like a common servant!"

"I don't want a new baby. I only want Marie. And she hasn't even got a head anymore!" Rosy's lower lip trembled. A tear splashed down her cheek. It was fortunate Richildis was out of the room or Janna would have been sorely tempted to drag the girl over to witness the hurt she'd caused.

"I know nothing can take the place of Marie." Janna gave Rosy a quick hug, and this time the child didn't pull away. "But you know, there might be a rag baby sitting in a stall somewhere, with beads for eyes just like your own baby. And I'll wager she's just longing for a little girl to look after her and give her a good home."

"Do you really think so?" Rosy looked up with a wet, hopeful face.

"I know so." Janna hoped she wouldn't be proved a liar. She turned to Blanche. "If it would ease your concern, my lady, perhaps one of the servants could accompany us?"

"Please, Maman? Please, may we go?" Rosy was brightening by the moment, recalling the adventure of their last walk out. "There's something else we can do," she added. "We can look for something nice to give to Richildis. She is soon to celebrate the day of her birth."

"I doubt you'll find anything suitable," said Blanche.

"Oh, Maman, I'm sure there'll be some wonderful things to choose," Rosy pleaded, now quite won over to Janna's proposal.

Blanche nodded a reluctant approval. "Take Gervase with you," she instructed. Janna hid a smile. After all they'd been through together, Gervase would be far more inclined to keep her secrets than spy on her for Blanche – which, no doubt, was her stepmother's intention.

But to Janna's great dismay, they could find no shops or stalls selling rag dolls, although just about everything else seemed to be out on display. A bright glitter stopped their footsteps, and they lingered to admire a small mirror in a goldsmith's shop front. As soon as he noticed their interest, the goldsmith hurried over. "My son brought this back from the fair at Provins." He picked up the mirror and held it out in front of Janna. Curious, she studied her reflection, for she didn't often get the chance to see herself in a proper mirror. Her hair was back to its normal color, but when she tilted her head and looked down her nose even she could see her resemblance to the empress. She quickly dropped her chin, then took the mirror from the goldsmith and gave it to Rosy. "See how beautiful you are," she said.

"I know." Rosy poked her tongue out at her mirror image and shrieked with laughter at the result.

Janna was struck by an idea. "Do you think Richildis might like this? We could give it to her for her birth celebration." Perhaps if

Richildis could see for herself how thin and pale she was, it might spur her to eat more and take better care of herself.

Rosy clapped her hands. "If we give it to Richildis, can I look in it too?"

Janna smiled. "That's for Richildis to decide, not me." And she turned to the shopkeeper to ask the cost.

His answer took her breath away. Even though she now received a generous allowance from her father, it was far more than she could afford. But Rosy was determined that they should have it. "My father, John fitz Henry, shall pay for it," she said grandly, and turned to Janna. "He'll want to give Richildis something pretty, I know he will."

Janna wondered if the gift would be enough to turn Richildis from the dark path she walked. It was certainly an expensive token of her father's regard, she reflected, as the merchant agreed to Rosy's suggestion. But when Rosy held out her hand to take the mirror from him, he said hastily, "This mirror is both costly and extremely fragile. It's far too dangerous for a young girl to carry it through the streets of Winchestre."

"Shall I carry it, my lady?" Gervase stepped forward.

"Yes, thank you, Gervase. Take it back to the house now, if you please, before any harm may come to it." Janna turned to the merchant. "My father, John fitz Henry of Alwarene Street, is presently away, but I shall make sure he sends a man with payment for the mirror on his return."

Janna hoped her father wouldn't object to the arrangement. The mirror was costly, true, but it might be money well spent if the gift reassured Richildis that she was loved and valued, especially if it shamed her into repentance for her past actions.

"Let's keep walking down the street," she said, once they'd left the shop. She was glad she'd found an excuse to send Gervase away, but still didn't want Rosy to know her intentions. She would rather have her believe it was mere chance that took them to Wolvesey Palace. "We may find some stalls selling rag babies further along." She caught a glimpse of the Bell and Bush in the distance and was sorely tempted to call in once more to tell Sybil of recent developments, but she knew Rosy would pass on the news if they did. It wasn't worth all the trouble it would surely cause. If only it was easier to escape the family to be on her own. She sorely needed a friend, particularly someone with the sound common sense of Sybil Taverner.

A ribbon seller stepped into their path, and Janna stopped to admire the pretty display. "Would you like a new ribbon for your hair, Rosy?" she asked, thinking to give the girl something else in lieu of the cloth baby.

"Ooh, yes!" The child seized hold of first one bright braid and then another. "What color shall I choose?" she asked, holding a fistful in front of Janna for her inspection.

"Let's choose a ribbon in every color of the rainbow!" That should lift Rosy's spirits, Janna thought. With a squeal of delight, Rosy pointed out her selection to the peddler, who cut them into lengths and folded them together into a lustrous loop. Well pleased with their purchases, Janna walked on. Rosy jigged beside her, anxiously scanning the streets for any signs of rag babies for sale.

"Look!" She pointed eagerly at a bent old woman who had spread a folded cloth out on the street. Janna's heart lifted in relief as she saw what the woman was pulling out of her pack: rag babies – big and little, fat and thin, with colored beads for eyes. She followed Rosy, who had already rushed to the old woman's side and was eagerly inspecting her wares.

"This is a little bit like Marie, isn't it, Johanna?" She thrust a fat rag baby under Janna's nose.

Janna admired the peddler's industry in turning cast-off rags into a child's treasure. "It's just like Marie," she agreed.

"Can I have it, then? Please?"

"Yes, of course you may." It was wonderful to have sufficient coins to buy gifts, Janna reflected, enjoying Rosy's pleasure as she fussed over her new baby. She just hoped the mirror would bring as much pleasure to Richildis; if not now, then perhaps in the future. The girl could be beautiful if only she took better care of herself. And, if she regained her spirits, her health and her confidence, perhaps she would regret her acts of spite – if indeed she was the one responsible for them.

With the rag baby paid for, Janna set off once more.

"Where are we going now? Can't we go home? I'm tired," Rosy whined.

Janna hesitated, searching for a convincing reason to visit Wolvesey. "We're almost at Wolvesey Palace, and as we're so close, I'd just like to call in and ask the cook for a recipe," she said slowly.

"What for?" Rosy eyed her suspiciously. Janna sighed. There was nothing the cook had made that had tempted her appetite, other than the fruit pastries. And they had been made to Blanche's specification.

"For a special birthday treat for Richildis," she improvised, making a mental note to ask the cook for such a thing while she questioned him.

In fact, he proved surprisingly cooperative, listing several sweetmeats for her consideration and obligingly telling her the ingredients once she'd made her choice. "And can you tell me one last thing," Janna said, wondering how to phrase her question without raising anyone's suspicions. "The fruit pastries? I've a mind to make those as well as the marchpane squares and candied aniseed. Were they made to Dame Blanche's recipe, or did Dame Richildis tell you what to do?"

"No, it were Dame Blanche's instructions I followed. The young lady said never a word about it, just watched what we did."

"I see. Thank you very much." Janna did not dare ask anything further, for Rosy was close beside her and listening, already wriggling with excitement at the prospect of the sweet treats to come. The cook's words confirmed that Richildis had been present, but nothing more. But at least they showed that her suspicion was feasible.

Janna pondered the problem on the way home and was still wondering how to show Richildis's hand in past events when she heard her father's voice out in the yard. She bid Rosy go upstairs to tell her mother they were safely returned, and rushed to meet him. She waited while he gave instructions to the groom and handed over his horse, for she wanted the chance to speak to him before his mind was poisoned against her by Blanche. Yet she hardly knew what to say or where to begin.

And then the thought came to her: It was time to trust her father, to tell him what she knew, what she'd found out, and also tell him about the past and the truth of how her mother had died. She was desperate now to get away from Winchestre and fulfill her destiny at Wiltune. Hopefully, what she had to say would convince her father that they should delay no longer.

Yet doubts assailed her on every side. Her father might not believe her account of her mother's death, nor trust her enough to act on her word alone. Set against those difficulties was the thought that, if she didn't speak out now, she might lose this chance for ever. Especially if her father decided to disinherit her – and worse, accompanied his family back to Normandy without ever seeing the king or visiting Wiltune.

"There's something I have to tell you, Papa," she said, at last prepared to put into words the reason she had tried so hard to find him.

"Then let us go inside to talk."

"No!" The last thing Janna wanted was the chance that the family might overhear what she was about to say. "It's about my mother," she added quickly, knowing that anything to do with Eadgyth would keep him by her side. "I told you that she died after drinking tainted wine. What I haven't told you is that the wine was deliberately poisoned. Nor have I told you who was responsible for her death."

"Are you saying your mother was murdered?" John looked at the grooms, who were busy attending the horses, and at the steward, who stood close by awaiting further instructions. "You may go," he told him. "I'll send for you later." He turned to Janna. "We'll go into the garden," he said. Without waiting for an answer, he took her by the hand and led her out of the yard and into the fragrant enclosure. He gestured to a turf bench studded with daisies, and waited until they were both seated before he said, "Tell me all you know – or suspect."

Clearly and logically, Janna described the dark days following her mother's death; how she had talked to everyone whom she suspected might know anything about what had occurred, and the clues she'd followed that had led her to the man guilty of murder: the lord of the manor, Robert of Babestoche. "I was just the daughter of a poor herb wife. I couldn't say anything to anyone," she continued, addressing her father's back, for he was now pacing about in agitation. "That's why I needed to find you." She proceeded to tell her father the rest of the story: that the priest had refused to bury Eadgyth in consecrated ground and how, incited by both Robert and the priest, the villagers had turned on Janna herself, and burned to the ground the cottage she'd shared with her mother.

"It was only after the fire that my mother's hiding place was uncovered. That was where I found your letter, and brooch and ring," Janna concluded.

By now John's face was red; he was shaking with rage. "By God!" He pounded his fist into his other hand. "I'll make them regret – "

But Janna had seen her chance and was quick to act on it. "Only one man believed in me through all that time. Godric," she said. "He helped me escape on more than one occasion. I owe him my life, Papa.

And I would so like to repay his kindness." *By marrying him, if you'll only agree to it.* She didn't dare put her hopes into words, not yet.

"And who is he, this Godric? Don't tell me he's Robert of Babestoche's son?"

"No, that's Hamo." Seeing her father's confusion, Janna hurried on. "You remember the young boy you met with me at the cathedral when Hugh was wed? Hugh is Hamo's cousin and nephew to Robert of Babestoche."

"And who is Godric?" John tried again.

"He..." Janna's courage almost failed her. "He is Hugh's highly trusted and capable steward," she said, putting the best gloss she could on Godric's status.

"As I understood it, Hugh has no property of his own. He married to acquire it."

"Yes." Janna nodded in agreement. "At present, he and his wife are living at the manor farm Hugh oversees for his aunt, Dame Alice."

"And that's where Godric is?"

"Yes," Janna agreed.

"Then I shall certainly reward him for coming to your aid. A purse of silver will suffice."

Janna's heart sank. Godric might welcome owning such a sum, but she was sure he would resent the reasoning behind it, might even believe that her father was buying him off.

"Have no fear, Johanna. I shall be making enquiries regarding your mother's death while I am in Wiltune with the king. I shall see justice done."

"The nuns at Ambresberie who told me about you, and about my mother, said that they would petition the abbess to have her body taken from unhallowed ground and reburied at their own abbey. But the abbess may not have allowed it."

"Then I shall also see that your mother's mortal remains, and her memory, are honored as they should be," John promised.

At his words, Janna felt some of the burden she had carried for so long lift from her shoulders. Yet there was still more she needed to accomplish, beginning with her father's permission to accompany him on his quest for justice. She knew negotiating that would take all the tact and persuasive powers she possessed.

"There's something else I have to tell you," she began. She took a breath and stood tall, looking him straight in the eye. "Several things have happened while you've been gone. Awful things; things for which your wife blames me."

Not giving her father any time to comment, Janna detailed everything that had happened in his absence. But, as she had no real proof that Richildis was responsible for at least some of the mischief, she did not tell him of her suspicions.

"I assure you on my mother's life that I have no knowledge of any of this," she concluded. "I have no need to steal anyone's possessions. You have been more than generous to me and I have everything I could want. Nor would I do anything to hurt Rosy. She, more than anyone, has made me welcome and shown me friendship. In fact, we've just been shopping in the town, looking for a new cloth baby to replace her Marie."

John nodded thoughtfully. "I shall speak to my wife," he said. "It is only fair that I hear what she has to say before I make any decisions about these incidents. What I do know is that we cannot go on as we are. Somehow or other, the culprit must be found and dealt with. Do you have any thoughts as to who is behind this?"

Janna searched his face for the trust and love she hoped to find there, but his expression was guarded and watchful. With a sinking heart, she realized that he was not entirely convinced by her protestations of innocence. "No," she said.

She watched him walk inside, her imagination already conjuring up the scene that would meet his arrival. Blanche, full of accusations and spite, her venom fueled no doubt by Richildis and Giles. She shivered.

If her father believed them, she was doomed. But if he defended her, she was also doomed. Richildis would have nothing to lose and everything to gain by continuing her campaign of hatred.

All Janna could do was watch and wait. But she greatly feared what might happen next. She pitied Richildis, and also her mother. A belief that they were unloved, and certainly not valued, must fuel their spite, along with a determination to keep all her father's property for themselves. But Janna knew she could not afford to feel pity. The family was united against her; they would do her down, and even do away with her, if they could. She had to protect herself, and if she stayed always in sight of them, they would not be able to accuse her of acting against them. Yet she longed to escape them all. She found their presence suffocating, and yearned for the days when she had been free to go where she pleased and see whom she pleased. Finding her father had caused more problems than she'd ever imagined; nevertheless, she was determined to court his favor, at least until she had carried out her promise to her mother.

After that? She would be reluctant to leave, for she had grown used to living well, to having servants perform the daily chores of life and put food regularly on the table for her. Set against that was her love for Godric – but if she left her father's household there was even less likelihood they could ever be together. She hurriedly thrust that disagreeable conclusion aside. For now, her priority must be to stay alive and somehow protect her reputation.

*

As the family went in to dinner, her father drew her aside. "I've been talking to my wife," he said gravely. "I know she holds you responsible for what's happened in my absence. I wondered if you had anything to add to what you've already told me, Johanna?"

Janna took some comfort from the fact that her father wasn't accusing her outright, that he was prepared to give her the chance to refute Blanche's allegations. She drew him out of sight and hearing of the rest of the family. "That poisoned fruit pastry was no accident. I am quite sure its purpose was to get me out of the way," she said, cutting straight to the heart of the matter. She heard an indrawn breath, but John said nothing. "The stolen brooch – that could have been taken either for someone's gain or to discredit me in your eyes. Probably the latter, for no servant would stash it in such an unlikely hiding place. For the other things that have gone missing?" Janna threw out her hands. A search of Richildis's belongings might turn them up, but she wouldn't mention that possibility just yet. "For gain, perhaps, but coupled with what followed makes me believe that the thefts were all part of the plan to discredit me." Janna paused to gather her thoughts, for now they were coming to the core of her argument. "Putting a spider in Giles's shoe and destroying Rosy's rag baby – those seem more like the tricks of a spiteful child," she continued

John heaved a weary sigh. "I'm inclined to agree with you."

"Please, Papa, please can we leave for Wiltune now, without further delay? Your family hates me, surely you must see that? And I – " Janna's voice shook as she made the admission, " – I fear what tricks may be played on me in the future, especially if you are not here to protect me. I fear there'll be another attempt on my life."

In the silence that followed, Janna thought that she had gone too far. She waited for her father's judgment – there was no more she could say in her own defense, not without proof of her accusations.

"Tell me, if Richildis comes to Wiltune with us, do you think the infirmarian at the abbey will be able to bring her back to health?" John said at last.

Surprised by the change of subject, Janna nodded without thinking. "I am sure Sister Anne would take good care of her," she said, before realizing with horror what her father was suggesting. But she'd gone too far to back out, even though having Richildis accompany them on their journey was something she most desperately wanted to prevent.

"Richildis tries too hard to please my wife," her father mused.

"And I suspect she believes that whatever she can do to harm me will please her mother," Janna added, taking the chance to speak her thoughts out loud.

"No!" John's denial was instinctive. Janna knew she could say no more. She glanced at him, waiting for permission to go in to dinner, but he seemed unaware of her, his brow furrowed in thought. Finally he spoke. "You'll have wondered why I've delayed our departure, but in truth I wanted to keep an eye on my daughter. We celebrate the time of her birth soon, and I wish to be here for that, for I am worried about her. In my absence she seems to have grown weaker. She is betrothed to a young lord in Normandy and is now of an age to be wed, but I fear she may not live long enough ever to find happiness as a wife and mother."

"She's not looking well," Janna agreed, thinking privately that the best thing for Richildis – for her health and her peace of mind – would be to get as far away from her mother as possible, and stay there.

It seemed that she and her father were thinking along the same lines. "I've decided that as soon as we have celebrated the time of her birth, she will come with us to Wiltune to meet the king," he said. "A change of air, a change of surroundings, will be good for her. And you have spoken so highly of Sister Anne that I shall ask her to look after Richildis. Perhaps she can make up some sort of tonic for her."

"I can give her a tonic, if that's what you wish," Janna said sharply, trying to hide the dismay she felt at her father's words.

"Ah, yes." John's gaze softened slightly. "You have your mother's healing touch, I believe. Nevertheless, I know my daughter. And my wife. And I think it would be best if we asked Sister Anne to prepare the medication."

Janna's spirits fell. This was surely proof that her father still did not trust her. In silence, she followed him in to dinner, to find the rest of the family already assembled and waiting for them. She rinsed her hands and sat down, not looking at any of them for fear of what she might read in their faces.

Her father recited the blessing. As the servants brought the food, he announced his intentions regarding Richildis. The girl's triumphant pleasure at the knowledge that she was to accompany her father to meet the king quickly turned into fury when she realized that Janna would also make up the party.

"I don't want to go. Not if she's going too!"

"It's a great honor to be presented to King Stephen, Richildis. You will not have another chance once we return to Normandy."

"I don't care. I'm not going anywhere with that lowborn – "

"Richildis!"

The girl pouted and turned her face from her father.

John cast a look of appeal at Janna. "Tell Richildis about Wiltune and the abbey there."

"You'll like it there, Richildis. Sister Anne is the infirmarian. She's very wise, and she'll give you a tonic that will soon put roses back in your cheeks."

"I don't need a tonic. There's nothing wrong with how I look."

Janna was tempted to tell the girl the truth, tempted also to tell her that Sister Anne wouldn't stand for any of her nonsense. Instead, she said, "You'll also meet Sister Ursel. She taught me how to read and write. You'll like her, Richildis. She's a gentle and loving friend." Which was just what Richildis needed. "When I last saw Sister Ursel, she was writing the life of St Edith and illuminating her manuscript most beautifully. Her work will long be treasured by the abbey."

Unimpressed, Richildis tossed her head. Janna shrugged. She'd done what she could.

"We shall celebrate your birth on the morrow, Richildis," their father said sternly. "Johanna and I will leave the day after that, and you *will* come with us. I want you fully recovered in both health and spirits before we return to Normandy. I shall not see you wed until I am sure you are well again."

Richildis glared at him. Janna waited for another explosion, but it didn't come. Instead, the girl pushed away her trencher and flounced out of the room.

"Look, Papa!" Rosy brandished her rag baby for everyone to see. "Johanna bought a new rag baby for me."

"Wherever did you find such an object?" Blanche looked down her nose at Janna.

"An old lady was selling them," Rosy answered, before Janna could say a word. "She let me choose which one I wanted. She was ever so nice. And we also bought a present for Richildis, but you have to pay for it, Papa. You have to send a man to the goldsmith's shop with the money. Gervase knows where to go."

John raised a questioning eyebrow and waited for an explanation.

"It's a beautiful mirror, but very costly," Janna explained.

"Most unsuitable." Blanche's face scrunched up in displeasure.

"I think it's a wonderful idea," John contradicted his wife. "And I shall give it to Richildis myself."

"And we also went to the bishop's palace."

"Why?" Blanche's voice was sharp with suspicion.

Janna sighed, wishing Rosy wasn't quite so forthcoming with information, and Rosy took the opportunity to answer.

"Johanna wants to make something nice for us to eat for Richildis's birth celebration."

Blanche turned her cold gaze on Janna. "You're being uncommonly kind to my daughter."

"Someone has to be." As soon as she said the words, Janna regretted them. Blanche gave an outraged sniff, but her father reacted differently.

"It is a kind and generous thought, Johanna. And you have our thanks for it."

His words brought the memory of a poisoned pastry into Janna's mind, the pastry with a heart on it. She considered her words carefully before she ventured to speak.

"Richildis has been kind to me in the past. Indeed, was it not her idea to put the heart on the fruit pastry that you ordered to welcome me?"

"How did you know that?" Blanche stared at her. Then, as the implications of Janna's question sank in, she puffed up, scarlet with fury. "What are you insinuating?"

Janna kept silent. So far as she was concerned, Richildis's guilt was now proven. Which meant that Blanche might well have been ignorant of her daughter's evil schemes. Even so, Janna could not warm to her stepmother, for she was sure it was Blanche's neglect and cruelty that had led Richildis to act as she had. The girl was desperate to win her mother's love and approval. Perhaps she'd thought the best way to succeed in that was by ridding their family of the one person who threatened both her mother's peace of mind and all their prospects. What troubled Janna was what her half-sister might try next, now that she was going to travel to Wiltune with them.

That night she lay awake listening to the quiet sobs coming from the girl lying beside her in the bed. Richildis had not returned to the table, nor had she appeared at the evening meal. It seemed she'd gone to bed early, for she was lying still, feigning sleep, when Janna and Rosy came in to the bedchamber. The crying had started later, perhaps when Richildis thought they were asleep and she would not be overheard. It was hard to find privacy to grieve; hard to find privacy for anything else either. Janna felt some sympathy, although not enough to risk starting an argument if she tried to comfort her.

She made sure to put on a bright face in the morning, and not let her suspicions show. "This marks the start of a new life for you, for you will soon be wed and will become mistress of your own demesne," she congratulated Richildis, once she saw that the girl had woken.

Richildis scowled at her and turned away, not bothering to acknowledge her greeting.

"Johanna and I chose your present, Richildis," Rosy piped up, "but Papa wants to give it to you himself. But we have something else for you." To Janna's surprise, she withdrew from under her pillow the rainbow of ribbons they'd chosen in the market place. "I've kept the red one, but you can have all these," she said, and thrust them into her sister's hands. "I chose them. There's something to match all your gowns, Richildis."

With a pleased smile, the girl took the ribbons from Rosy and unfurled them over the bed in a cascade of bright color. "Thank you," she said, and held them up to admire them. Janna thought how attractive she looked when she was pleased and animated rather than sullen and withdrawn, and wondered if having a mirror to see the difference in her expression might prompt the girl to change her ways.

Her father came in then, alerted to the fact that they were awake by the sound of their voices. He bent down to kiss Richildis, and handed over a bulky package.

She took it and hurriedly unwrapped it, flinging aside the woolly fleece that had protected the delicate object. She gasped with pleasure as the mirror was revealed, and held it up to peer at herself, her eyes widening with wonder. Then, with an angry cry, she threw it across the room. It hit the stone wall; the glass shattered on impact.

"Richildis! Daughter, what are you thinking? Why did you do that?" John rushed forward, but Richildis shrank away from him.

"I know I am ugly, too ugly to be wed! Why do you mock me so?" The girl's voice was raw with pain as she shrieked the words.

"Mock you?" Janna found her voice with an effort. "Oh, Richildis, can't you see how beautiful you are? You were." The words were coming out all wrong. "How beautiful you could be, if only you would smile more and start eating properly?"

"Why should I?" Richildis glared at her, her eyes huge and haunted in her thin face. "I was Papa's favorite until you came along," she hissed, glancing swiftly at her father before turning back to Janna. "Now he does not notice me. Nor does Maman. You've come between us and my father, and now all Papa thinks about is you. Finding *you* a husband, making *you* a good match, introducing *you* to the king. He doesn't care about me anymore. No-one does!" Distraught, she covered her eyes with her hands, curled up into a small ball on the bed and began to rock back and forth, crying all the while.

"You know that's not true, Richildis." John moved swiftly to sit next to her. "You are my daughter and I love you," he said, taking her hands in his and rubbing them gently. "I want to take care of you, but I can't do that if I leave you behind when I go to Wiltune. That's why I want you to come with me."

Richildis stared at him doubtfully. Rosy, however, was highly indignant. "She's bad. Wicked! She doesn't deserve to go with you, Papa. Look what she's done!" And she pointed at the smashed remains of the mirror lying on the floor.

John looked at the bright shards of glass, and then turned to his daughters. "Johanna. Rohesia. Will you leave us, please?"

Janna led the way out with alacrity, relieved to escape. Rosy trailed after her, obviously longing to witness whatever came next.

It was a greatly subdued Richildis who joined them later at the dinner table. Her eyes were red-rimmed from weeping; her face was haggard with despair. She sat with her head down, not looking at anyone, even when her mother and brother produced gifts to mark her passage to womanhood. In spite of all the grief she'd caused, Janna couldn't help feeling sorry for Richildis, especially when, with trembling hands, she unwrapped the gift from her mother to reveal an unbecoming cloak of dark brown velvet that would age her far beyond her years. Chosen with great care, Janna had no doubt, although Richildis did her best to sound pleased with the gift as she stammered her thanks.

"I think Richildis has something else to say to us," John prompted gently, once the girl had fallen silent.

"I apologize for breaking the mirror. It – it was an accident." Richildis's voice faltered on the lie.

"You threw it at the wall!" Rosy shouted indignantly.

"We'll say no more about it," John said firmly, and gestured to the servants to serve the food.

It seemed that, in spite of Richildis's willful act, she was still to travel to Wiltune with them. Janna wondered if she should voice her misgivings, but a few moments' reflection led her to think that her father already knew what she suspected. She would keep silent – and watchful. It was all she could do.

Chapter 6

For this journey to Wiltune, John took with him a sizable escort, as befitted his position, and made no effort to hide his identity. Their passage also differed in other ways, for it was summer, and instead of winter storms and biting winds they traveled along muddy roads hemmed with high hedgerows of sweet-smelling roses and briars, and the jeweled colors of wildflowers bright among grass that was rapidly fading from green to gold. Shady trees gave protection from the midday sun or the sudden showers that occasionally swept across the sky. As they traveled further west, Janna began to notice familiar landmarks, and felt her stomach roil with a mix of excitement and fear. Her agitation grew as they came ever closer to their destination, which left her little time to worry about what Richildis might try next. Her mind was wholly taken up with the prospect of seeing Godric again, and what might come of it.

Their first stop was at Wiltune Abbey. Janna was puzzled to find that the whole town had been heavily fortified, while the abbey itself looked more like a military garrison than a house dedicated to God. "I had heard that Stephen and his troops are staying here as guests of the abbey while a new castle is being built nearby," her father explained when she asked him about it. His face set in grim lines as he continued, "Judging from what I see here, I suspect that once he has secured Wiltune as a stronghold to fall back on, he will march against the castle at Sarisberie, which remains loyal to my half-sister. Strategically, capturing the castle is crucial to Stephen, for it would break my sister's hold over the West Country."

"But – " Janna's alarm was partly assuaged as her father interrupted her.

"I don't know if Robert of Gloucestre is aware of Stephen's plans and how far his preparations have progressed, but I shall certainly send a message to him to prepare to defend Sarisberie."

In spite of her father's assurance, the scene before her gave Janna a deep feeling of disquiet. She hoped with all her heart that the king would take his quarrel to Sarisberie before it met him here, for she knew only too well how devastating these sieges could be.

The abbess was all smiles and obsequiousness as she greeted Janna's father and welcomed his party. Her smile turned into a puzzled frown when John introduced his daughter. Her puzzlement grew as John explained that Sister Emanuelle was Janna's mother, that they had been wed at the time of her conception, and that his daughter was his legitimate heir.

"You knew my mother as Eadgyth, the *wortwyf*," Janna explained, realizing that the abbess had no idea either of who she was or what John was talking about. "You gave her a cot to live in, a cot that was burned down by the villagers at the urging of the priest and Robert of Babestoche. I was lucky to escape with my life." She felt safe in telling the truth at last, now that her father was here to support her. The abbess opened her mouth but apparently could not find voice to speak. She stared at Janna in shocked disbelief.

"You gave me shelter here for a time," Janna continued helpfully. "You might remember that I served in the infirmary with Sister Anne."

The abbess gulped and nodded. "You are welcome," she said faintly. "Most welcome. Sister Anne will be glad to see you again, as will Sister Ursel. You are fondly remembered here, my child."

Janna couldn't help a smile spreading across her face. After all she'd endured on her journey to find her father, all the setbacks and sneers, it was sweet indeed to have such praise from the abbess. Even if the abbess's words were prompted by the presence of her father, Janna was determined to savor the moment. Her pleasure was momentarily dimmed by the expression on Richildis's face. Such envy. Such malice. Truly, the girl was in urgent need of repair.

It seemed that John was thinking along the same lines. "This is my younger daughter, Richildis," he said, drawing her forward. "I have fears for her health, Mother Abbess. I understand from Johanna that your infirmarian is greatly skilled as a healer, and I wonder if I may leave my daughter here at the abbey in her care once we travel on to attend to…certain matters."

"Of course you may. We shall be delighted to have her here. In fact, let me take her to Sister Anne at once." After a moment's hesitation, the abbess put her arm around Richildis's shoulder. The girl made a small movement to pull away, but John's hand at her back stayed her.

"There is another matter I wish to discuss with you," he said. "I understand that the priest refused to bury my wife, Johanna's mother, in consecrated ground. If her body has not yet been taken to Ambresberie, then it is my wish that her remains be removed from where she now rests and that she be buried here in the abbey without delay."

Janna thought of her proud, free mother being laid to rest within the confines of the abbey. "Not inside the abbey," she said quickly. "I am sure my mother would prefer to lie outside, under the sky."

John raised his eyebrows.

"Toward the end of her life my mother did not go to church." Janna shot a glance at the abbess, who remained silent although her expression betrayed her conflicting emotions. Janna was tempted to explain that her mother had lost faith in the church partly because of her treatment by the abbess, but also because of the attitude of the new priest, who would not tolerate any deviation from his own orthodoxy and who denigrated Eadgyth at every opportunity. But she needed all the support she could muster to fulfill her promise and so she held her peace. "My mother used to talk about 'God's great garden' and how there was no need to go to church to worship Him when there are signs of His presence all around us," she said instead.

John gave a grudging nod. "You knew your mother best of all," he said gruffly, as if it hurt him to admit as much. "It shall be as you say. My daughter shall choose my wife's last resting place within the confines of the abbey grounds. And I want a commemorative requiem mass to be said here, at the abbey, in her honor."

John paused, perhaps waiting for the abbess's assent. Janna thought she could not dare refuse. But the abbess was the liege lord of her demesne; that might give her the right to decide.

"You are aware, sire, that your…your wife died unshriven, and by her own hand? It was for that reason that I rejected the request from Ambresberie Abbey."

"She may have died unshriven, but she was murdered. She did *not* take her own life!"

"But – "

"And the murderer will be brought to justice. That is a promise I intend to keep."

The abbess's mouth opened and then closed. She raised a hand as if in protest.

"You will find me generous toward the abbey, once my wife's soul is able to rest in peace," John offered, as an added inducement.

"Of course, my lord. I shall make sure your wishes are carried out."

Janna exhaled a quiet breath of relief. This was part of what she had hoped to achieve when first she'd set out to find her father.

How easy he made it all seem, and how grateful she was to him for gaining the abbess's consent to his plans. Truly, anything was possible for those who had the wealth and power to demand that their wishes be met. She hoped that the rest of her quest might be achieved so easily: that Robert of Babestoche would be brought to justice, and her father would consent to let her choose her own husband.

She stood quietly while he made arrangements for the exhumation and return of his wife's remains, and also for Richildis's welfare. That done, he took leave from the abbess and motioned for Janna to follow him to the guest house.

After making her own obeisance, and with a last glance at Richildis, Janna left the abbess's parlor. Her heart was wrung with pity as she noted the girl's anguish. She had grown up in a family born to wealth and prestige, and yet she seemed entirely alone, whereas Janna, who'd had no-one at the start, could now count on numerous friends and allies for support, along with a father who seemed determined to do his best for her. Could that be because she had been loved by her mother and therefore had grown into confident womanhood, whereas Richildis seemed neither loved nor valued by anyone? Or had she found good fortune because she'd had the freedom to act, to follow her own will, to make mistakes and learn from them, while Richildis was completely confined and shaped by her family?

Richildis would never have the freedom to follow her own desires, for her future was bound entirely by her father's wishes. A further thought gave Janna cold shudders of fear: Unless she could find some way to extricate herself from her father's ambitions for her own future, she was now trapped just like Richildis.

*

"I heard you'd returned to Wiltune! Oh, Janna, I'm so pleased to see you!"

Janna and her father were standing in the outer courtyard of the abbey after attending High Mass. It felt strange being an honored guest rather than a lowly lay sister; she was still getting used to her new position. She had lingered, hoping to catch sight of some of the sisters who had befriended her in the past, and now it took her a moment to recognize the portly figure who lumbered across the yard and threw her arms around her, hugging her so tightly she could barely breathe.

"Agnes!" She drew back and surveyed her friend with great pleasure, and some satisfaction. The last time she'd seen Agnes, the girl was planning to sever her ties with the abbey in order to wed the bailiff. Now here she was, and swollen with a child that, if the size of her belly was anything to go by, was imminently due. "How are you? Are you happy now you've left the abbey?" she asked, even though the evidence was before her in her friend's shining face and changed appearance.

"So happy, you have no idea! And it's all thanks to you. If you hadn't given me such a great push…" Agnes laughed, and set her hands on either side of her stomach. "If it's a girl I shall name her after you. Johanna." A sudden realization brought a flush to her cheek and a stammered apology. "I beg your pardon, my lady. I have heard also of your changed circumstances, your great good fortune." She cast a quick, shy glance at Janna's father, and bobbed a hasty curtsy to them both.

"To you, and to all my friends, I am still Janna. Nothing's changed," Janna said firmly. She drew her father forward. "Look, Agnes, I found him, just as I'd hoped. This is my father, Sire John." She turned as she heard her name called out, and gladly greeted Sister Ursel and Sister Anne. Once she'd performed the introductions, Sister Anne drew her father away to consult with him about Richildis's welfare, leaving Janna free to talk to Ursel and Agnes.

"How is the life of St Edith coming along?" she asked, pleased to note Sister Ursel's happy and confident demeanor.

"S-splendidly! I am almost f-finished my manuscript, and already one of the postulants has been set to m-making a copy. You remember our lay sister, Sister Martha, I'm sure?"

Agnes gave a snort of mirth. "The gnat," she reminded Janna.

Janna's eyes widened as she recalled the lengths to which the young woman had gone in her determination to report even the smallest lapse and infraction of the Rule whenever the nuns assembled at Chapter.

"She has shown great aptitude in learning her letters, and has an uncommon gift for d-drawing and lettering. I am giving her extra t-tuition," Sister Ursel continued. "She's coming along very well. I am so proud of her." She permitted herself a small smile. "Sister Martha has become happier and more amenable now that she has something she values to occupy her time, along with her new position in the abbey as a postulant."

"I am so glad she's found something more worthy to fulfill her life." Janna exchanged a wry grin with Agnes.

"The abbess spoke true, Johanna. You have made many friends during your journey to find me." Janna's father had rejoined them, along with Sister Anne.

"Johanna is intelligent and loving, and has a generous heart." The words were kind, but Sister Anne's tone conveyed something more. Janna wondered what she'd been saying about Richildis, for it sounded as if a comparison was being made. Had her father told the infirmarian about Richildis's tricks, or was Sister Anne making her own judgment, based on the girl's appearance and behavior? She longed to ask, for she felt genuine concern over her half-sister's welfare, but knew that now was not the right time to air such intimate family matters.

"I'm going to visit Richildis with Sister Anne," John told Janna, while Sister Ursel also bade them a reluctant farewell in order to attend to her duties.

"Oh, Janna, I am so glad to have the chance to talk to you alone," Agnes said, as soon as they'd left. "A terrible thing has happened, and you're just the person to set things right."

"Me? What do you mean?"

"You worked out who was stealing pages from Sister Ursel's manuscript and spoiling them, and also who attacked Lord Hugh in the market place. You even solved the mystery of the lilies – and changed my future! You're clever at finding out the truth when things go wrong."

Janna could only hope Agnes's faith in her was not misplaced. "Tell me what's happened."

"A young girl has drowned in the millrace. She was caught on the wheel and badly battered, poor thing. Maybe it was an accident, maybe she was trapping eels or some such. Or it may have been suicide, for it seems she was with child, though she was unwed. But a man is being held for murder, although he swears he is not guilty and others say he speaks the truth. If it was murder, then his crime is a double sin, for an unborn child has died as well as its mother." Agnes shuddered, and cupped her hands across her stomach in an unconscious gesture of protection.

"Who is looking into the matter?"

"Robert of Babestoche. The girl was the daughter of one of Dame Alice's villeins."

Robert! Janna was filled with immediate suspicion. "Is anything known about the father of the unborn child?" she asked carefully.

Agnes shook her head. "She never said who he was, but she was seen with someone shortly before she died. That is the man who's been taken in for questioning."

"When did she die? How long ago?" From what she'd been told and her own observation, Janna knew that it was possible to tell from an examination of the body whether death was from drowning or due to some other means. She wondered if it was still possible to view the girl's body.

"I know not when she died, but news of it came only yesterday. The man they suspect of murder actually comes from Dame Alice's manor farm, the one that is overseen by Sire Hugh. You'll remember him, of course?" Agnes's eyes twinkled; they both remembered the attraction that had flared between the injured Hugh and Janna, who had nursed him back to health at the abbey. "Sire Hugh is one of those who believes the man is not guilty, and he came himself to ask the abbess to stay proceedings until the man's guilt can be proven. He's very troubled by the whole affair. Oh, Janna, you will help him find out the truth, won't you?"

"Was the girl from Sire Hugh's demesne, or did she live at Babestoche?" Janna cast her mind back to the time when, seeking refuge, she had passed herself off as a boy and labored on Hugh's farm. She couldn't think of anyone who would be so cruel as to woo and bed a girl and then drown her in a desperate effort to hide the evidence – anyone other than a man who was already wed.

"She came from Babestoche. But the accused visited Dame Alice's demesne from time to time and he was seen with his arm around the girl shortly before she died."

"Do you know the name of the accused?"

"His name is Godric. He is – or he was – Sire Hugh's steward."

"Godric? No!" Janna stared at Agnes in growing horror, sure she must have misheard. "That can't be right!"

"Do you remember him?" Agnes looked a little puzzled. "I think he came to visit Sire Hugh while the lord was recuperating here in the infirmary."

"Yes, I remember him. I know him well." Janna could hardly think straight, she was so upset.

But Agnes was still following her own train of thought, her brow wrinkled into a frown of concern. "You do know...that is, have you heard that Sire Hugh is now wed?"

"Yes. Yes, I know all about it."

"You're not heartsick about it?"

"Heartsick?" Janna stared at Agnes.

"I-I thought you cared for him. I know he came to care for you while you looked after him."

Janna blinked. It was true, yet so much had happened since that time, so much that had opened her mind to the secrets of her heart.

"No, I don't care for Hugh." She brushed off Agnes's concerns. "I saw him wed in Winchestre, and I truly wish him great happiness. But it's Godric I love, Agnes, although it's taken me a long time to understand my own heart. I do not believe for one moment that he is responsible for this foul crime."

"Then you must do all you can to prove it, for Robert of Babestoche is determined to hang him."

"Hang him?" Janna's face went white. "No!" Her mind spun with sickening fear. How could she find out the truth of the girl's death before it was too late? If the girl had been murdered, Janna had a fair idea who was responsible – and who would be in a great hurry to cover his tracks by laying the blame on someone else.

"Will you help him?" Agnes asked anxiously. "Robert wanted to hang him immediately, but the abbess has ordered that proceedings be delayed until the matter is fully investigated and a report prepared."

Janna nodded, panicking and frantic. "He cannot be hanged. I'll do all I can to save him." She must call on her father; they must leave immediately. Then she paused as she considered the reality of the situation. She could not tell him the real reason for her haste, for she needed to present Godric as a worthy suitor for her hand. Somehow she had to find a way to implicate Robert of Babestoche. He would not be able to act against Godric if he himself was facing a charge of murder: the murder of Janna's mother and – if Janna could only prove her suspicions – the murder of this young girl who had died at his demesne.

"Was the young girl known to Dame Alice and Sire Robert?" she asked.

Agnes thought for a moment. "I believe she was a servant in the dame's household. But I can't be sure."

So far as Janna was concerned, Robert's guilt was now assured, but she knew also that it wouldn't be long before he came up with "proof" enough to hang Godric in his stead. What she needed was time: time to ask questions about the girl's death; time to prove Godric innocent.

As soon as her father was alone, she approached him with the request that they leave Wiltune at once. But John was determined that she must first meet the king, to sort out the matter of her inheritance and also her marriage. Although this was the last thing on Janna's mind, and the last thing she wanted, she could not openly defy him. Nor would he countenance leaving until after the requiem mass was held in her mother's honor. In truth, Janna would not have wanted to miss it. So, in spite of her anxiety, she put on a brave face and resigned herself to staying at the abbey for several more days.

Bearing in mind her father's instruction to act as unlike the empress as possible, she donned her dowdiest gown and her meekest demeanor for her meeting with the king. They had only to walk as far as the newly enlarged gatehouse, for it was there that he was housed, along with his men. Richildis accompanied them, and pushed herself forward to stand beside her father as they waited for the king to receive them. Janna was happy to stay in the background; her stomach was roiling with unease although her father seemed calm enough.

King Stephen strode into the small chamber into which they'd been shown. To Janna's horror, his brother Henry, Bishop of Winchestre, followed him. Dry mouthed, Janna stared at him. Her heart raced, her senses were in turmoil as memories of Ralph came rushing back. Although she'd met him before, albeit briefly, she wondered if he'd found out more about the travelers who had intercepted his message to his brother the king, and the young woman who had brought about the death of his spy. Had he guessed that she might also be behind the empress's escape? Acutely aware of the danger she faced, she ducked her head and sank into a deep curtsy.

She sneaked a quick glance at the king. He too was surveying her with an appraising stare. As her father performed the introductions, the bishop's glance sharpened. Janna waited for him to say something to his brother but he kept silent, hiding his thoughts behind a bland expression. She kept her eyes downcast, wishing she could disappear from their sight.

"I can see the family resemblance," the king commented dryly. Janna passed a hand over her damp forehead and wiped it down her gown. It was a hot summer's day. Hopefully the king would think she was merely warm; that this was not the sweat of fear. If he knew even half of what she'd done to thwart his campaign against the empress, he would have her placed in irons and imprisoned for a very long time.

"I've been giving some thought to your request for a husband for your daughter." The king addressed his remark to John. A cold dread settled on Janna, made worse when he continued, "There is a baron in my retinue whom I wish to reward. He is some years older than Johanna, with two children. His wife died three years ago while giving birth to their third child, who also died."

Janna closed her eyes. She wondered if her father remembered her request that any prospective suitor must be young, handsome and rich. She wondered how she could get out of this arrangement, even if most of her criteria were met.

"His name is William of Marsford. He is of good birth, with some property to his name, and he has served me faithfully during these trying times against my cousin. Your half-sister, John." The king's gaze was still on Janna's father as his tone had hardened.

John inclined his head. "We have other business to attend to before I can give time to seeing my daughter married, sire," he said, "but I would like to know that the matter is settled. I have informed my daughter that I wish her to inherit all my property here in England on my death. I hope that meets with your consent?"

The king nodded. Greatly relieved, Janna stole a glance at the bishop, conscious of his critical stare. Unable to meet his eyes, she looked away.

"While I trust my daughter's ability to manage my affairs here in England, I would also see her wed before she comes into her inheritance. As a wealthy heiress she will need the protection of a good husband. Is William of Marsford my daughter's equal in this?"

"Indeed he is."

"Then I'd like my daughter to meet her prospective husband as soon as possible, if that can be arranged."

"You can meet William now, if you wish." Not waiting for a reply, the king snapped his fingers and a minion hurried over to do his bidding. Janna waited in great trepidation. She knew, well enough, that unless she could secure her father's agreement for the man of her choice, her future lay with the king's choice instead. Which made her future bleak indeed, for so far as her father was concerned, a landless serf could never match the favorite of a king.

"I mentioned, my liege, that I wish to make Johanna the heir of my properties here in England." John pulled a sheet of parchment from his scrip and handed it to the king. "I've set down my thoughts on the matter, along with a full account of what I own. I'd be most grateful if you would hold this for safekeeping, for I intend to move my family back to Normandy once my affairs are settled here."

Stephen took the parchment and quickly read it. His eyes narrowed as he looked at Janna. "Your fortune comes at a cost to others, it would seem," he commented dryly.

"It is no more than her worth," John said sharply.

Stephen grunted and handed the paper to his steward. "The matter of her marriage needs to be resolved first," he said, and raised his hand to beckon the man whom he'd selected for Janna.

Her first glance at the figure silhouetted against the sunlight streaming through the window showed her suitor as a fine, upstanding man. But a closer inspection as he hurried forward to kneel before the king revealed a receding hairline and a small paunch. There was about him the faint odor of wet dog. Janna recoiled, then tried to cover the instinctive movement with a fit of coughing.

How could she bear it? It was a huge effort to stand calmly rather than racing out of the room to freedom. Trying to hide a shudder of distaste, she held out a hand, which was grasped and kissed.

"This is Johanna, daughter of John fitz Henry," the king told the knight.

"*Ma dame. Mon sieur.*" He swept a bow, then straightened to survey Janna with bright, dark eyes. Struggling against despair, Janna sought to find something, anything, good about him. His voice was deep, pleasing to the ear. He smiled at her, a kindly smile, she thought, and she did her best to ignore a prominent snaggletooth as she returned the gesture. She wondered if he knew the king's plans and thought perhaps he did not, for he seemed slightly puzzled as he waited for whatever was to follow.

"John fitz Henry is looking for a husband for his daughter," the king enlightened him, and stood up. "I shall leave you all to become better acquainted," he said, and strode from the room. The bishop subjected Janna to a last searching glance before he followed his brother. Janna wondered if, once outside, he would waste no time in making his suspicions known to the king, if indeed the king didn't already harbor suspicions of his own.

She wished she could have the chance to talk to her father, to beg for release without William being present, but realized she had no choice but to go along with his plans, at least for the moment. In fact, once she'd moved past William's somewhat unprepossessing physical appearance, she found him to be well-informed and with a dry sense of humor that once or twice had her laughing in spite of herself. Nevertheless, she longed for the ordeal to be over, and was immensely grateful when her father finally dismissed the baron from their presence without committing either of them to a second meeting.

"Not quite what I would have wished for you," John commented, once the baron had left them. Janna could have wept with relief. She was about to speak of her true feelings when her father continued thoughtfully, "But he seems a good-hearted soul, and would treat you well, I believe. You could do worse, Johanna."

"I could also do so much better!" *Godric, oh Godric*, she thought with despair.

"You must remember that I have a son who will inherit the bulk of my property, Johanna." John shot her a sharp glance. "Even though you are my legitimate daughter and will inherit a sizable fortune, you cannot afford to be too particular. More importantly, you should remember that this man is in the king's favor – and it's the king's favor you will need once I am back in Normandy."

"I know what you say is true, sire, but I – " Janna remembered Godric's circumstances, and choked to a stop.

"You need time to get used to the idea," John said kindly. "While you think about it, will you come with me to where your mother was buried? The abbess is sending some men with a cart and I've decided to accompany them, to make sure your mother's remains are treated with respect. It would help if you could show us exactly where she lies."

Janna nodded. "I planted some rosemary on her grave, as a token that I would remember her always and that I would avenge her death," she said, feeling a bitter jubilation at the thought of finally bringing Robert of Babestoche to justice.

"And so you have, and so you will." Janna looked up to meet his steady gaze. "You're an astonishing young woman," he told her, and she flushed with pleasure at his compliment.

"Papa says the man I'm to marry is young and handsome – and rich," Richildis whispered behind John's back as they made their way across the courtyard. "Papa might flatter you with pretty words, but you'll be stuck with that fat old man while I'm the one who will have a happy life with the man of my dreams."

Janna ignored her, too sick at heart to respond. With all her heart she wanted to leave Wiltune and fly to Godric's side. She couldn't care less what her half-sister thought. But she needed her father, and for that reason alone she was prepared to offer her obedience to his wishes.

*

Janna and her father rode beside the horse and cart to Berford, going straight to the wasteland of unhallowed ground adjacent to the small church where Eadgyth had been buried. To Janna's surprise, the area around the rosemary bush she'd planted on her mother's grave had been fenced with small sharpened stakes which now were covered with a tangle of sweet-smelling honeysuckle. Someone must be tending the grave on a regular basis, for the enclosure was neat and tidy, unlike the surrounding wasteland. Godric? She could think of no-one else who cared enough to carry out this small service for her and her mother, and her heart swelled with love and gratitude.

The rosemary bush had flourished, and she picked several sprigs from it to plant at the site of her mother's new grave. She and her father stood witness to the gravediggers as they dug down until they reached the rough shroud that contained her mother's body. Janna turned aside, fighting tears and an overwhelming desire to run so that she would not have to look on her mother's pitiful remains. But the muddy shroud was immediately placed into a stout, lead-lined coffin and all was hidden from sight.

Eadgyth's coffin was placed in the chapel on their return, and Janna and her father kept vigil overnight. In the morning of the following day, the coffin was removed to a site carefully chosen by Janna, where splashes of sunlight pebbled the green grass through the boughs of a leafy oak. There Eagyth's body was interred once more, with the priest intoning the funeral rites in front of a large crowd of mourners that included all members of the abbey as well as the king and his entourage. The coffin was lowered into the ground and John threw onto it the first clod of earth. As he did so, he began to weep.

Richildis drew apart in a gesture of distaste, but Janna tucked her arm through her father's. She had grieved for her mother at the time of her death, and her heart again was full of sorrow, but she felt also a sense of satisfaction that she had managed to fulfill the promise she had made so long ago. She threw the next clod of earth onto the coffin, after which the gravediggers took over the task. Once they were done, Janna planted the sprigs of rosemary at the head and foot of the grave, pushing them deep into the damp, loose soil while she murmured her own prayers.

The requiem mass, said for the repose of Eadgyth's soul, followed the burial. Sister Ursel had told Janna what to expect, but Janna drew also on her tuition in the language of the church so that she could translate the proceedings into words that made sense to her. *Requiem aeternam*: the plea for mercy and eternal rest, a solemn, reflective refrain. *Dies irae*, the day of wrath and judgment, followed by a plea for forgiveness and salvation. Janna felt peace settle in her heart as the words of comfort sang softly in her ear. For years she'd tormented herself with the memory of the last bitter words she'd exchanged with her mother, an argument she'd had no time to repair before her mother's death. The knowledge that forgiveness was possible was a balm to her soul, as was the realization that, although Eadgyth may have turned her back on the church, this at last was the church's acknowledgment of her mother's worth.

Tears dripped down her cheeks as she listened to the last words of the mass: *Agnus Dei, qui tollis peccata mundi, dona eis requiem sempiternam; Lux aeterna luceat eis, Domine.* Lamb of God, who takest away the sins of the world, grant them eternal rest; may eternal light shine upon them, oh Lord.

And upon us all, Janna prayed, as the mass came to an end. She sneaked a look at her father, who knelt beside her on the cold stone flagging. Whatever differences lay between them, whatever difficulties still lay ahead of them, they would always be joined by love for each other, and by the strong bond of the woman who had loved them both.

*

Janna was on fire with anxiety, desperate to leave for Babestoche, but there was still the matter of Richildis to sort out when they visited her in the infirmary to say goodbye. With all her heart, Janna hoped that they could leave her behind at the abbey, but Richildis clung to her father and begged to be allowed to come with them.

"Sister Anne believes your health will be better served if you stay here for a time," her father told her, putting the onus of the decision onto the infirmarian.

Richildis immediately began to sob bitterly. "You don't love me," she screeched. "If you did, you'd take me with you."

"Richildis!" John sat down next to his daughter and put his arms around her, while casting a worried glance at Janna over her head. "I want only what's best for you, you know that."

"Then you'll take me with you." The girl raised a triumphant, tear-stained face to smirk at Janna.

"No, he won't." Sister Anne bustled in, alerted by the noise. "With respect, sire, your daughter's interests will be better served if she stays here with me."

Richildis let out a loud shriek. John stood up, looking undecided. Richildis clung to his hand and would not let him go.

Sister Anne tightened her lips. "May I speak to you in private, sire?"

John freed himself from Richildis's grasp and followed the nun out. Janna and Richildis looked at each other.

"I *will* come with you," the girl hissed. "I won't let you take him away from me again."

Janna sighed, feeling both impatience and concern over her half-sister's histrionics, and alarm on her own account, should Richildis get her own way. She couldn't afford the distraction of having to watch her back all the time if she accompanied them. Freeing Godric was her priority; she didn't have time to deal with the girl's poisonous resentment.

"Sister Anne is right. You need help," she said mildly. "It's better if you stay here."

"Sister Anne is in league with you."

"Nonsense!"

Richildis raised herself from her bed and leaned toward Janna. "You won't get away with this. If you say anything against me, I'll tell my father that you are a thief and…and I'll say you tried to harm me!"

Shocked, Janna took a hasty step back and stared at her half-sister. A simmering rage shook her as the hurtful words sank in. "You'll do no such thing, for I already know the truth about you, Richildis. And so does our father." *Even if he won't admit it.* "We found the phial that contained the hemlock outside the kitchen window where you threw it," she continued. "We also know whose idea it was to mark the poisoned pastry with the heart."

Richildis drew in a breath with a sudden hiss.

"As for the spider in Giles's shoe? And Rosy's rag baby? Those are a child's tricks," Janna continued remorselessly. "A mean, vindictive child, and not a very clever one either, when it came to hiding your mother's brooch among my possessions. Did you really think I'd take the blame and not try to find out the truth?"

140

Richildis didn't answer. Her face was white, her eyes burning with rage. She began to shake.

"And the other things that went missing – I'm sure you can tell us where they are?" Still Richildis stayed silent. "No?" Janna took a step closer and glared at her. "It's time you looked into your heart, Richildis. It's time to see yourself for what you really are: a spoilt, spiteful little – "

"That's enough!" John's thunderous roar from the doorway stopped Janna mid-flow. At once she felt shame that he'd witnessed her assessment of her half-sister's character, yet she could not take back what she'd just said. Nor, she reflected, did she really want to do so. It was time the truth was spoken, so that her father could see how badly damaged Richildis was.

"Is this the truth?"

Richildis quaked before her father's icy glare. The silence lengthened; finally she nodded.

"Good God! Why?"

"I think you already know the reason." Sister Anne had been standing behind John, listening, but now she came forward and fixed Richildis with a glare of her own. "It's best if you stay here with me, and let your half-sister and father go about their business in peace," she said firmly. "While you are here, you can assist me, for I have need of an extra pair of hands. I've found in the past that making oneself useful in the service of our Lord can mend most upsets of the heart and the mind, and it seems to me that, in your case, there is a great deal of mending to be done."

Richildis looked from her father to the infirmarian, then stared down at her feet, mute with rage and hostility.

"Goodbye, Sister Anne." Janna bid the nun a hasty farewell. She said nothing to Richildis, for she couldn't think of anything to say. She left, hoping her father would follow her. She was desperate to be gone before anything happened to change his mind about leaving Richildis behind.

To her relief, she heard his footsteps behind her. She kept on walking, but he quickly caught up with her. "Did you know all along that Richildis was to blame for trying to discredit you? To bring about your death?" he queried.

"No. I blamed your wife." Janna wondered if she should tell him she still wasn't sure if Richildis had been acting on Blanche's instructions some of the time.

"I had no idea." John put his arm around Janna's shoulders. "I'm so very sorry that my family have made you so unwelcome, that they've been so unpleasant to you," he said awkwardly, as they came out into the courtyard and made their way to the stables.

Janna shrugged. "I expect I would have felt the same in their position," she admitted.

"I shall make it up to you once we return home, I promise you that." John's mouth tightened into a grim line. "And I shall ensure justice and reparation for your mother's death when I haul Robert of Babestoche before the abbess and her court."

Chapter 7

There were only a few miles to ride between Wiltune and Babestoche, and Janna spent all of them tormented by the one question that had haunted her ever since she first heard the news: What if she was too late and Godric was already dead, hanged for a crime he didn't commit? She trotted decorously beside her father while all the time she wanted to urge her horse into a wild gallop, to reach Dame Alice's manor as quickly as possible and find out the worst, although she dreaded what she might find once she got there. Her emotions were coiled into a tight spring; it took all her self-control not to burst apart.

"You realize I cannot just walk in and accuse this man." Her father broke the silence that had fallen between them. "This young woman must bear witness against him. Cecily? Is that her name?"

Janna nodded. "I don't know if I can persuade her to speak out," she said. "She is very loyal to Dame Alice. She won't wish to hurt her by telling the truth of her liaison with the dame's husband, and its consequences. Nor will she want to jeopardize her chances with – with any future husband. She's also very frightened of Robert."

"I don't suppose she wants to admit her shame either," John commented dryly.

"I doubt she had much choice in the matter, once Robert singled her out," Janna snapped, annoyed that her father automatically blamed Cecily for the affair.

"True."

"Besides, she truly believed that he loved her and that she loved him." Janna hesitated, wondering how she should broach the matter of the dead girl, or even if it was wise to do so. "Papa," she began, "I have been told of another young woman at the manor who was expecting a child, and who is now dead."

"Do you believe this same man is responsible?"

"I think it likely. But someone else has been blamed for the girl's death." Janna paused, conscious of the need to keep Godric's name out of her account. "She was found drowned in the millrace, caught up in the wheel. Her death may even have been an accident. Or suicide. I-I would like to see her body, if that is possible, for my mother taught me ways to ascertain the true nature of death, and it may be that I can help shed light on what really happened to her." She took a breath. "I also need to talk to the man they accuse of this foul deed. I am told that most people think he is innocent of this crime, but he may have some useful information. Can you help me with this, Papa?" Just the thought of Godric being held in captivity brought her close to tears, but she could not let her father see how much this meant to her, how much was at stake.

He was watching her, and it seemed he understood that there was more to this enquiry than mere curiosity. "Why?" he asked bluntly.

"I'm told that Robert of Babestoche is in a hurry to see this man hang for the crime. I find that suspicious in itself. I want to be sure that justice is done."

"Very well. But you do understand that I cannot accuse the lord without proof, and I'm relying on you to provide it." John nudged his mount with his heels and they rode on, skirting the great forest where once Janna had roamed with her mother, gathering wild herbs and flowers and even trapping birds and small animals to sustain them through the lean and hungry months. They passed through the centers of Bredecumbe and Berford, where once they had traded goods in the market place. Janna felt the clutch and tug of painful memories as she guided her horse past wandering livestock, avoiding where she could the steaming piles of dung and scraps of waste that littered the narrow streets. She was fairly sure that any who had known her in the past would not recognize her now, but kept her head bent, just in case. There was no time to waste on greetings and explanations.

Hurry, hurry, hurry. The word beat a soft refrain in her mind as they rode on to Babestoche. She recognized that she was riding into danger, for Robert hated and feared her and had tried on several occasions to have her silenced forever. But his assassin was now in prison, so either he must find another and at once, or else be prepared to act himself. Would he have the courage, now that she was under her father's protection?

Yes, she decided, for his life and his livelihood were at stake. It was his word against hers, and it would certainly benefit him if she was no longer alive to bear witness. She would have to be alert and on guard at all times.

They were brought first into Dame Alice's presence, and she gave Janna's father a courteous and respectful welcome, which broadened into pleasure as she turned to Janna. "Hugh told me that you'd found your father, my lady," she said, with a quick glance at John. "I am so sorry we did not know of him before."

Janna knew they were both thinking of how badly her mother had been treated. Yet she still felt kindly toward the dame, who had done her best to champion her in difficult circumstances. So she made no comment, but instead asked anxiously, "I am told that Hugh's steward has been accused of murder. Is it possible to see him, please?"

She closed her eyes and waited, with nerves aquiver, for Dame Alice's response. *Please*, she prayed silently, *please don't tell me I'm too late.*

"Of course, you knew him in the past, didn't you?"

Janna's relief that the dame hadn't mentioned Godric by name was tempered by the sinking realization that she hadn't answered her question either. "May I see him?"

Dame Alice inclined her head. Janna went limp with relief. She wasn't too late after all.

"But you shall not see him on your own!" John said sharply. "The man is up on a criminal charge. I shall come with you, Johanna."

"No!" Realizing how close she was to giving herself away, Janna tried for a better answer. "Is your nephew here with you, my lady?" she asked, hoping that Hugh would not have deserted Godric. "Perhaps he could come with me instead? He knows the accused very well, whereas you do not, Papa."

"I shall be honored to accompany you." Hugh was standing in the shadows behind his aunt; Janna hadn't noticed him come in and his voice gave her a sharp jolt of surprise.

"Hugh! My lord." The honorific came automatically, from long usage.

"My lady." He bowed to her, and Janna realized how far their respective statuses had been reversed.

"It is a great pleasure to see you again." She held out her hand, felt it grasped and held tight. He looked into her eyes and she read in his expression his love and longing, and also his regret at having lost her. She freed her hand, hardening her heart against him. "Are you well?" she asked, adding a gentle reminder: "And your wife? How does she fare?"

"She is with child." A momentary gleam lightened Hugh's face into something resembling happiness.

"That is good news indeed." Janna was genuinely delighted. She quickly introduced Hugh to her father, while reminding him that he'd attended Hugh's marriage to Eleanor in Winchestre. "Shall we go now to talk to...to your steward?"

"I should prefer to come with you," John fretted.

"No, Papa. Stay and – and speak to Dame Alice. And her husband, *Lord Robert*." Janna hoped her father had noted her emphasis, and that he would take this opportunity to learn more about the man behind her mother's murder.

"My husband will be pleased to welcome you, sire," the dame said quickly. "Perhaps I can offer you some refreshments while we wait for him? He's out speaking to our reeve, but I expect him back within the hour."

John hesitated, then agreed. Wasting no more time, Janna left the solar, followed by Hugh.

"How is Godric?" she asked anxiously, once they were out of hearing.

"Swearing his innocence. But it doesn't look good," Hugh answered tersely.

"On what grounds? Surely anyone who knows him cannot believe – "

"He was seen with his arm around the girl, in a close and loving position."

For a moment Janna felt her heart constrict as she imagined Godric embracing another woman. But he had told her that he loved her and no-one else. She trusted him, would trust him with her life as well as her love. So, no matter how things might have appeared, the witness had misinterpreted the scene and Godric's arrest was a nonsense. Besides, she knew how kind he was; if he had his arm around the young woman it was because she was distressed and in need of comfort. But why? Janna needed to find the answer, for Godric's life depended on it.

"Who saw Godric with the young woman?"

"One of my aunt's attendants. She claims she's seen Godric with the dead girl on more than one occasion."

"How can that be, when Godric spends his time at your manor rather than here?"

Hugh shrugged. "It is usually Godric who brings reports of our manor to my aunt, and carries back her instructions. In truth, I have come to trust him in everything, my lady."

"For the Lord's sake, call me Janna. Or Johanna, if you prefer." Janna thought for a moment. "Have you ever heard Godric speak of the dead girl? What's her name?"

"Her name is Isabel. Was Isabel. And no, I've not heard Godric mention her name – until now."

"Was – was Godric courting her?" It was a question she had to ask, even though she couldn't believe it to be true. Not after the kiss they'd shared at Winchestre; not after the vows of love and fidelity they'd exchanged.

"Godric says he hardly knows her. If he's courting anyone, it would be Cecily." The answer came promptly, but then Hugh frowned. "That is, I know Cecily would like to wed Godric, but he has never spoken of her or of anyone else."

Godric would need to ask Hugh's permission to wed if it was on his mind. In spite of her anxiety, Janna smiled. Godric was still true to her.

"Has Isabel's name been linked with anyone else?"

"Not that I've heard. Perhaps we should ask Godric that question." While they'd been talking, Hugh had led Janna across the yard to a collection of barns and outbuildings, and now he paused beside a door that was secured with a padlock. A key stuck out of it. Janna's heart was hammering so hard she wondered if she was about to swoon. She leaned against the wall and braced herself.

Hugh turned the key, and Janna followed him into the shed. It took her a moment to become accustomed to the darkness, but then she saw the figure of a man standing beside the far wall. A well-remembered voice said, "My lord?" and she pushed forward, unable to bear the space between them any longer. She seized his hands.

"Godric!" His gaze met hers, and she read in his eyes all the love and longing she was sure were reflected in her own. But there was also a growing sense of loss, and something else which she couldn't name or understand.

"My lady." He loosed his hands and bowed to her.

Janna couldn't speak, she was so shaken by his gesture. She stared at him with hungry eyes, absorbing every detail of the man she'd feared she might never see again. She remembered Godric's confident air that had always told the world he was his own man, and comfortable within his skin. But now his shoulders were slumped; his eyes had shuttered against her, while his backward step put more than a mile of distance between them.

Hugh broke the tense silence. "It's such a surprise to see you here at Babestoche, my lady. I can't think of anyone better to help you out of this coil, can you, Godric?"

"Janna. My name is Janna." She was still staring at Godric. "I've longed to see you again," she said, desperate to reignite the flame that had once burned between them.

"You have no place here, my lady."

"Godric!" Janna couldn't believe what she was hearing. "I want to be here, with you! There's no place else I'd rather be."

"I've been accused of a crime, my lady; a crime for which I shall hang. Please – " his tone was desperate now, " – *please* go away!"

"No!" Janna's heart was wrung by his words. "I won't leave until you tell me everything you know about this girl's death. I know you're innocent of this charge and I will not rest until I have found out the truth."

Godric's head came up. There was fire in his eyes as he retorted, "You are the daughter of a nobleman, with a fine future ahead of you. It's not seemly for you to involve yourself in the affairs of a common serf. I won't have it!"

"It's not for you to say what I shall and shall not do," Janna retorted just as sharply. "Your life is at stake, Godric, and I care about that! I will not let you be blamed for something you didn't do."

Godric glared at her. Janna glared back at him. Hugh looked from one to the other in confusion.

"You must tell me everything, Godric," Janna insisted. "Where you went and what you did on the day that Isabel died. Tell me also what you know about the dead girl."

"I didn't kill her, my lady."

"For the Lord Christ's sake, Godric, my name is Janna! And I know you didn't kill her. What we have to do is find out who did. But the first question to ask is: Could her death have been an accident?"

"Why are you so determined to concern yourself in my affairs when I am sure your father would not wish you to do so?"

Because I love you and I plan to marry you! Janna couldn't say what was uppermost in her mind, so she said instead, "You have helped me so often in the past, Godric. This is my chance to repay that debt. So please, let's not waste any more time. Tell me what you know."

Godric's lips tightened. He began a close study of a wasp's nest stuck to one corner of the shed. "It's true I saw Isabel shortly before she died," he muttered. "She was walking by the river in the direction of the mill stream. She seemed in great distress. I put my arm about her, I tried to comfort her. When I asked what ailed her, she sobbed most bitterly. She told me she was in great trouble, that she was with child and feared the father of the child would not marry her."

"Why not?"

Godric shrugged. "She would not say who he was, but I suspect he was already married."

"Could she have been going to meet him, do you think?" Janna's mind was racing ahead, seeing possibilities that she could only hope she would be able to prove.

"I don't know." Godric thought about it. "Maybe," he said slowly. "She was dressed very fine, almost as if she was going to church."

"Would you wear your best dress if you were going to drown yourself?"

"Suicide, not murder? Is that what you're thinking?"

"I'd know more if I could examine her body. Has she been buried yet?"

"No." It was Hugh who answered Janna's question. "I can take you to her, if you like. She lies in the manor's chapel. It's not far from here. My aunt has sent word to Isabel's family, but as yet they have not arrived to claim her."

"Very well." But Janna was reluctant to leave Godric quite so soon. She longed to feel his arms around her, his lips on her own. She leaned into him, and was mortified when he took another step back.

"Are you well, Godric? Are you happy to see me?" Stupid question, she thought, as he finally looked at her once more; how could he possibly be happy in these circumstances? "I've thought of you so often these past months," she said quickly, wanting to reassure him that no matter his circumstances now, her feelings for him hadn't changed at all. But his expression filled her with dismay. How cold and remote he seemed, when all of her was on fire with wanting him.

Godric stayed silent. Beside her, Hugh drew in a breath. Janna was conscious of his suddenly sharpened gaze moving from her to Godric, and back again. But he said nothing, and she was grateful for it.

"You told me once that you would come to me any time I called, and that you would stay true," Janna tried again.

"That was a long time ago, when you had no-one to protect you," Godric said gruffly. "Our circumstances are very different now. Everything has changed."

"But my regard for you has not." Janna paused, wishing that she was alone with him, that Hugh was not there as witness to what she had to say.

"There is no future for you here. Better that you go and be an obedient daughter to your father, and live the life he plans for you."

"I will not!" Janna swallowed hard over the sudden lump that came into her throat. Godric had risen from humble beginnings to his present station as Hugh's steward; she had seen his pride in his achievement when she'd met up with him again at the tavern: he, the consort of a nobleman, while she was just a common serving wench. It had made no difference to his treatment of her at the time; it would make no difference to her treatment of him now that their fortunes had reversed in so unexpected a fashion. Godric might feel shame that she should see him cast so low, but she didn't care about that at all. He'd given his word that he would always love her, and she'd believed him then as she did now. At last she had the chance to prove to him her own love, trust and loyalty.

Panic churned in her belly. It would all go for naught unless she could solve the riddle of the girl's death and bring the real culprit to justice before Robert carried out his threat. Godric's life and her own future depended on it.

She made an effort to rein in her emotions and order her thoughts. "You say you were seen with Isabel. What do you know about the witness?"

"I don't know anything about her at all."

"Her name is Amy," Hugh interposed. "She's only been with my aunt a short time, but she's set quite a few hearts aflutter already, I believe."

Amy. Janna determined to interview the girl as soon as possible. "And what was she doing near the millrace, did she say?"

"She says she was on her way home from visiting her family who live nearby."

"And what about you, Godric?" Janna kept her voice steady with an effort, for so much depended on his answer. "After you spoke to Isabel, where did you go? What did you do? Can anyone vouch that they saw you elsewhere after your meeting with Isabel?"

"No, my lady." It seemed that Godric was determined to make the most of the huge gulf between them. "My business here was finished and so I traveled back to Sire Hugh's manor," he continued. "I was alone. I rode part way along the river, then turned and went through the forest, taking the short way. I saw no-one." He glanced at Janna. She wondered if he was remembering their meeting in the forest when he had saved her from being gored by a wild boar. He had kissed her then, the first of several kisses they had shared. The thought of Godric's kisses was enough to turn Janna's bones to water.

"No witnesses, then." Janna held his gaze, willing him to remember what had passed between them in the forest. It was Godric who looked away first.

"No-one has come forward to say they saw him on the journey," Hugh said. "I've asked around, both here and at my own manor."

Janna turned to him. "Is there anything at all you can tell me about Isabel?" She knew she was chasing phantoms, but knew also that uncovering the real facts of the matter meant having to unravel a tangle of threads, one by one, before she could weave them into a new pattern, the pattern of truth.

Hugh hesitated. "I know nothing of Isabel, but I questioned Amy once I arrived here, after I heard that Godric had been arrested. I must say I was unimpressed by her testimony. It wasn't anything she said so much as the way she said it. As if she knew more than she was telling, almost as if she was glad that her words spelled Godric's doom."

"And what can you tell me about Amy, Godric?"

"Nothing, for I don't know her. Nor is there any reason why she should hold a grudge against me. Indeed, she tells the truth of what she saw, but she greatly mistakes the reasoning behind it."

"And on that small point your fate rests." She would go and find Amy just as soon as she'd examined Isabel's body.

"I'll come again to see you," she promised Godric, as they took their leave. He didn't say anything, only bobbed his head in an awkward gesture of obeisance. Saddened, Janna left him. Their meeting had not gone at all as she'd expected; nevertheless, she hoped he found some comfort in knowing that he had someone else on his side, determined to prove his innocence. She looked at her companion, glad of his presence. She knew that Hugh would do all in his power to help his trusted steward.

The small chapel was deserted when they walked in. Hugh guided Janna to a stone slab half-hidden in the shadows at the back of the chapel, where the girl's body lay. It was fortunate that, although it was summer, the interior remained pleasantly cool, or decomposition would be more advanced than it already was. Even so, there was an unpleasant odor about the body. As she lifted the shroud, Janna saw that flies had already laid their eggs and maggots had begun to feast on the dead girl's flesh.

At the sight, Hugh recoiled and began to retch. "Go outside," Janna told him, even though her stomach was also churning in protest. It was a relief to be left alone with the girl, for she needed to strip off her clothes for a closer inspection.

She set to work as soon as Hugh had gone, wincing as the long gown and undergarments came off and the full extent of the girl's injuries was revealed. Isabel's body had been battered and broken on the huge wheel. Janna realized now that it would be impossible to tell if any of the wounds had been made before she went into the water.

Mindful of what she'd done some years ago, when she'd pulled Hamo from the river and pushed on his chest to get the water out of his lungs so that he could breathe again, she pressed down lightly on the girl's chest. Nothing happened, so she pressed harder. And frowned, not knowing whether to feel glad or fearful. The girl's lungs, if she'd drowned, should have been full of water, water that should have gushed out of nose and mouth when she'd applied pressure to the girl's chest. Instead, there was...nothing. The girl hadn't drowned at all. She must have been dead before she went into the millrace, before her body was pulled downstream and broken on the great wheel. Not suicide, then, nor was it an accident. It was murder.

Her finding must be in Godric's favor; he would not have been comforting her if, moments later, he planned to kill her and throw her body into the millrace. But how to find evidence pointing to the real killer? Once more, Janna made a careful examination of Isabel's body. The small bump that defined the child growing in the girl's belly brought a rush of pity. She laid her hands on it, and whispered a quiet prayer for the repose of the child's soul as well as the soul of its mother. No-one deserved to die like this, not least an unborn child, she thought fiercely, and continued her examination.

At last she straightened, feeling defeated. The body was lacerated and horribly bruised; the girl's limbs were broken and possibly also her backbone. All of those injuries could have been caused once Isabel was caught on the wheel. There was nothing Janna could point to as evidence of a blow severe enough to kill the girl before she entered the millrace.

She embarked on another careful examination, then turned the body over so that she could scrutinize the girl's back. But she found nothing untoward among the bruises and lacerations caused by the wheel.

She clicked her tongue in frustration, wishing Sister Anne was present. She needed an extra pair of eyes to see what she might be missing. As she pondered the problem, she smoothed the girl's long hair and began to pick out the bits of weed and twigs caught within the snarled tresses. It suddenly seemed important that Isabel's family should not see their daughter in such disarray. She wished she had a comb, or even a dried teasel head to help unravel the tangles, for despite her best efforts, the hair still looked unkempt once she was done. Resolving to braid it into tidiness, she lifted up its heavy mass and parted it into three sections. Her action exposed the girl's thin, fragile neck which, at the hairline, was marred by a small, deep wound. Janna bent close to inspect it, and realized that fortune had worked in her favor, for she had found what she'd been seeking.

The cut wasn't wide, but a gentle probing revealed that it was deep enough to be fatal. Janna shuddered as her mind constructed the scene: The innocent girl possibly held in a close embrace, or with her back turned to the murderer as he wielded the dagger. A quick thrust and then a shove into the millrace. Was it chance that the girl had died before she hit the water? It was certainly chance that had led Janna to the truth.

A small, very thin blade. Or was it a spike, some sort of farming implement? Janna thought that Hugh might know. Before she went outside to summon him, she dressed Isabel, unwilling to subject the girl's naked body to anyone else's gaze. Dressing an inert body was difficult and took much longer than she'd expected, but as soon as Isabel looked decent once more, Janna hurried out of the chapel to find Hugh.

He gave a long, low whistle when Janna showed him the wound at Isabel's neck and explained her ideas to him of what had probably happened. Unlike Janna, he had no trouble identifying the weapon. "I suspect it was a misericord," he told her, going on to explain that the long, narrow knife was used to deliver a "mercy stroke" in battle. "It's thin and sharp enough to penetrate through holes or weak points in armor and put a seriously wounded knight out of his agony," he said, adding grimly, "not that it was used for that purpose on this occasion."

"Would Godric have such a weapon?" The question had to be asked.

"No. This is a weapon such as a knight would carry. A soldier." Hugh's mouth thinned into a grim line. "I own a knife like this...and so does my uncle."

Robert of Babestoche. It always came back to him. But to be fair, Janna had to ask another question. "I'm assuming it's not your knife, Hugh. Would anyone other than Sire Robert own such an object?"

Hugh thought a moment, frowned, and slowly shook his head. "But my uncle will deny everything, of course," he said, adding bitterly, "as he always does."

What did Hugh mean? How much did he know of his uncle's philandering? For that matter, how much did Dame Alice know? Janna was tempted to tell Hugh about Cecily, and the truth of her own mother's death. There was so much at stake, and she was sure Hugh would champion her if only he knew. Loyalty to Cecily made her hesitate, along with the knowledge that without Cecily's co-operation she would be placing Hugh in an impossible position unless she could also convince his aunt. But that meant convincing Dame Alice that she was wed to a philanderer and murderer who also happened to be the father of her only beloved son, Hamo.

No. She couldn't speak, not yet. So she said only, "I shall go now to talk to Amy."

"I'll come with you."

"No, please do not. I'm sure she'll speak more freely to me if you are not present. It's – it's women's affairs we need to discuss."

Hugh nodded his understanding. "Then I shall go and tell Godric what we've found. What you have found." He paused. "You care deeply for Godric, do you not?"

Janna felt her face flame into an embarrassing blush. "Yes, I do. I love him with all my heart."

"So that was why you didn't mention your father to me when I told you of my marriage plans?"

Janna was about to contradict him, to say that on the contrary, believing that Godric was lost to her, she'd been testing how much he truly loved her, daring him to choose her, who had no prospects at the time, over the wealthy woman who had now become his wife. Instead, she decided to spare his feelings. He had failed that test – and she was glad that he had. It had taken her a long time to understand the true secrets of her heart, but she was certain now that she would never love another as she loved Godric, nor was she prepared to wed anyone other than him.

"I intend to do all in my power to save Godric's life, and I'd welcome your help," she told him. "While I'm talking to Amy, will you question your uncle – if you can find some way to do so without rousing his suspicion?"

Hugh nodded. "I'll ask if I can compare the girth of his misericord with mine. And I'll look very closely for bloodstains, that I promise you."

"There would have been a lot of blood." Janna made a mental note to speak to the laundress. But there was something more urgent to address. "Where is Cecily? Where does she live now?" she asked. "I know she was living on your manor while your nephew was there, but he's – "

"She's still at my manor, although Hamo is now living with my wife's parents, just as I did when I was his age." Hugh gave a grim smile. "Cecily stayed on with me. I suspect my aunt believes she's safer there than here."

Safer away from Robert. Janna wondered anew just how much the dame knew of her husband's affairs, and if he'd continued to have liaisons with other women after Cecily left. It seemed likely enough. "Could you send for her?" she asked. "Would she come?"

Puzzled, Hugh looked at her. "She may be able to help us," Janna hinted, determined that, if Cecily came, she would put the utmost pressure on her to tell the truth, might even force her to it, if it would save Godric from being hanged.

"Very well, I'll send a servant to fetch her." Hugh studied her with narrowed eyes. "You know more than you're saying about all this, don't you?"

Janna gave a wry smile. "I'll do anything – *anything* – to clear Godric's name."

But before speaking to Amy, perhaps her first task should be to speak to the servants? Kitchen tattle, while often malicious, sometimes held a grain of truth, and truth was what she needed right now. Truth about the dead girl's life. Truth about Amy. Accordingly, Janna made her way to the kitchen, well remembered from the time she'd tried, unsuccessfully, to brew a mix that might revive Dame Alice's newborn babe. Then, the cook had chased her out of the kitchen with a besom. Now, it seemed, she did not recognize Janna, and was so politely formal that Janna began to despair of ever hearing anything of interest at all.

"You don't remember me, do you?" she asked at last, growing tired of having her every question met with blank incomprehension. The cook had been busy kneading dough to bake bread. Her hands were sticky and now she tried to wipe them clean on her apron as she stared at Janna.

"There is something about you, my lady," she began hesitantly.

"I am the daughter of Eadgyth, the *wortwyf* whom your mistress asked to assist with the birth of her babe."

"You?" The cook gazed at her with open suspicion.

Janna hoped she hadn't made a mistake in revealing herself, for she'd been treated with great hostility at the time. "I am here to help Godric, my friend. I want to clear his name, for I do not believe he is responsible for Isabel's death."

"Neither do I!" The cook's unexpected vehemence gave Janna's spirits a welcome boost.

"In that case, please will you tell me all you know about Isabel, and about Amy."

"Why do you want to know about Amy?"

Janna shrugged, trying to make light of her questions so as not to arouse the cook's suspicions as to where her thoughts really lay. "She was a witness to the meeting between Godric and Isabel, that's all."

The cook sniffed. "Coming home from seeing her family, so she says. I say she spends more time visiting them than she does serving her mistress. But she's had to change her ways now that Isabel is dead."

"Are you saying that Isabel spent more time here with Dame Alice than Amy does?" Janna resolved to visit Amy's family, to see for herself if the girl was always where she said she was.

The cook thought for a moment. "Not so much at first," she admitted. "In fact, rumor was that Isabel was seeing someone on the sly.

Well, we know that for a fact now, don't we?" She pursed her lips. "Pity these girls who don't learn the value of a marriage vow before they spread their favors around."

"Who was Isabel seeing? Do you know?"

The cook shook her head. "She was ever close-mouthed about her business. But it came to a sad end, everyone could see that. The girl took to moping about and crying in corners. And now we know why."

"So you believe she killed herself?"

The cook nodded vigorously. "Stands to reason," she said. "A babe on the way and no husband to support her. Mind you, she could have gone to Dame Alice, for I'm sure the dame would have helped her in her distress." She shook her head sadly. "I liked Isabel. She was a good'un, if somewhat lacking in judgment. Not like that Amy, with her fancy ways, her airs and graces. Looking down her nose at everyone as if *she's* so fine!"

"What do you know of her?" Janna would rather have asked what the cook had against the girl, but that seemed a little too direct. Nevertheless, she was keen to make the most of the cook's seeming ill-will.

"Not much," the cook said grudgingly. "She hasn't been here very long. Another close-mouthed one, but thinks herself very fine, she does. Always dressed up and strutting about. She pretends she can't see the men on my lady's demesne looking at her, lusting after her, but she loves it, loves the attention, don't tell me she doesn't."

"And does she have anyone special in her life?"

"It wouldn't surprise me if she has half a dozen of 'em!" The cook thought for a moment. "No, that's not true," she said slowly. "I would say she fancies herself too special to go with just anyone. But if she does have a lover?" She turned her attention back to kneading the dough, slapping and pounding it vigorously. "I wouldn't know who he is."

"Where does her family live?" Janna asked.

"Domnitone. Just past that water mill where Isabel was found."

She would visit them first, Janna decided, and see if their story squared with Amy's excuses for her frequent absences. The more she knew about Amy before she interrogated her, the more likely she was to get straight answers from the girl. Having asked directions from the cook, she was about to set out, thinking to walk past the millrace where Isabel had died so that she could examine the site for clues, when she was intercepted by Hugh.

"I was asked to find you and bring you in to dinner," he said.

Janna took his arm, accepting that her mission would have to wait until later.

To her dismay, the first person they met as they walked to the hall was Robert. He loomed over her and stared down. "My lady," he said, making the two words sound as insolent as he dared. "So we meet again."

"And in very different circumstances," Janna retorted coolly, even though her heart was pounding with remembered fright.

"I had thought never to see you again."

"I have come back here to seek justice. I would not wish a man to hang for a crime he did not commit." Janna met his cold stare without flinching. Robert was the first to look away. She followed him into the hall and found everyone else already assembled. At once she went to stand beside her father, reminding Robert of her new status and connection to royalty.

John greeted her with a smile. "You are just in time," he said.

"May I introduce you to Amy," Dame Alice said, drawing a young woman forward. "She is new to our household."

Janna eyed the girl with interest, and continued to keep a close watch on her once they'd sat down at a table on a raised platform at one end of the hall. She and her father were seated beside Dame Alice, Robert and Hugh. Amy was further down the table. Janna noticed that her eyes kept straying to Robert, although he seemed determined to ignore her. His attention was all on Janna's father, flattering him in so obsequious a manner that Janna surmised he understood the purpose underlying their visit, and sought to ingratiate himself to such a degree as to make any accusation impossible.

"Did you find Godric well?" Dame Alice's low-voiced question caught her attention.

"Well enough, but he shouldn't be where he is," Janna said fiercely, but quietly, so that her father couldn't hear her.

Dame Alice nodded and sighed. Janna noticed her glance also straying toward the young girl seated further down, and wondered anew how much the dame suspected of her husband's liaisons. Would she bear witness against him if Janna could prove his hand in this new calamity as well as in her mother's death? She followed the dame's gaze, acknowledging the truth of the cook's comment that Amy was beautiful enough to turn anyone's head. And the girl knew it – her awareness of the lustful glances from the workers seated at the tables below was obvious.

The meal seemed interminable, with a succession of poultry, fishes and meats in a variety of sauces, all served with a seemingly inexhaustible supply of wine. It was obvious that Dame Alice was out to impress. Janna determined to speak with Amy once the last fruit and honey pastry was consumed and she was free to leave the table, but to her dismay, the girl seemed to have disappeared. She looked around more carefully, and noticed that Robert had also vanished.

"Dreadful man." Her father materialized at her side, pulling a grimace of distaste. "I can well believe him capable of anything, for all he has the oily smoothness of a – an eel." Janna smiled at him, pleased that her father seemed in agreement with her.

"I have asked Hugh to send for Cecily," she told him. "I'll do my best to persuade her to tell the truth."

As there was no sign of Amy, Janna made her excuses to her father and left the manor house to walk down across the fields to the river. She followed its course until she came to where the narrow millrace branched off. Janna traced the roaring, rushing waters down toward the huge wheel. She looked at the paddles beating through the water, and shivered with horror as she imagined how it would feel to be caught on them and dragged down and around. It would be a dreadful way to die. In some ways, the murderer had done Isabel a good turn by killing her first.

She kept a close eye on the path as she neared the wheel, and at last she spied the signs she'd been hoping to find: a patch of trampled grass. At once she followed the faint trail to a screening thatch of reeds. A careful inspection around and behind the screen revealed rusty splatters of blood, silent witness to what had occurred there. The wheel was only a few yards further along the millrace. The roar of the water would have drowned out any cries for help, while the reeds would have hidden the act until the girl was dragged back to the stream and swept almost instantly onto the wheel.

Janna could not believe the girl's death was the result of an accidental encounter. Someone had arranged to meet her, and had come prepared. She was sure she knew who that someone was, but proving it might well be impossible.

She retraced her steps and walked on then to the small village of Domnitone. It comprised a few cots straggled around a muddy street that was populated by dogs, pigs, geese and hens with their chicks. A couple of ragged children directed Janna to Amy's home. There she found a haggard woman, old before her time, with several young children underfoot, the youngest just a baby. They were eating their dinner, but their trenchers were rapidly snatched up and hidden when they noticed Janna at the door. She sniffed the air, surprised to identify the rich scent of roasted meat. From their guilty looks, Janna concluded that the food had been a gift from Amy, probably purloined without Dame Alice's knowledge. Unless a family member had poached a boar from the forest? But that was a crime incurring such serious punishment if the miscreant was caught by the king's forester that Janna was willing to wager it was more likely an illicit gift from the daughter.

She pretended not to notice, for she did not want them on guard against her. Instead, she said gaily, "Amy has told me all about you and, as I was passing by this way, she suggested I step in and pay my compliments." She wished she'd thought to bring a gift of food to smooth her path.

"You're a friend of our Amy?" The woman's manner thawed somewhat.

Telling herself that Godric's life depended on the truth, even if it was arrived at through deception, Janna nodded. "You're lucky to have such a good and dutiful daughter."

At once the woman stiffened into wariness again. Janna sought to allay her fears. "Dame Alice is always happy to give her leave to visit you and bring you gifts," she lied.

Amy's mother sniffed. "I don't know about that. Amy did call in a few days back, and brought us a haunch of mutton and a wedge of bacon. Otherwise we hardly ever see her. The dame keeps her far too busy to visit us."

Janna pricked up her ears. Amy's mother couldn't know that she'd just shown her daughter to be a liar and possibly also a thief. To hide her interest, she picked up the baby, who had started to cry, and sat down to calm it, using the child as an excuse to talk to its siblings and mother about Amy. But she learned little more of interest, and finally she bid them farewell, pressing a silver coin into the woman's hand as she left. Although she felt uneasy at the betrayal to come, she soothed her conscience with thoughts of Godric and her need to set him free.

She was close to the millrace once more when she noticed a figure walking toward her in the heat of late afternoon. A woman. As she came closer, she realized it was Amy. This was the opportunity she'd been waiting for. She hurried to meet her with a smile on her face and caution in her heart.

"My lady." The girl bobbed a curtsy.

"Amy. I was hoping to have a quiet word with you," she said. She noticed that the girl looked ill at ease. Guilty conscience, Janna thought, and wondered what she could be hiding behind her back. Was she on the way to see her family with more purloined food for them? But it was none of Janna's business; indeed, she was pleased the girl was becoming more attentive, for she'd felt pity for her gaunt, downtrodden mother. Nevertheless, she was determined to find out what she could before letting Amy go on her way.

"I believe you knew Isabel? Was she a friend of yours?" she asked.

"Yes. We were very close." Amy raised a hand to wipe away an imaginary tear. "I still can't believe she's dead. That villain deserves to die for what he did to her."

Janna bit back an angry defense of Godric and instead said carefully, "I believe you saw Godric with Isabel shortly before she died. But did you actually see him push her into the millrace? Did you see her drown?"

"N-no." The girl flicked a quick glance at Janna, then looked away. "But that's what must have happened. Everyone says so. She was caught on the wheel and she drowned before the miller could block off the millrace and rescue her."

It sounded as though Amy genuinely believed what she was saying, what everyone was saying. Nevertheless, Janna suspected Amy knew more than she was telling.

"Why was Isabel there, do you know? What was she doing at the millrace?"

"She was meeting Godric, of course."

"But he didn't meet her there. He met her walking along the river, where you saw them together."

"Then they walked on to the millrace after." But the girl wouldn't look at Janna. She shifted uncomfortably. Janna thought she was probably anxious to get on her way before her disappearance was noted.

"You know Isabel was with child? Who was the father, do you know?"

Amy shrugged. "Must've been that Godric."

"She didn't tell you who was courting her, even though you were close friends?"

"Not that close."

"Did you see anyone else by the river that day?"

"No."

"So if it came to bearing witness, really you saw nothing of how Isabel died, or who might have caused her death."

"We all know who caused her death." Amy's mouth clamped into an obstinate line.

Janna sighed. She was going nowhere with this, but maybe she could frighten the girl into telling her what she wanted to know. "And where were you going when you saw Godric with Isabel?"

"To visit my mother."

"I've just been speaking to your mother. She was grateful for the food you brought her, and I'm sure she was glad to see you, for it seems you don't often visit your home even though the cook told me you spend a great deal of time away from the manor house."

Amy looked suddenly frightened. "Why are you questioning everyone about me?"

Janna returned her gaze, but didn't answer.

"I've done nothing wrong! You can't prove anything against me."

Janna smiled, but stayed silent.

"What does it matter to you anyway? My life is none of your business!"

"Oh, but it is," Janna said softly. "Where are you going now? To visit your family again?"

"No. It's getting late. I'll come back to the manor with you." Amy stepped out of the way, indicating that Janna should go ahead of her along the narrow path.

Surprised that the girl would still want to keep her company after such an uncomfortable interrogation, Janna began walking. Amy fell in behind her. Janna felt a prickling unease as she mulled over their conversation and its unlikely outcome. Had Amy been sent to find her – and if so, why? The path had left the river and was now winding through a belt of trees and thick scrub toward the manor house. All was silent. They were quite alone. Janna's unease deepened. She tried to comfort herself with the knowledge that she was safe; the assassin Robert had sent after her on previous occasions was now imprisoned in Winchestre. He would not come after her again.

But someone else might! She whirled around to confront Amy in time to see the girl's arm upraised and ready to strike. The thin blade she'd concealed behind her back flashed down, aimed now at Janna's heart instead of her back. Panic-stricken, Janna threw herself sideways and the blade caught her arm instead, a glancing blow that sliced through her sleeve and into her flesh.

Caught off-balance by Janna's sudden movement, Amy stumbled. Her grip tightened around the knife, her gaze fixed on her target as she righted herself. But Janna had sprung to her feet and, within the space of a heartbeat, she bunched up her skirt and kicked out, aiming for the knife in Amy's hand. Her boot connected with a satisfying crunch and the girl cried out in pain. But she still kept tight hold of the knife, thrusting forward to make sure of Janna's death.

Remembering the defensive moves that the runaway, Edwin, had shown her so long ago, and thankful that it was her left arm that had been injured, Janna launched herself at Amy, driving the forked fingers of her right hand straight into the girl's eyes. She felt the knife slice into her side, but ignored the pain as she followed through with a quick chop to Amy's throat, using her hand like a blade.

Amy screamed and fell back, dropping the knife. "Help me!" she croaked. But Janna had already scooped up the weapon and was running for her life. One hand was clamped to her side in a vain effort to staunch the blood that leaked between her fingers. In her other hand she gripped the long, thin knife, the misericord that she was sure had been used to silence Isabel, but had failed to silence her. She felt a great sense of triumph, overlaid by the fear that she would not live long enough to tell what she knew. She wasn't sure whether anything vital had been damaged, but knew that she was losing a great deal of blood. A fierce pain in her side and a growing weakness slowed her steps and made each breath more labored, but she was coming close now to the manor. And she prayed that it wouldn't be Robert who saw her first, for she knew he would stop at nothing to finish what his leman had started.

Chapter 8

Janna came to her senses to find herself stretched out on a bed, with Aldith in attendance. Her first thought was to give thanks that she was still alive, but her elation quickly gave way to alarm as she recognized the woman who was busy applying a salve to the deep wound in her side.

She remembered the midwife, and with recognition came the recollection that Aldith was not always scrupulous about cleanliness. She was about to send Aldith away, but realized suddenly that the midwife's apron was clean and the salve felt cool and comforting. She cleared her throat. "Hello, Aldith," she said weakly, speaking in the language of her childhood.

"Janna! You're awake at last!" The genuine pleasure on the woman's face quickly tightened into reserve. "Mistress Johanna," she amended.

"Janna. And I thank you for looking after me." Concern overrode courtesy. "How bad is the wound?"

"It's narrow, but deep. You've lost a lot of blood, but I don't think the knife pierced anything vital. I've cleansed the wound with water betony and sanicle, and this is a salve of woundwort and comfrey." Aldith hesitated. "I've taken your mother's advice and instructions to heart, my lady. And those in my care have benefited from it – most especially those women in childbirth," she added with some pride.

"I can see I'm in the best of hands," Janna said gratefully.

"It's fortunate I was already here, helping the reeve's wife give birth to her babe. You were – " Before she could finish speaking, the door flung open and Janna's father stormed into the room. At once Aldith drew back, but John had no eyes for the midwife. Instead, he fell on his knees beside the bed and grasped Janna's hand in his own.

"You are alive!" he said hoarsely. "I thank God for it! But how…who…?" And he glanced around the room as if the answer lurked somewhere in the shadowy corners.

"It was Amy, Dame Alice's serving woman, who attacked me. She waylaid me on the track leading down to the river and – " Janna sat up straighter, wincing at the pain in her side, " – she may still be there. I'm afraid I may have blinded her while trying to defend myself. And she will certainly have a bruised neck as a reward for her actions. Someone should go out and look for her."

"I'll see to it." John stood up and strode out. They heard his voice barking commands before he returned to the room.

"Where's the knife?" Janna asked Aldith. "Did you find the knife?"

"You mean this?" Aldith took the thin blade from the basin of bloodied water and wiped it clean. She held it up for Janna to see. "I had to prize it from you, you were clutching it so tight."

Janna smiled her thanks, and fell back against the bolster on the bed. "Find the owner and you find out who was responsible both for killing Isabel and for ordering my death." But there was no doubt whatsoever in her mind. *Robert.*

"I suspect the misericord belongs to my husband." A cool voice drew their attention to the doorway and to Dame Alice who stood there. She stepped forward. "I heard what had happened to you," she told Janna. "I came to see for myself if it was true." She hesitated.

"I would speak with you in private, if I may?" She sent a glance of appeal to John, who nodded. He walked out, followed by Aldith.

"Please, tell me what happened. Why were you attacked?" the dame demanded, as soon as they were left alone.

Janna had no wish to either alarm or distress Dame Alice, but Godric's life was at stake and she knew that it was time, now, for the truth. And so she told the dame all that had happened, leaving nothing out save the information about Cecily and her own mother, for by his actions Robert was already condemned. She understood, from the dame's darkening expression, how difficult the information must be to hear, but foremost in Janna's mind was Godric. Saving him was more important than fostering any illusions the dame might harbor regarding her husband's fidelity.

Dame Alice took the dagger from Janna and scrutinized it carefully, perhaps hoping even now that it might, after all, belong to someone else. "I've known about Robert's dalliances for years," she said then, breaking the silence that had fallen between them. "Your friend Cecily wasn't the first, but Amy will certainly be the last." Her lips tightened as she contemplated her husband's fate.

That Dame Alice knew about Cecily came as no surprise to Janna; she had long suspected it. She wondered if the dame was aware that Cecily had also been pregnant, even if she couldn't know the consequences of that pregnancy. Janna couldn't bring herself to mention it. In spite of the dame's brave words, Robert's betrayals must have hurt her pride and destroyed any last vestige of affection she might once have felt for him, while his punishment would shame and disgrace her in the eyes of the world. Even worse, Janna knew how desperately Dame Alice longed to bear another child. That another woman could lie with her husband and conceive so easily would cut deep indeed.

Putting aside her sympathy for the dame, she went to the heart of her concern. "What about Godric?" she asked. "Will you arrange for his release?"

Dame Alice hesitated. "I would like to see for myself the fatal wound that led you to suspect that Isabel had been murdered before she was pushed into the river."

Janna made to rise, but the dame bid her rest. "You tell me Hugh saw it too. I shall ask him to show me," she said, and took her leave. Janna wasn't sure whether or not the dame believed her story, but could understand how desperately she would clutch at the hope that, after all, someone else might have been responsible for Isabel's death.

After Dame Alice left the room, her father and Aldith came in once more. The midwife wasted no time in finishing her ministrations, wrapping Janna's wound with clean linen and binding it tight before turning her attention to the superficial cut on Janna's arm. "Thank you." Janna lay back, feeling easy in her mind that the midwife was doing exactly what she herself would have done. She turned to her father. "What about the dame's husband?" she asked, knowing her father would understand her meaning.

"My men are keeping an eye on him for the moment," John answered grimly. "I shall interrogate the girl, once she's been found and brought back here, and after that I shall speak to Robert." There was no need for him to say any more; Janna knew they understood each other perfectly.

A sharp knock surprised them all. Aldith went to the door and Hugh practically fell into the room, followed by Godric. His agonized expression smoothed into relief as he noted that Janna had apparently suffered no lasting harm. She ventured a smile in his direction, which he returned. It warmed her heart and brought a flush to her pale cheeks.

"The manor is buzzing with rumors," Hugh said, as he bowed to Janna's father. "How do you fare, my lady?"

"Very well, I thank you." Janna was amused at his mode of address, suspecting that it was more for her father's benefit than her own.

"We've heard what happened. That girl, Amy, has been brought back to the manor. She claims that you were both waylaid and attacked by a fugitive from the forest."

"Nonsense! You can go back and tell her that I'm still alive and that I have told the truth of what transpired between us. The truth is that she tried to kill me."

"But...why?"

"You must look to your aunt's husband for an answer to that," Janna said shortly.

"Robert?" Hugh's tone was flat with disgust.

Janna wished she could explain the full extent of Robert's villainy, but she knew it would have to wait until Cecily's confession. "I can tell you what I suspect," she said at last. "I believe your uncle made Isabel pregnant, but he needed to hide the evidence."

"So he sent Amy after her, just as he sent her after you?"

"I don't think so. Yes, she was certainly out along the river bank on that day, but it's more likely that she decided to go and visit her family because she was not meeting Robert as usual. No, I'm fairly sure Robert was behind Isabel's death, for two reasons. One, he wouldn't risk telling Amy why he wanted Isabel dead, not when his new mistress could well find herself in a similar predicament."

"And the second reason?" Janna's father asked.

"Isabel was wearing her finest dress when she was killed."

"So?"

"So I suspect Isabel must have told Robert about the baby, and already suffered his wrath. Certainly she was in great fear and distress over her predicament. The cook told me so, and so did you." Janna turned to Godric, careful not to mention his name for fear that her father would remember it. Godric's eyes met hers in a straight gaze but his expression was inscrutable. "I think Robert arranged to meet her along the river bank, and so she dressed for the occasion. Perhaps she hoped that he'd changed his mind and that he would look after her and do the right thing by her. But he'd decided to kill her instead." Just as he'd once meant to dispose of Cecily. But this time he'd chosen a more foolproof method. "Perhaps he'd already started a liaison with Amy by then. Certainly he needed to eliminate the danger of being found out, but I expect he assumed everyone would believe Isabel's death was an accident.

"Instead, and fortunately for Robert, Amy saw you with Isabel," she continued, looking directly at Godric. "No doubt it was Robert's suggestion that you two were lovers, so that he could accuse you of his own crime and make you the scapegoat."

"But why did Amy go after you with a knife? Why would she see you as any sort of threat?" Hugh asked.

"Robert believes I have knowledge of something that threatens his safety, and he wants me silenced. He sent Mus after me on more than one occasion, and he hasn't given up yet. I suspect he may have told Amy that I was here to look into Cecily's death and that I'd been asking questions about her testimony. He may even have warned her that, if their liaison became known, I would report her behavior to Dame Alice and she would be dismissed - unless she could silence me. He would know that I'd be on my guard if I encountered him along the river, but he would imagine that I'd feel safe with Amy – as indeed I did. To Amy's credit, she did seem somewhat unsure of me until my questions confirmed what Robert may have told her."

"I thank God that devil has been found out!" John said fervently. "I will make sure he hangs, and that young woman with him." He turned to Godric. "It seems you've had a lucky escape from the gallows, young man. What is your name?"

Don't answer! But Godric had no intimation of danger as he calmly said his name.

"Godric?" John frowned, puzzling for a moment before turning to Janna. "Is this the young man whom you say was helpful to you on past occasions?"

Janna closed her eyes and groaned inwardly. All the warmth engendered by Godric's smile drained out of her as she whispered a wretched, "Yes, Papa."

"I wish to reward you for your services to my daughter." John was unfastening his scrip as he spoke.

"No!" Janna and Godric spoke in unison.

"No?" Perplexed, John looked from Godric to Janna. "I thought you felt some gratitude toward this young man?"

Not only gratitude – love! Janna tried desperately to find the right words to pacify her father while telling Godric what was in her heart. Before she could speak, Godric intervened.

"I've been privileged to serve your daughter in the past, but with no expectation of any reward, sire. Nor do I want one."

"Don't be ridiculous, man. Take the money, I pray you." John held out a fistful of silver coins.

Godric took a step backward. "Please excuse me," he muttered, and left the room.

"Extraordinary." John shook his head.

Hugh exchanged a sympathetic glance with Janna.

"Will you speak to him?" Janna found her voice at last, addressing Hugh.

But John answered her. "I can try if you wish, but he seems very stiff-necked and arrogant. I'm surprised you tolerate that sort of attitude in a servant, Hugh."

"He's not – " Janna began, but Hugh spoke over her.

"I can assure you, sire, that Godric is the very best of men, despite his humble origins. I've learned that I can count on him in all things. In fact, I would trust him with my very life. He's the sort of man, sire, whom you would be proud to call your son if only you knew him as I know him."

Janna held her breath, wondering whether her father would chastise Hugh for his insolence. She was grateful beyond measure for

Hugh's testimony, and knew that it was a mark of his regard for her as well as for Godric that he would risk speaking out so boldly.

Her father stayed silent, his gaze moving from Janna to Hugh and back again. Janna felt her cheeks burn under his regard, but she said nothing. The silence lengthened between them. Finally, it was broken by Hugh.

"I apologize if I have spoken out of turn, sire. I just wanted you to know how grateful I am that my steward has been exonerated from this crime, although I deeply regret that your daughter was wounded as a result."

John nodded, and turned on his heel. "It's time for me to interrogate that young woman, and I will then speak to your uncle," he said grimly, and left the room.

"Thank you for your defense of Godric. Could you...would you ask him to come back here and speak to me?" Janna asked, as soon as her father was out of hearing.

Hugh smiled down at her with wry humor. "Oh, Johanna; I shall always wish that you had the same regard for me." His knuckles stroked her cheek in a brief and gentle caress. "And of course I shall do as you ask."

Left alone with Aldith, Janna wondered if she should take the midwife into her confidence. It was at times like these that she most missed her mother's presence and the comfort of her advice. She'd made such a muddle of things in the past, first believing herself in love with Hugh, and then transferring her affection to the charismatic Ralph, whose death had left a scar that had taken quite some time to heal. It had always been her mother's dearest wish that she and Godric would marry; a request that Janna had furiously rejected at the time. And when Godric had expressed the same desire, she'd dismissed him out of hand. It was only now that she'd grown into womanhood that she'd come to understand Godric's true worth, and her own love for him – a love he'd reciprocated when he thought of her as lowly born like himself, but withheld now that he knew about her father. How could she change Godric's mind? And how could she persuade her father to accept him as her husband? Wanting him was driving her to distraction. She had to know what was in his heart, for the thought that she might lose him forever cast her into black despair.

"So you're in love with that young man. That Godric." Aldith's voice broke into her thoughts.

"How did...?"

"Plain to anyone with eyes and a brain." Aldith gave a gleeful cackle. "Your mother would be so happy to know you've finally come around to her way of thinking."

Janna bobbed her head in acknowledgment. "But I think it may be too late now, for our circumstances have changed so greatly," she said mournfully.

"Nonsense! I saw how he looked at you – and how you looked at him. And your father saw it too."

"My father?" Janna jolted upright in alarm, then groaned with pain at the movement.

"Lie easy." Aldith helped settle her down once more. "You can only speak what is in your heart, and hope that your father will listen to you," she advised. "As to Godric – he's come far from his humble birth, but not so far as you, of course. He's a good choice for a husband, but he's proud, Janna. You'd do well to remember that." She patted Janna's hand. "Speak your heart," she said. "It's always best to start with the truth." And with a final reassuring pat, she left the room as Godric entered.

He was alone. Janna was glad of it. She beckoned him forward. "Thank you for coming," she said huskily.

He took a couple of steps closer and bowed his head in respectful obeisance, taking care to keep some distance between them. Janna wished she could get up and close the gap, but was wary of movement now, and so stayed still. They looked at each other.

Godric's face gave nothing away. He held himself taut, his stance betraying that every part of him was under stringent control. There was nothing left of the easy familiarity there had once been between them, nor of the ardor that had led to his offer of marriage. Janna wondered what to say that might convince him that she was prepared to abandon everything, if only she could be with him. She remembered Aldith's advice, and knew it was wise – knew also that she would never have a better chance than this to speak her mind. But her mouth was dry and her heart hammered so violently she could hardly think. She was panic-stricken that a careless comment might widen the gulf between them, might drive Godric away forever. She took a deep breath.

"There's no easy way to say this," she began, "but you once asked me to wed you."

"Twice."

It was true. Janna wondered if he meant it as a reminder of his affection or if it was a grievance on his part.

"Twice," she agreed. "But I was not ready, then, to think of marriage, of settling down with a husband and having children."

"Just as well, for you have found your family and a fortune that might otherwise have been lost to you."

It was a gentle reminder, said without bitterness, yet his words hurt worse than a hornet's sting.

"Not marrying you is my greatest regret, Godric," Janna said. "At the time, all I could think of was trying to find my father in order to avenge my mother's death, so that she might rest in peace. I made the promise at her grave, and I felt it was my duty to see it through. Of course, I had no way of knowing who my father was, or even if my quest would succeed. But I do know now what I didn't know before: that I wish with all my heart that you had shared this journey with me."

"Ah, Janna." Godric's voice was gentle as he continued. "For so many years I longed to hear those words from you, and longed to be with you. But it's too late now. You saw what your father thinks of me. Someone to be paid off for services rendered to his daughter – and those services most certainly do not include taking her as a wife!"

"If we were wed without asking my father's permission, he could do little to prevent the match after the event. After all, that's how he wed my mother!"

"A powerful and noble lord marrying a woman of lowly birth is a very different situation from ours. Your father would disown you, should you do such a thing."

"It's what Dame Alice did when she wanted to marry Robert."

"And look how *that* match has ended!"

Janna flinched at the scorn in Godric's voice. "But you are nothing like Robert," she protested, wishing she'd never raised his name. "You are honorable, I know that."

"Too honorable to sneak off and wed the granddaughter of a king!" Godric shook his head. "Janna, I – " For a moment his mask slipped, revealing something of his true thoughts before he put on the mantle of indifference once more. "You must forget me," he said. "All your life is before you and it will go well and be happy if you pay heed to your father's wishes."

"No! Never!" But Janna's protest went unheard for, without waiting for her dismissal, Godric hurried from the room.

Janna stared at the empty spot where once he had stood, too upset and shaken even to cry. She was sure she hadn't misread the agony of loss on his face, just in that fleeting moment. She was equally sure he was quite determined that he could not and would not marry her. She folded her arms around her body in an instinctive gesture of comfort, and began to rock to and fro. She tried to cheer herself with the thought that she had saved Godric from the hangman and was about to avenge her mother's death, yet even those triumphs paled beside the enormity of her loss.

*

She had fallen into a restless sleep when Cecily was shown into her room. She roused herself to welcome the young woman, and quickly set about trying to persuade her to add her testimony to that already supplied by Amy: to confess that she'd also been seduced by Robert.

"Like Isabel, you too became pregnant," Janna reminded Cecily, who had turned her face away as soon as Janna raised the subject. Janna could see that she was upset, and trying to hide it, but she pressed on. "But you were luckier than Isabel. You survived, even though Robert tried to get you out of the way too – with a bottle of poisoned wine. The wine you gave to my mother. The wine that killed her."

"But I had no knowledge that the wine was poisoned." Cecily turned her tear-stained face to Janna. "I'm so sorry that it happened, but it wasn't my fault. It was Robert's doing."

"Yes. And that's what I want you to tell Dame Alice and my father."

"I can't!" Cecily drew back, tears forgotten as she faced this new threat. "I asked you before not to meddle, Janna. I begged you! You know that it would jeopardize my chance of marrying Godric and our future together attending Sire Hugh and his wife."

"Godric is not going to marry you, Cecily." Janna was remorseless in her determination to make Cecily tell the truth. "If you wish to wed, you must look elsewhere. But I want my father to know the truth about my mother's death, and why Robert was responsible for it. It's time for Robert to be called to account for everything he's done. But that won't happen unless you add your evidence against him. I should tell you that Dame Alice already knows that her husband stabbed Isabel to prevent her pregnancy becoming known."

"Stabbed? But I thought she – "

"Dame Alice also knows that her husband has had several other liaisons, including his dalliance with you."

180

"She knows about me?" Aghast, Cecily jumped up from the stool on which she'd been sitting, and began to pace the room.

"Why do you think she sent you to stay with Hugh? And why do you think she did not ask you to return?"

"I never meant to hurt the dame." Now Cecily was wringing her hands as she paced. "You know that I loved Robert, and that I acted in good faith that he would treat me honorably."

"I expect he told all his mistresses the same thing," Janna said dryly.

"But it's even worse than that. I know how the dame longs to conceive and bear another child. I can't tell her...I can't let her know..." Cecily gulped, and began to cry again.

Janna watched her, feeling sympathy for her distress although she was still determined to have her way. "She's already had to face that knowledge with Isabel."

"I don't want her thinking badly of me, any more so than she does already." Cecily wiped away her tears and faced Janna. "You say Godric won't marry me, but I know that he can't marry you. Our future lies with Sire Hugh, and once you are gone again you can be sure that I'll do everything in my power to change Godric's mind. You can't ask me to risk my home and my only chance of happiness by saying things that will only cause great harm and misery to everyone. It's best to forget the past, Janna, when the future shines so bright."

"Best for everyone – except me and my father, Cecily," Janna said tartly, furious at the implied threat behind Cecily's words. "I will speak, even if you won't. I've waited a long time to bring my mother's killer to justice and I will have him publicly condemned for his deed – with or without your help." Even though she knew she was justified in her demands, nevertheless she felt some unease at achieving her goal at Cecily's expense. And it seemed that she'd made a new enemy as a result, for Cecily's face hardened in anger.

"By your leave, my lady," she said coldly, and hastened out of the room without waiting for Janna's reply.

Chapter 9

As soon as Janna was healed enough to ride without discomfort, her father ordered Robert to be taken to Wiltune under guard. He would be tried before the abbess who, as liege lord of her realm, had the power to dispense justice within it. Janna had warned her father that Cecily still refused to tell the truth about what had happened to her, but he had only pursed his lips and said, "You can leave that young woman to me." And so, traveling in the party were also Dame Alice and Cecily, along with Hugh and Godric. Aldith came too, to look after Janna.

Janna felt awkward riding alongside her father at the head of the train, and wished she could ride with Godric and Hugh, or even with Cecily, so that she could try one last time to persuade her to speak out. She wondered if Cecily was even now trying to win Godric to her side and glanced behind her. Yes, they were riding close together, the pair of them, and deep in conversation. She turned her face forward, determined not to let either of them see how upset and fearful she was.

It didn't help that she was welcomed back to Wiltune by William of Marsford, who came rushing across from the king's quarters at the gatehouse to greet her when they turned into the yard of the abbey's guest quarters. As soon as she'd dismounted, he bowed before her and seized hold of her hand to bestow a kiss. Janna cringed, sure that Godric and Cecily would be watching closely.

Richildis had also hurried out into the yard. Janna wondered if she'd spent all her time watching out for them while they'd been away, and felt a twinge of pity for the young girl. Richildis waited until her father had finished making arrangements for Robert to be held under guard in the abbey before casting herself into his arms. "I hate it here!" she sobbed. "That Sister Anne is making me work like the worst sort of servant."

Janna smothered a grin and went back to trying to discourage the attentions of her intended husband. But he would not listen to her hints, until finally she was obliged to tell him that the journey had exhausted her and she must rest. Fortunately, Aldith was close by and wasted no time in escorting Janna to the bedchamber that had been prepared for her use.

In view of the urgency of the matter, the abbess had agreed to preside over an informal court at the abbey, with the king present to make sure that justice was done. While arrangements were under way for Robert to be tried, including a search for those who might speak out in his favor as well as those who would bear witness to his crimes, Janna's father asked Sister Ursel to add an extra passage to his last will and testament that would make known his intention to leave all his property in England to his daughter and her husband.

When she found out what he was about, Janna had a quiet and private word with Sister Ursel as to the exact wording of the passage. "Is it about my proposed marriage to William? Has my father named him as my husband?" she demanded, as soon as she could get Sister Ursel on her own.

Sister Ursel nodded. "Yes. He's made his intentions very clear to me, Janna." She blushed, looking suddenly flustered. "M-my apologies. I should have called you m-m-my lady."

"You must call me Janna," Janna insisted, concerned to notice how Sister Ursel's stammer returned when she felt uncertain. She patted the nun's arm to reassure her, and hastily snatched back her hand when she recalled that touching was frowned on in the abbey.

"Janna." Sister Ursel relaxed and her face broke into a beaming smile. "I am so p-pleased you've succeeded in finding your father. It must be a great comfort to you. And, of course, you're going to be a very w-wealthy woman one day."

"But I hope my father will live for a long, long time!"

"Of course." Sister Ursel was quick to agree. "It touches my heart to see the love he bears for you. That you bear for each other." She leaned closer to Janna. "But that other daughter of his has been touched by the d-devil," she said seriously.

"Why? What has Richildis done?"

"Tears and tantrums when you left. And d-downright insubordination when our infirmarian asks for her help with anything. I swear, Sister Anne is at her wits' end as to how to deal with her." Ursel clapped a hand to her mouth. "I shouldn't have said 'swear,'" she apologized.

Janna grinned. "Richildis is enough to make anyone curse," she agreed. "But she's looking better. She seems to be eating properly again."

"Like a little pig – except when her father's around," Ursel said shrewdly. "If you ask me, this starving herself is a bid to capture his attention, and to come first in his care. She's very j-jealous of you, Janna. You should take care in your dealings with her."

"I know." Janna was kind enough not to share with Ursel the lengths to which Richildis had already gone to discredit her in the eyes of her father and his family. Instead, she cut back to her main concern. "Sister Ursel, could I ask you for a favor?"

"Of course. Anything!" The nun's promise was heartfelt. Janna remembered the stolen pages from Ursel's beautifully illuminated manuscript of St Edith's life and how she'd solved the mystery of their disappearance. She must remember to ask the nun to show her how the work progressed. But first things first.

"Instead of naming William of Marsford, could you just write 'husband' and leave it at that?"

"But your father's made his wishes most clear." Sister Ursel looked troubled.

"It may be my father's wish, but it's not mine." Janna hesitated, wondering whether it was wise to confide in the nun. "I love Sire Hugh's steward, Godric, with all my heart. He's the man I wish to marry."

"And does he love you?"

"Yes."

"But your father will not permit the match?"

"No." Janna gave a strained smile. "Even though I know my own mind, there are two men whom I still have to convince."

"I'll do what I can," Ursel promised.

But Ursel's effort ended in failure, for John noticed the missing words at once and, speaking over her stammered apologies, ordered her to add them. And so it was that when Janna, in company with her father and Richildis, presented herself once more to the king, William was named as her husband in her father's last will and testament.

Janna was relieved that, this time, the bishop was absent from the gathering. Yet it seemed he'd had more than enough time to convey his suspicions, for there was no doubt in her mind that the king's manner had changed since they'd last met. Although he welcomed Richildis into his presence, he seemed cool once he turned his attention to Janna and her father. Perhaps sensing trouble ahead, John made a flattering speech before handing over the amended document to the king. Stephen scanned the parchment briefly, and frowned at John. "I see no provision here for your wife and your other children," he said sternly. "I would need to be satisfied that they, too, will be looked after."

John frowned. "My liege," he said. Janna could sense his anger at having to explain himself to his cousin. "They will inherit my property and a sizable fortune in Normandy. I was not aware that I needed your permission to witness my intentions across the water."

It was a sharp reminder to the king of his misfortune in losing Normandy to Geoffrey of Anjou, the empress's husband. And it was clear from Stephen's thunderous expression that he did not value the reminder. "Tell me something," he said sharply. "When you came to me at Oxeneford, did you bring your eldest daughter with you?"

Janna's heart sank. She sneaked a sideways glance at her father, wondering if he'd tell his cousin and king the truth. Just how much did Stephen know – or suspect? John's face had flushed somewhat, but he answered, after only a slight pause, "Yes, my liege. She came with me."

"The nuns at Godstow Abbey gave me shelter in my father's absence, sire, while he came into Oxeneford to pay his respects to you," Janna said hastily. It was almost the truth, after all.

"She bears a remarkable resemblance to your half-sister. My enemy, the empress." The king frowned at Janna, taking her measure. She wondered if he was thinking back to an icy winter's night when the empress was seen abroad yet somehow managed to escape the king's troops.

"But the color of my hair is quite different, sire," she said quickly. "I am fair like my mother, who was a Saxon woman."

Stephen grunted and turned back to John. "Leave this document with me," he said. "I need to make further enquiries about...several matters." His eyes were bright with suspicion as he watched them take their leave.

Janna wondered if he'd worked out the possibility of her deception for himself, or if he and the bishop had shared information to help him arrive at the truth. She was fairly sure that there was a real purpose behind both his question and his observation.

Richildis, while unaware of the real reason behind Stephen's prevarication, was quick to put on it her own interpretation. "He's much more interested in doing right by my mother and our family than rewarding a nobody like you," she said gleefully, once their father had left them alone in the yard. "He won't witness Papa's document because he thinks you're not worthy of William."

"I don't think I'm worthy of William either," Janna snapped, anxious to silence her. The girl was as persistent and annoying as a midge in summer.

"You're not worthy of having a noble husband at all!" Richildis placed her hands on her hips and surveyed the crowded yard. The abbey's servants had been busy collecting produce from outlying properties, bringing it in from barns to the undercroft within the abbey so as to provide for the king and his army, those unwelcome guests who now occupied the gatehouse and who needed board as well as beds. Merchants came and went, everyone from the lowliest faggot seller to rich craftsmen hoping to interest the king and his barons in the goods they brought with them for sale.

Janna stiffened as she watched Hugh traverse the yard, followed closely by Godric. It seemed they were on their way to the stables. Seeing Janna, Hugh checked and started toward them. Godric plucked at his sleeve, perhaps with the idea of dissuading him, but Hugh kept on. With pounding heart, Janna stared at Godric. And Richildis watched her, watched them both, while her lips curled into a spiteful sneer.

"My lady. Johanna," Hugh greeted her. Godric bobbed his head but said nothing.

"Hello, Hugh. Richildis, this is Sire Hugh and his steward, Godric. My half-sister, Richildis."

Richildis made no response, just surveyed the two men with a scornful expression. Then she pointed at Godric. "You should be marrying someone lowly like him, not a baron like William of Marsford," she told Janna.

A rush of shock and shame swept over Janna, rendering her speechless. But Hugh had sized up the situation and was quick to respond. "Godric would make an excellent husband for any woman, my lady. Even for someone like you." Janna wondered if Richildis recognized his words for the insult she was sure was intended. She gazed at Godric in mute apology. And Richildis saw that too.

"But she's betrothed to William now," she said. "My father has seen to it." She smiled with bitter amusement. "My half-sister is to wed a man twice her age, who's already been wed before and has several brats to show for it."

Richildis's cruelty took Janna's breath away. Still she stayed silent, registering the shock on the faces of the men in front of her.

"My – my congratulations on your betrothal, my lady." Hugh cleared his throat. "I have met William of Marsford. He is a fine...soldier."

Still Godric said nothing. After an awkward pause, Hugh took his leave and the two men set off in the direction of the stables. Janna turned on Richildis as soon as they were out of earshot.

"You little hellspawn!"

"Why? What have I done?" The girl's voice was full of whining self-pity, but a gleam in her eyes told Janna she knew exactly the mischief she had caused.

"Go to hell, and may the devil keep you company!" Janna stamped away, keen to put as much distance as possible between her and her half-sister.

"I'll tell my father on you!"

Janna ignored the shouted threat and kept going, thinking that Sister Ursel was closer to the truth than she'd realized. Indeed, the girl seemed to have been touched by the devil. So much malice and spite! Where once she'd felt sorry for Richildis, now she felt only aggravation and a desperate wish that her father would send the girl home, and take himself with her.

Finding him had caused so many problems. Her heart and future happiness were in jeopardy because of her father. And yet she knew that the promise of having her own home in Winchestre was enough for her to want to keep him on side, for the future she longed for was inextricably tied up with the property there. But overlying all other considerations was the fact that she'd come to genuinely care for him as a daughter should for her father.

She felt bereft as she recalled Richildis's spiteful remark, and the shock it had caused. And yet, if she could not have Godric, perhaps she should please her father and agree to the match? After all, what other choice did she have? But every instinct rebelled against it. In her heart, Janna knew that asking Ursel to omit the name of her husband on the testament had been with the last, desperate hope that she might persuade John to her way of thinking. All Janna wanted to do now was weep for the past, for everything she'd thrown away when she'd dismissed Godric so carelessly from her life. This, now, was her future. Marriage to a man she did not love; passing from her father's control into the control of a husband she didn't know and certainly didn't care about.

Was it really too late? Janna's tears checked as she considered the question. As Richildis had so gleefully pointed out, the king had not yet ratified her father's wishes on the matter of a husband. And until the deed was done, there must always be hope. It was a flicker of comfort to set against the cold dread that had settled on her heart.

*

But her problems were not yet over for, true to her word, Richildis continued with her mischief-making. The first intimation Janna had of the problem was John's request for a private word with her after they'd broken their fast the next day.

"I think it was not a good idea to bring Richildis to Wiltune," he said, as he steered her out to the abbey's gardens and the orchard beyond. "Sister Anne tells me she has not settled here; that she is rude and insubordinate."

"But she's looking better in herself. You must encourage her to eat, Father. She will do so if she thinks it will please you." It was the only positive comment Janna could make about her half-sister.

"Yes, Sister Anne has already had much to say on that matter." John sighed. "I'm only now beginning to understand the depths of her hatred of you, Johanna. For example, she tells me you are in love with that man who was accused of murder. Godric. I've told her she is mistaken, but she was most insistent."

Janna stole a glance at her father. The expression on his face gave nothing away.

"I recall that you were over-anxious to come to his aid, to prove his innocence," John continued. "I suspected there might be some attachment between you from the past, but I told myself you had more sense than to harbor such feelings now, given your new situation."

Janna took a breath, giving herself time to order her thoughts. She remembered Aldith's advice to speak from the heart, and Sister Ursel's comment on the love she'd witnessed between her father and Janna. Would love be enough to persuade him to her way of thinking?

"Richildis speaks the truth, Papa." Something else Aldith had said came into Janna's mind. "It was always my mother's dearest wish that Godric and I would make a match together. She believed he would make a good husband for me." It was the single most compelling argument she could come up with to convince her father.

"That was when you had no money and no prospects, Johanna. Things are very different now." Janna thought she detected some sympathy in her father's voice. It encouraged her to continue.

"Not so different, Papa. Regardless of his station in life, I love him, just as you once loved my mother. I'll always love him, just as I suspect you love my mother still, in spite of your marriage to Dame Blanche."

"You have your mother's knack of turning an argument to your own benefit," John told her. "But our situation was different from yours, Johanna. Your mother married wisely when she married me, because I could offer her wealth and status as well as love. And I would see you safely wed to a nobleman in a similar position."

"Godric will look after me!"

"Godric has no property of his own. He is in no position to offer you the sort of future that befits the granddaughter of a king."

"But you have wealth and status, Papa, and you have said you will confer some of your property on me. Surely that is enough for both of us!"

"And has he asked for your hand, even knowing that you are to be betrothed to another? Is he as anxious for the match as you seem to be?"

Janna hesitated. "Godric loves me, Papa, as I love him. I've suggested that we marry without your consent, or even that we should run away together. But he is honorable, and he will not agree to it. He did not know about my betrothal until Richildis told him yesterday, but even before then he argued that the difference in our station in life is too great for you to agree to the match."

"I'll give him credit for some sense, then." John surveyed his daughter with narrowed eyes. "It's a different matter altogether when a man marries a woman in order to gain her property and status. You have two examples right in front of you: the tragedy of Dame Alice's match with Robert of Babestoche, and your friend Hugh's loveless marriage to Eleanor." He smiled, amused by Janna's surprise. "I see more than you might realize," he said dryly. "You may believe yourself in love with Godric, but I know that Hugh loves you far more than he loves his wife."

191

"That may be, but Godric loves me for myself, not for my prospects."

"Even my half-sister's marriage is a disaster," John spoke over her protest. "Geoffrey of Anjou was never the right choice for Matilda, no matter what my father might have thought."

"But your father dictated that match just as you would dictate mine!" Angry now, Janna faced her father. "Have you considered that perhaps the mistake lies with the man rather than with his circumstances? I can't answer for Geoffrey of Anjou because I don't know him, but Robert of Babestoche would never have been a good match for Dame Alice even if he'd been born a baron. Hugh, on the other hand, is an honorable man and will make his wife happy even if he loves her not. And Godric is honorable too. He may not be a baron, but he will make me a good husband, Father. I know it."

"And you say that he loves you as you love him?"

"He has told me so and I believe him." Janna turned her head lest her father read her fear that Godric's pride would not let him consent to the match even if it did have her father's blessing.

John put his arm around her in a brief embrace. "I see you love him now, but William is a far more suitable match for you. I've been making enquiries about him. It seems that his first marriage was a happy one; he was considered a dutiful and attentive husband and a good father to his children. He's also an upright and honorable man. The men under his command think very highly of him. I am sure you will grow to love him in time."

"If the king gives his permission for the match." It was the last argument Janna could muster. "I suspect the bishop has told him of my role in intercepting his message and taking it to Robert of Gloucestre. And I also think the king suspects what really happened on the night the empress made her escape from Oxeneford."

"You may well be right." John was silent for a time as he mulled over Janna's words. "But suspicion is one thing, proof quite another, and he has none. Besides, he is my cousin. I have known him since childhood and I am confident he will do as I ask, especially if he thinks he can buy my loyalty that way. You must reconcile yourself to marriage with William, Johanna. He will protect you and your estates here in England, and I am sure he will prove an attentive and loving consort. You will grow to care for him in time, even if you cannot believe that now."

Never! But Janna kept her thoughts to herself, knowing that further argument was useless. It seemed that her future was assured. That it was not to her liking was not important, for she had no say in the matter, none at all.

That night she lay awake, tossing and restless in her narrow bed in the guest quarters of the abbey. She heard the great bell of the abbey chime to wake the nuns for their devotions, and pictured them rousing from their beds, half asleep and yawning, donning their slippers and filing into the church for Matins and Lauds. She was of half a mind to join them, in the hope that quiet communion with God might help her find some measure of peace. She sat up and swiveled her feet to the floor, but paused as she heard a patter of footsteps and a sudden urgent knock on her door.

"Yes? What is it?" she called, and fumbled for the tinder box and candle beside her bed.

"Please, my lady, can you come quickly?" A dark shape stood at the door, panting and distressed.

"What's the trouble?"

"It's Agnes, my lady. Her time has come, but the baby...the baby..." The high, girlish voice faltered into silence. After a few strikes at the tinder box, Janna had succeeded in lighting the candle. Now she held it aloft and recognized Susanna, the bailiff's daughter from his first marriage. Distraught and disheveled, forgetting propriety in her distress, she tugged at Janna's arm. "Agnes asked me to fetch you. Please make haste," she implored.

Together they hurried through the abbey gates to the home farm where the bailiff had his residence. Even as she ran beside the girl, Janna berated herself for not thinking to alert Sister Anne to the problem, or even to ask the infirmarian for any medicaments she might need. Her steps faltered as she faced the enormity of what she was about to do: assist a woman in a difficult childbirth when she had no idea what that entailed. True, she'd attended births with her mother in the past, but on those occasions, Janna had merely observed while her mother did all that was required.

"Hurry, my lady!" the girl urged her on. But Janna stood still, knowing there were others more suited to the task this night, even though it hurt her pride to admit it.

"Go back to the abbey," she told Susanna. "Ask for Mistress Aldith, the midwife, and bid her come with you to your stepmother. But first explain the problem to her, and also tell her that the infirmarian, Sister Anne, will give her all the medicaments she might need. Say that you have spoken to me and these are my instructions."

"But Agnes asked for you, my lady."

"And I shall go to her. But you must go back and find Mistress Aldith. Hurry, Susanna. Run!"

Pausing only long enough to ensure that the girl was doing as she was bid, Janna hastened on to the bailiff's cottage. She found Master Will outside, sweating and anxious as he paced about. His children huddled around him, pasty faced and frightened as they listened to the moans and cries coming from within. Janna knew the bailiff's first wife had died of sickness after childbirth, and she understood their fear. She bid him a swift good evening and rushed inside to find her friend.

Agnes was in great distress, shuddering and groaning as she doubled over with the pains of giving birth. One of the local women was with her, but seemed incapable of any action other than wringing her hands and fluttering about the bed.

Janna pushed her aside. "Bring me some warmed oil, and make sure there's plenty of clean linen," she said, and leaned over Agnes.

"Janna! Thank God you've come," Agnes panted, quieting momentarily as she grabbed Janna's hand in relief. "Please, help me," she begged. Her body convulsed in another contraction and she moaned piteously as she strained to push the baby out.

"How long has this been going on?" Janna withdrew her hand and parted Agnes's thighs, hoping that the baby's head was visible. But there was no sign of it.

"Hours." Tears leaked into Agnes's eyes as the contraction passed and her body relaxed in a brief respite. "I push...and push...but the baby won't come."

Janna tried to hide her concern. She knew enough to understand that babies were supposed to present head first down the birth canal, and that complications and even death could occur if, for some reason, they did not. Her mother had used warm oil to massage the woman's stomach in an effort to turn the baby around if there was a problem, but Janna had never done such a thing before. She stared at Agnes's bloated belly. She was sure that if she went about it the wrong way, she might make matters worse. She shuddered as she recalled one birth she had witnessed. The baby had been born dead, with the birth cord wrapped around its neck.

She cursed her lack of knowledge as she took hold of her friend's hand and held it tight. "I think the baby is in the wrong position to come," she said steadily, "but I have sent for Aldith, the midwife. She will know what to do."

"No!" Agnes reared up in alarm. "I will not have her!"

"You have nothing to fear." Janna pushed her gently back onto the bed. "Aldith has learned much while I've been away. She tended my wound after I was stabbed, and I could not fault her care."

"Stabbed?" Agnes reared up once more, her own troubles temporarily forgotten. "In God's name, Janna, what happened to you? Are you all right?"

"Yes, no lasting harm," Janna reassured her. She seized the basin of warm oil from the fluttering attendant and began to gently massage her friend's swollen stomach, not attempting to turn the baby but hoping merely to calm her and bring some relief until Aldith arrived. "The attack marks the end of a long story, Agnes, but my quest to bring a killer to justice is complete and the culprit will be tried at the abbess's court soon enough."

"Tell me all about it. It might take my mind off my travail." Agnes subsided back on to the bed. "I'm not going anywhere in a hurry," she added, with a weak smile.

Janna was nearing the end of her recital when she heard the sound of voices coming closer. Breathing a sigh of relief, for she was becoming increasingly alarmed by Agnes's weakening state, she threw open the door to welcome in not only Aldith but also Sister Anne.

"I need your help," she admitted, but Aldith had already thrust a bag into her arms and extracted a small phial of oil from it. Janna and Sister Anne exchanged glances, ruefully acknowledging their lack of experience when it came down to this most basic of human activities. After carefully washing her hands in a basin of clean water and drying them on a cloth, Aldith applied a dab of the oil, which smelt faintly of roses. With her eyes closed, she began to palpate Agnes's stomach almost as if trying to determine the shape of what lay inside. Finally she gave a small grunt and turned her attention to the birth canal, feeling inside Agnes with a deft, slippery hand. Janna watched closely, for she needed to remedy this gap in her knowledge. It was vital to know all she could about childbirth if she was to achieve her dream for the future.

"The baby's lying in the wrong position," Aldith commented at last. "I'm hoping it hasn't moved too far down into the birth canal and that I may still be able to turn it."

Janna nodded, taking some comfort from the fact that at least she'd diagnosed the problem correctly. But she remembered enough from the past to know that Agnes would be in real trouble if Aldith couldn't turn the child. The midwife washed and dried her hands once more, and again smoothed them over with oil. Then she placed her hands on Agnes's distended stomach and began to push and rotate, just as Janna remembered her mother doing in the past.

"Janna, there's mugwort and birthwort in my bag. Mix the mugwort with warm ale and give it to Agnes to drink," Aldith instructed, as her hands moved rhythmically. "Mix the birthwort with wine – or ale if there is none. The drink will help the afterbirth to come away after the baby is born."

Aldith's confidence and her calm instructions, plus having something to do, helped give Janna heart. Looking at her friend, she could see that Agnes seemed calmer, until she was shaken by another contraction.

"Try not to push! Not yet," Aldith said sharply. "Take long, deep breaths and say a prayer to our Lord for the safe birth of your babe."

Sister Anne began to pray, and after a few moments Agnes joined in, her words punctuated by her labored breaths and choked-back moans. Janna returned to the bed. She raised Agnes's head so that she could drink the concoction, and Agnes gulped it down gratefully. Needing something else to do to take her mind off her fears, Janna fetched a basin of cool water and began to bathe her friend's face. She had an awful feeling that time was running out for Agnes, who was growing visibly weaker.

"If it comes feet first there's a chance both mother and baby will survive, but if its bottom is stuck…" Aldith shook her head, although her busy hands did not break their rhythm.

"You could cut me open to save the baby." Agnes's whisper broke the silence that had followed Aldith's pronouncement.

"No!" Janna knew that such a procedure spelled danger for the baby and certain death for the mother.

"We're nowhere near having to do that yet," Aldith soothed. Her careful hands, massaging and pushing, told Janna that she was not going to give up without a fight.

"Are you sure you're not harming the baby?" Agnes asked fretfully. "I've got an awful squirming feeling inside."

For a moment Aldith relaxed and a smile lit her grim features. "That's good. It means the baby's turning," she said, and bent to her task once more. Agnes's breathing was growing more ragged. Her face showed the strain she was under, while her lips were bitten raw. Finally she could not hold on any longer.

"Aarghh!" Her whole body convulsed in a violent contraction.

"Push!" Aldith shouted. Her hands were still busy but now had changed direction, pressing downward, pushing, pushing, helping Agnes to push the baby out.

"Aarghh!" Agnes screamed again. Janna caught her breath and resolved that she would never, ever have a child, not if it meant going through this. And yet, when the birth finally happened, it happened so quickly that afterward it just seemed like a blur of sound and movement. The crown of the baby's head emerged, blood staining Aldith's hands as she gently held and supported its weight, until the whole body was suddenly expelled in a rush. They huddled around for an anxious inspection of the inert blue form while Aldith quickly tied the birth cord and clipped it.

"It's a little girl." Aldith blew up the baby's nose and put her finger in its mouth to clear out the air passages. Then she turned the baby over and gave its bottom a hearty smack.

"No!" Agnes's wail of protest was caught short as they all heard an indrawn breath followed by a thin, quavering cry. By now, tears were coursing down Janna's cheeks. She glanced at Agnes, whose cheeks were as wet but whose smile equaled the brightness of a thousand suns. The new mother stretched out her arms to take the child from Aldith, and cuddled it to her breast, while her tears dripped onto the child's bloodied head.

"Johanna." Agnes smiled up at Janna, and then reached a hand in gratitude to the midwife. "Johanna Aldith."

Chapter 10

The abbess's court was finally convened some days later. It was held in the chapter house where, by custom, the abbey sisters met every morning for prayers and to discuss matters pertaining to the abbey. Now only the most senior members of the convent were present, but still the room was crowded. Most of those present were witnesses both for and against Robert of Babestoche, but there were also men of prominence from the town. Although she knew the evidence against him was overwhelming, Janna felt her heart speed up as she entered the court, flanked by her father and Richildis. Facing them across the room was Robert, looking proud and defiant. Amy sat close beside him. All her fine airs were gone now; she seemed cowed and frightened as she huddled into herself.

Dame Alice sat on her own, face turned away from her husband. The dame's head was tilted at a proud angle; it was difficult to read the expression on her face. Janna wondered if she would give evidence on his behalf or against him.

The abbess swept in through the door, and those inside the room surged to their feet and waited for her to be seated. But she did not take the high chair at the center. Instead, she stood beside it until the

pl0x

pl0x

king entered some moments later and seated himself, a wave of his hand indicating that everyone else might now sit down. There was a murmuring buzz until the abbess held up her hands, after which an expectant hush fell over the room.

Janna leaned forward, and the trial began.

Although the king sat in pride of place, it soon became obvious that the abbess was in charge, as her sergeant-at-arms came forward to present the cases against both Amy and Robert. At his appearance, Robert surged to his feet. *"Miserere mei, Deus. Secundum misericordiam tuam – "* he began. Janna recognized the words of the psalm, often quoted by miscreants in an attempt to save their necks by pleading benefit of the clergy so that they could be tried in the more lenient clerical court instead. But it did him no good in this instance, for the abbess interrupted him.

"You showed little mercy for your victims when you preyed upon them. Do not presume to ask for God's mercy in this court." And she gestured for her sergeant-at-arms to proceed.

Janna was first to be called on to give evidence, which she did, beginning with her investigation into the death of Isabel, followed by Amy's attempt to silence her. She was about to go on to tell the court about Mus, the assassin who, on Robert's instructions, had tried several times to kill her, but was forestalled by the abbess, who thanked her and bade her take her seat. Janna wondered if those present knew of her past life, and whether it was her father's wish that her employment at the tavern be kept secret. She sat down, regretting the lost opportunity to speak of Cecily's liaison with Robert, and the death of her mother that had resulted from it.

Amy came next. She wasted no time in turning against her former lover, portraying herself as an innocent victim of his lust and an unwilling accomplice to his plans. It was not a convincing performance, and when Dame Alice took the stand the court's sympathy immediately swung toward the betrayed wife. She held herself erect and gave her evidence against her husband and his past infidelities in a clear voice and without a quaver. Janna could only guess at the cost to the dame's pride and to her heart, and admired her greatly for her courage. When Robert followed his wife, it was apparent to everyone that he had already been judged and found guilty.

It seemed that a verdict must surely follow, but then Janna's father rose to his feet and asked for permission to address the court. Janna glanced at Cecily, knowing what was to come. Cecily knew it too, for she turned pale as whey. She and Godric were sitting together, and Janna watched as she leaned aside to murmur in his ear and he patted her hand in a comforting gesture. Even as he did so, he glanced across at Janna. She thought she read compassion rather than judgment in his expression, but she felt very uncomfortable nevertheless.

"I wish the court to be apprised of what else I know about the accused," John began, and Janna sat back as the damning indictment unfolded. John's voice faltered only once, as he spoke of the death of his beloved Sister Emanuelle: "My wife, whom you all knew as Eadgyth," he said, with a fond glance at Janna. She understood what was behind his words. He was ensuring that everyone present knew that her father and mother had been wed, and that her birth was therefore legitimate.

Robert's air of defiance had collapsed. Now he looked like a fox caught at bay by a pack of hounds, knowing that death was imminent and that it would be agonizing.

And then it was Janna's turn once more to give evidence, this time implicating Cecily in the death of her mother. Janna could only guess how the young woman was feeling, and was sorry that she was forced to relive her shame in public. But there was comfort in finally setting the record straight. "Robert of Babestoche did not intend to kill my mother," Janna concluded, "but he certainly intended to silence any who might bear witness against him." She flashed a quick glance at

Cecily and then hurried on, hoping to distract the court's attention from the unhappy young woman with her further disclosures. "Once he realized his plan had failed, that my mother had died instead of his intended victim, and that I'd discovered the truth of the matter, he incited the villagers to burn down my home while I was still inside. It was only by the grace of God that I managed to escape. And, indeed, once the accused found out that I was still alive, he then sent Alan, known as Mus, his servant, after me on several other occasions, to silence me before I could give evidence against him."

A faint gasp, quickly stifled, told Janna that the news had come as a shock to Dame Alice. Before she could continue with her testimony, the dame was on her feet and pointing a shaking finger at her husband. "I can vouch for part of that statement, my liege," she spat. "I was unaware of the circumstances behind all the misfortunes that befell this young woman, but I do know that she speaks the truth of at least some of what has happened to her in the past."

"I, too, am aware of at least one attack on Dame Johanna," the abbess said coolly, without bothering to rise from her chair. "Fortunately she is a young woman of spirit, and she fought off her attacker with great courage."

"I, too, can vouch for that, my lord, for I was a witness."

Janna turned, surprised to see Will and Agnes among the throng. Agnes was pale, still recovering from the ordeal of childbirth. She clutched her child to her bosom as if it was a rare and precious object. If she was aware she was breaking convention or endangering her health by appearing in public so soon after giving birth, she gave little sign of it. She was supported by her husband on one side; Wat, eldest of the bailiff's children, stood on the other. She faced the king, determined to put in a word for her friend.

"Let your husband speak for you," the abbess reproved her sternly. And so Will stepped forward and gave evidence for both of them, for they had both been there, out in the fields, when the first attack had taken place. The bailiff might not have understood what lay behind it at the time, but by now he was obviously well briefed by his wife.

"So you have proved more than a match for an armed assassin? It seems you are brave as well as resourceful," the king interrupted. Janna was only too aware of the guilty color staining her face as she recalled her adventures in Oxeneford. She was sure the king had received a full report of the chase after the so-called empress before she seemingly vanished into thin air. How much did he know? How much did he suspect? She forced her attention back to the matter at hand, in time to hear the abbess pronounce the verdict against Robert: he was to hang for his crimes. Amy was convicted and would spend several years in prison, but at least she had escaped with her life.

And then it was all over, and they were free to go. Janna felt a surge of mixed feelings as she left the chapter house. She'd done all she'd set out to do: she'd avenged her mother's death, set the record straight, and her mother had been given a proper, Christian burial. And Godric had been publicly exonerated of all blame for Isabel's death. But instead of feeling triumphant, she felt instead as if she'd been ripped in two, as if only half of her was walking out of the chapter house.

The other half was with Godric. She watched him with Cecily. He had a steadying hand under the girl's arm, supporting her as they emerged into the harsh sunlight of high summer. Janna joined the crowd as everyone traversed the quiet cloister and entered into the yard of the guest quarters. But she couldn't help glancing back over her shoulder, each glimpse reinforcing anew, and with the sharp sting of an arrow, Godric's care and concern for Cecily. She knew Godric wasn't in love with Cecily, that he was merely being kind to a woman in distress, just as he'd once been kind to Isabel. Nevertheless, it hurt Janna that she was not able to take comfort from Godric herself when she needed him so desperately.

She stopped in the yard, yearning for a word with him, or even a look to acknowledge her presence. As she watched, an older man stepped forward to speak to Cecily. At once, Godric moved back as if to give the man all the space he needed to make his presence felt. Janna's interest quickened. Was this Hugh's new reeve? What was his interest in Cecily? The two conversed for a few moments, their words too quiet for Janna to hear, and then Cecily shook her head and the older man walked on. Cecily and Godric were left alone once more.

She ventured a smile, hoping even now that it might be possible to speak to him. But he merely bobbed his head to her and walked away, dragging Cecily away with him. Janna saw that he was aiming for Hugh, who stood with his arm around his aunt, apparently consoling her. Janna felt a stab of remorse. While she'd achieved what she'd set out to do, her ambition had come at great cost to several people, not least the dame herself. Did they all hate her for it?

She tried to console herself with the thought that all might yet turn out well. Freed of Robert, it was possible that Dame Alice might find happiness with a kindly man who would love and cherish her as her first husband had never done. And freed of her secrets at last, Cecily might also find happiness, perhaps with the older man, if not Godric. They both had some prospect of happiness in the future. Janna sighed as the image of William came into her mind. For her, and for Godric, there seemed to be no way out.

"Your young man seems more interested in the dame's companion than in you," her father observed as he came to Janna's side, closely followed by Richildis. The girl's sullen expression lifted into a smirk of triumph as she followed John's gaze.

"He would wed me tomorrow if you would only give your permission, Papa." It was her last chance to speak out, and Janna seized it. "You see now that he's been found innocent of any crime, and you've seen the esteem in which his liege lord holds him. He's a good man, Papa. He's the finest man I know!" In her agitation,

Janna took her father's hand and clasped it tight. "You recognized my mother's worth when you met her, and you married for love. Please, *please*, give thought to my happiness and let me do the same."

John stayed silent, gazing thoughtfully at the group clustered around Dame Alice. Then he sighed and shook his head. "It won't do, Johanna. I'm sorry, but it just won't do."

"*Please!*" Janna's desperate appeal rang out above the buzz of conversation in the yard. Several people turned to stare. John gripped her arm and forced her to walk on with him.

"Tomorrow we shall leave for Winchestre," he said firmly. "It is too late to pack up and go today, but I would like you to be ready by first light tomorrow, Johanna. We have delayed here long enough, I think."

Defeated, Janna let herself be dragged along by her father. It occurred to her that her father's new testament had not yet been acknowledged by the king. Janna wondered if her father deemed it more expedient to leave matters until the king's suspicions had time to die down, and felt a slight easing of anxiety. Anything that meant a delay in her betrothal and marriage was more than welcome.

"Why does she have to come back with us?" Richildis whined. "I thought she was going to stay in Wiltune and marry that smelly old man."

"Earl William is not a smelly old man," John contradicted sharply. "Curb your tongue, Richildis. It ill becomes you to speak like a common fishwife."

Richildis shot a glance of pure venom at Janna. "Why don't you let her stay and marry that peasant, then?" she said sulkily.

"That's enough!" John subjected his daughter to an icy glare before striding off. Janna wondered at Richildis's stupidity. If what the girl most wanted was to win her father's affection, she was certainly going about it the wrong way. But she said nothing, for she knew her half-sister would not listen anyway.

She was about to follow her father, to start packing up her things, when a thought stopped her. This might be her only opportunity to say goodbye to Godric, for unless he would run away with her, she would probably never see him again. The prospect of life without Godric wrung her heart; she could not bear to say goodbye. She had to take this one last chance to persuade him that they should try to turn their fate around.

She looked across to where Godric had been standing with Hugh and his family. But they had gone, in a hurry, perhaps, to return to their respective manors.

Should she follow them to the stable? Janna shook her head. No. She'd told Godric what was in her heart, and he'd given his reasons why their circumstances, their positions in life, and their obligations, must keep them apart. From his recent demeanor, he'd made it clear he would not change his mind. Better, perhaps, to stay away so that she would not have to witness Cecily's triumph at having Godric to herself at last.

With new determination, Janna whirled around and went to pack up her belongings. She told herself that the pain of living without Godric would pass. She told herself that she would make a good wife to William, and that she would make her father proud of her. She told herself that she had achieved her quest to avenge her mother, and that finding her father meant more to her than marrying the man of her choice.

She told herself many things, but she didn't believe any of them, because in her heart they counted for nothing against the enormity of losing Godric. The pain was indescribable; she felt as if she'd been flayed alive. All she had left was courage, and a determination to carry on to the best of her ability in the hope that somehow, somewhere, she might find some joy along the way. But that hope was an infinitesimal flicker of comfort on this, the blackest day of her life.

The sultry afternoon was giving way to evening when Janna became aware of movement and shouting outside in the yard. The tocsin shrilled an alarm, alerting everyone within the abbey of impending danger. Stephen's men responded by pouring out of the gatehouse, but they were too late to secure the gates of the abbey against the onslaught. By the time Janna and her father had rushed out to see what was happening, the yard was already full of men in armor, some on foot and some on horseback, all fighting for the crown and for their lives.

One horrified glance told John all he needed to know, and he turned to his daughter. "You must run," he said crisply, giving her a shove in the direction of the stables. "Don't stop for anything or anyone. Quickly get your horse and go out through the side gate, across the fields. I pray to God that the way is still safe."

"But Papa – "

"I'll follow you. But I need to find Richildis first."

"Surely we can seek sanctuary within the abbey itself?" Janna was horrified at the thought of taking her chances outside, for where could they gain a safe haven if not here? But what most unsettled her was the question of why her father was set to run like a coward rather than staying to fight for his beliefs. A hasty glance showed her the answer; her father would be no match against the heavily armored warriors who, even now, were thrusting deeper into the abbey grounds, carving their way through the king's army with clashing swords and shouted oaths, accompanied by the screams of the dying. They'd set fire to the gatehouse as they'd entered. Smoke billowed out, partly obscuring the melee in the yard and adding to the confusion of men and horses.

"We should stay within the abbey," Janna insisted.

"No! Do as I say, girl. This is no place for us!" Janna's father gave her a hard shove, which sent her flying. She tripped, lost her footing and fell to the ground. She struggled to her feet just in time to see a helmeted soldier surge forward and plunge his sword into her father's chest.

"No!" she screamed, but the man ignored her and charged on to find his next victim, too crazed for blood and thirsty for the kill, and too intent on protecting his own life to care whom he cut down.

"Papa!" Tears coursed down Janna's cheeks as, disregarding the danger all around her, she dropped to her knees beside her father. "Papa!" Desperately she willed him to speak to her, to reassure her that all was well, that it was a scratch and nothing more. But although his eyes fluttered open, and his gaze fixed on her in mute appeal, the only sound was a desperate choking as he struggled to breathe. Janna was frantic, casting about for something, anything she might do to save him, but even as she clutched his hand and willed him to be strong, she knew that his life was slipping away. She began to pray desperately for his soul, for she realized he was incapable now of speech and that he would die unshriven. Although there was nothing she could do for him, still she hoped for a miracle, that somehow he might survive, that there might be more time for them to be together after the long and lonely years she had spent without him.

She looked about for Richildis or anyone else who might help her shift her father out of harm's way. But there was no sign of the girl or the nuns, all of whom must now be safely locked inside the church. There was no-one whom she could ask for assistance, and as Janna looked down once more at her father, she knew anyway that it was too late and he had gone beyond earthly care. Hardly aware of the battle being waged around her, or of the tears pouring down her cheeks, intent only on protecting her father's body, she hooked her hands under his armpits and began to drag him into the shelter of the stables. She was almost there when there was another surge forward and she found herself caught up in a scrum of fighting men.

The thatched roof of the stables had been torched; horses screamed and stamped in panic, and kicked at their stalls in a vain effort to escape to safety. Smoke billowed out, stinging Janna's eyes and making her cough. She found herself fighting for breath. The noise was deafening. There was nowhere she could go, nowhere safe to leave her father's body. Nowhere safe for her either, for soldiers swarmed all around, shouting oaths at her and at each other. Steel clashed on steel and she was buffeted and shoved as she propped her father's body against a stout pillar and then tried to crawl out of the way.

A loud shout caught her attention; a horse and rider were bearing down on her. She made a desperate leap to the side in an effort to avoid them, but the rider swerved and caught her up in his arms. He clasped her hard in front of him, and galloped on with hardly a pause. Wild with fear, Janna struggled to fight free but his arms tightened around her.

"Let me go!" she shrieked, clutching wildly at the horse's mane in an effort to keep her balance on the swiftly moving steed.

"Janna! Keep still! I have you safe."

Godric! Hardly daring to believe it was his voice she'd heard, Janna sagged back against him. They flew on toward a small gate in the newly fortified abbey walls; it was closed but not manned, for everyone had rushed to the main gatehouse when the tocsin had sounded. Godric leaped down and quickly opened it, then remounted and drove his horse on once more. He didn't speak and neither did Janna. She was beyond speech; overwhelmed by the events that, almost in a heartbeat, had overturned her whole life.

My father is dead. The words drummed through her mind like a funeral dirge; they scoured her heart, left her aching and empty. *My father is dead.* It seemed like the end of the world as she'd known it.

*

Once they left the abbey, Godric rode at full gallop, keeping to fields and country lanes where, with luck, their passage would not be remarked on. Janna realized he was heading for Hugh's manor, but was too distraught to question their destination and the reception they might find there. They were still some distance away when Godric finally reined in their exhausted steed and dismounted. He turned and held up his hands to help her down.

She slid into his arms and felt them close around her. In spite of her distress, she had the sensation that she had, at last, come home. Exhausted, she leaned against him, savoring the touch of his lips on her hair, on her cheek. She tilted her head sideways, and his lips found hers in a lingering kiss, soft and sweet enough to ignite a fire in her heart, her belly, her loins. She clung to him, desperate to convince him of her love, to erase the misunderstandings and difficulties that had kept them apart for so long.

But he let her go, and took her hand. "Come, let's sit down. My horse needs to rest for a while," he said, and led her to a grassy spot. He sat, and patted the ground beside him. "I'm sorry I have no cloak to protect your fine dress from grass stains," he said with a half-smile that yet held a tinge of bitterness.

Uncaring, Janna sank down beside him. "My father is dead." Reality had come crashing in as soon as she'd left the safety of his arms. Tears flooded down her cheeks, and she choked back a sob.

"I know. I saw him die, and I am sorry for it."

"You saw?" Janna suddenly became aware that Godric was wearing the padded gambeson that offered protection to those soldiers unable to afford a full suit of armor.

Godric nodded. "Lord Hugh had been told that the earl was mustering an army to defend the castle at Sarisberie. We were preparing to join him just as soon as the case against Robert of Babestoche was heard. But we met the earl's troops along the way. They were already close to Wiltune and on a forced march, aiming to take the king and his men by surprise and settle this dispute for the crown once and for all."

"You certainly caught us all by surprise! But – oh, Godric, why did my father have to die? He wasn't armed. He was no threat to anyone. I don't even know whose side that soldier supported! And he could have had no way of knowing whether Papa was on the same side as him or not."

Godric shook his head. "Men get caught up in the heat of battle and the crisis of the moment. They don't have time to wonder if they're confronted by friend or foe. It's more a matter of kill or be killed. And unfortunately your father got in the way." He took Janna's hand and held it to his heart in an effort to bring her comfort.

"And my father is gone now, gone forever." Janna began to weep once more, shuddering with sobs as loss and grief caught up with her.

At once Godric moved closer and put his arms around her. "Don't despair, Janna. I'm here, and I'll keep you safe."

"But you shouldn't be here!" The realization brought her upright; she struggled to free herself from Godric's embrace. "Surely you should be with the earl's army, supporting your lord in battle? You must go back, Godric, or pay the penalty for desertion!"

"I'm acting under Sire Hugh's instructions, Janna. As soon as we realized the earl's intentions, his one thought was to keep you safe. He told me to look out for you, even to put my life on the line if necessary. As soon as I saw your father wounded I ran to secure a horse to take you to safety."

Janna drew a shuddering breath. Their situation hadn't changed. Godric had only saved her because Hugh had instructed him to do so.

"You have done your duty, then. You can go back to your lord now." She stood up and brushed herself down, trying to control her churning emotions.

"I wasn't rescuing you out of duty, Janna. I intended to find you even without Sire Hugh's instructions." Godric ventured a small smile as he stood and faced her. "I don't know whether Earl Robert will understand my position or not, but keeping you safe is all I care about right now."

Chastened at having misunderstood his motives, Janna bowed her head. "If you go back quickly, you might not be missed. Only take care, Godric, I pray you." She took his hand and grasped it tight. "You are my life. My heart is in your keeping."

"But you are betrothed to another," Godric reminded her. "I don't know if he'll survive the earl's attack, or how the king's fortunes might turn after today, but your safety is my immediate concern. I cannot leave you here on your own, Janna."

"There's no danger." Janna's arm made a wide sweep of the peaceful countryside to illustrate her point. "I can walk from here to Hugh's manor, and I'll ask Hugh's wife to take me in for the night. After that I shall return to Winchestre."

"Winchestre? Why?"

"My father is dead." Janna's breath caught in her throat; she swallowed hard. Leaving Godric would be the hardest thing in the world, yet she knew that duty must come first. "My father's family must be told, and so must his daughter, who is still at the abbey in Wiltune. We must make arrangements for his funeral. You have carried out Hugh's orders, Godric. Please, go back, and make sure Earl Robert takes note of your presence as if you had never left the abbey."

"No, Janna. I shall escort you safely to the manor." Godric went to the horse, which had taken the opportunity to graze on the soft green grass. "But there's no need for you to travel to Winchestre. Dame Eleanor can arrange for messengers to be sent, both to your half-sister at Wiltune and also to Winchestre." He didn't look at her, but instead busied himself making some small readjustment to the stirrups. "You've had an appalling shock and you need to rest. I shall speak to Dame Eleanor on your behalf. She can take care of whatever needs to be done."

The temptation to go along with what Godric had suggested was overwhelming. Exhaustion washed over Janna; she found she could barely stand. She nodded, and Godric helped her to mount. *Let me have tonight with him*, she thought wearily. *Tomorrow I will become a dutiful daughter once more – even if my father is not here to see it.* Her throat constricted in sorrow as she began to understand the full horror of her loss, and all that it meant for her future. Godric's arms around her, his solid presence, were her only source of comfort as they rode on.

*

There was yet another ordeal to endure once they arrived. There had been many changes to Hugh's manor, Janna noticed; changes bearing the unmistakable stamp of a woman's touch. Cushions and colored hangings brightened the solar where they were told to wait for Dame Eleanor to receive them. There was the scent of sweet new rushes and strewn herbs in the air. Janna gratefully sank down onto a seat.

The lady's expression changed from the warmth of welcoming Godric to a freezing stare when she noticed Janna. "Where is Hugh?" she asked sharply, and listened intently as Godric supplied the answer. Her forehead creased in a worried frown as he went on to describe the earl's attack on the fortified abbey and the killing and confusion that had followed.

"So why have you deserted your lord? And why have you brought *her* into my home?" Eleanor smoothed her swollen stomach as if to reassure herself of her husband's love and fidelity. Janna estimated that the baby was only a month or two from being born. Knowing they were both condemned if Godric told Eleanor about Hugh's orders, and reluctant to cause Eleanor distress in her advanced state of pregnancy, she stepped quickly into the breach.

"My father died in the battle," she said, making a supreme effort to keep her voice steady as she mustered an explanation that might dispel Eleanor's suspicions. "I tried to drag his body to safety, but suddenly found myself in the middle of the fighting. It was my great good fortune that Godric noticed me and swept me up on his horse and carried me off to safety." She clutched Godric's arm, hoping that the dame could see the love she bore for him, hoping that in this way she could prove she was not a threat to the dame's own marriage. Yet still Eleanor watched her with a frosty glare.

"I beg you, give me refuge just for tonight, my lady," Janna continued. "I must cast myself on your charity, for now that my father is dead, I have nothing left. I am no-one without him."

"You are your father's legitimate daughter and the granddaughter of a king, my lady," Godric reminded her.

"You don't understand! My father is dead, and his family all hate me. They will go to the ends of the earth to deny my legitimacy and any claim I might have on his estate." Janna noticed the disbelief on their faces. "In spite of my father's request, the king delayed giving his agreement to my father's testament, which bequeaths all his property in England to me," she explained carefully. "Now that my father is dead, I am certain the king will not honor his wishes regarding my inheritance. Neither will my father's family, for they greatly resent me and the affection he bore me. So you see, I have nothing to offer you or anyone else, my lady. No wealth, no prospects. Nothing. I need to get back to Winchestre and find employment there."

As she thought of the manor house built to her specifications, and her burgeoning herb garden waiting for her attention, it was all Janna could do not to burst into bitter tears, to weep for her lost hopes, her dream of founding a hospitium where those in need might find shelter and healing. With difficulty, she brought her straying thoughts back to the duty still awaiting her. "But I must first return to Wiltune, just as soon as it is safe to do so, for my half-sister is at the abbey, and she will be devastated to hear of her father's death." She could not stop herself from adding bitterly, "No doubt their sorrow will be lightened somewhat by the fact that all of my father's property will now stay safely in their hands."

"But you are betrothed to William of Marsford," Godric protested. "He is a brave soldier and I've heard that he is a good and honest man. You have no need for despair, my lady, nor have you any need to seek employment. William will take care of you, I am sure."

William of Marsford! In one dizzying second Janna realized that she was free of him, for there was no father to insist on a marriage, nor would William want her now that her prospects had taken such a turn for the worse.

"We were never betrothed and I shall never wed him, whether or not he still wants me for a wife – which I doubt," she said fiercely.

Beside her, Godric drew a deep, shuddering sigh. "You truly believe you have no prospects of advancement now that your father is dead?"

Janna shook her head, hardly daring to hope that the new warmth she heard in his voice might signal something more.

Godric took her hand. "You could have a future with me, if you'd have me for a husband." He leaned back a little the better to observe her, to watch her reaction and wait for her answer.

Janna stilled, listening to the echo of his words in her mind. Did he mean it? Or was he just feeling sorry for her?

"But I have nothing to offer you, Godric, except myself."

"And that is why I'm free to speak to you at last," Godric said quietly. "All I want from you, Janna, all I've ever wanted, is your love."

"And you have it, you have all my heart." Janna wished that Eleanor was not present to witness Godric's declaration. She had waited so long for this moment; she ached to feel Godric's arms around her once more. Yet perhaps it was for the best, for Eleanor's tense wariness was gone now, replaced by a smile of pleasure that her worst fears had proved unfounded.

"But I can offer you nothing of the honor and status you've already known," Godric reminded her. "I am a working man, dependent on Sire Hugh for employment."

"I don't care about honor and status! I only care about you." It would mean they'd have to make their life here, with Hugh and Eleanor, which would not be to the lady's liking at all. Janna shot a quick glance at Eleanor, and was encouraged by what she saw there: sympathy, and something more – admiration?

"But Sire Hugh wishes you to marry Cecily," Janna reminded Godric, wanting to be reassured that all obstacles to their match could be safely set aside.

"You can leave my husband's wishes out of this, and you can leave Cecily to me." Eleanor's cool voice broke the tension between them. "I shall give some thought to your future and what might be best." She stood up. "It's late," she said, "and I'm sure, after all that has befallen you, Johanna, you need to rest." She turned to Godric. "Before you retire, please see to it that a messenger is sent, without delay, to Johanna's family in Winchestre to tell them of her father's death. And send another messenger to Wiltune, for I would have news of my husband as soon as possible. Ask him also to make enquiries regarding the safety of Johanna's half-sister."

"Yes, my lady." Godric left the room. Janna longed to follow after him, wanting to savor his presence and his kisses now that their future was finally assured.

"Come with me, Johanna." Eleanor sounded quite friendly now that Janna was no longer a candidate for her husband's affection. Even so, she could not resist a final check. "How long have you and Godric loved each other?"

"Since first we ever met." It was true, Janna thought, although it had taken her long enough to realize it. She remembered how she'd been dazzled by Hugh, and also by Ralph, so dazzled she'd been unable to appreciate the rough diamond so close to her hand and to her heart.

"Then why – ?"

"I was too young to understand his worth, and too impatient to fulfill a promise I had made to my mother. And so I rejected his offer of marriage and set out to find my unknown father in order to avenge my mother's death. It's taken me all these years to understand what I now know: that my life can only be complete if he is by my side."

"You set out on your own to find your father? That was a courageous thing to do, Johanna."

Unsure how to respond, Janna stayed silent.

"And now you have lost everything."

Janna winced at the pity in Eleanor's voice, while at the same time hearing also her relief that not only had Janna been cast down, but that she had given her heart to another and not to Hugh.

Janna felt sympathy for Eleanor's jealousy, for she'd shared just such an emotion when she'd first seen Godric and Cecily together, and had misunderstood the situation. She hadn't been able to put a name to her disquiet at the time, but now she knew exactly how the dame felt.

Cecily. Janna felt a stab of guilt at the thought of the young woman whose secret had been laid bare in court, and who had also lost the man she loved. Truly, she must curse the day she met Janna, and blame her for all her subsequent misfortune. And yet Cecily's misfortune had begun when first she'd trusted Robert's false promises and had lain with him. Everything had flowed from that: the death of Eadgyth, Janna's quest to find out the truth, and her return to her home to seek justice and revenge, a quest that had resulted in her father's death. But Janna's loss of father and fortune had also brought about the end of Cecily's hopes. Truly, the wheel of fate brought happiness and despair as it turned and turned again, while the actions of those caught up on it had repercussions far beyond what might have seemed apparent at the time.

Chapter 11

The new day brought with it the return of Hugh and some of those men who had accompanied him into battle. Two of his retinue had been killed, while Hugh himself had been wounded.

Janna immediately raided the manor's herb garden, relieved to find it well stocked with the sorts of plants she needed both to make a cleansing wash for the long gash in Hugh's arm and a soothing ointment to help it heal. Eleanor accompanied her, watching her every move. Janna wasn't sure if it was so that she could learn for herself how to treat wounds, or whether it was to make sure that nothing untoward passed between her husband and Janna.

They had exchanged complicit smiles as she brought the basin and cloth to him. Both remembered the last time Janna had nursed him to health after a similar injury had placed him in her care.

"Good news, Hugh. Johanna and Godric are to be wed," Eleanor announced as she followed Janna into their bedchamber.

"Godric? But I thought – "

Janna realized then that he couldn't know what had happened to change her circumstances. "My father died in the battle, my lord," she explained, grimly amused at how their roles had been reversed once more. "And with him died his plans to marry me off to William of Marsford, and for me to inherit his property here in England."

"Your father is dead? I am so sorry to hear that, Johanna." Hugh took her hand and pressed it in sympathy, ignoring his wife's glare as he did so. His words stabbed Janna with a new sense of loss. She blinked quickly to dispel the hot tears that swelled in her eyes.

"Godric rescued me and brought me here." Janna withdrew her hand from his. "He saved my life."

"I am greatly relieved to find you safe." Hugh didn't mention that Godric was following his orders.

"Godric should not have deserted you, no matter how pressing the cause!" Eleanor's sharp retort betrayed her concern.

Janna thought it best to divert their attention. "Did you see anything of my half-sister Richildis before you left Wiltune, my lord?" Much as she disliked the girl, Janna hoped that she had come safely through the firestorm.

"Aarghh!" Hugh groaned as Janna unwrapped his wound and began to bathe it. His face set in grim lines as he thought back to the madness of the previous day. "I didn't see Richildis. I'm sorry, Johanna, I didn't think to look for her. In fact, I was lucky to escape with my own life." He was silent for a moment. Janna could see how the memory troubled him.

"It was like a scene from the pits of hell," Hugh said slowly. "The king had only a task force with him at the abbey. They were greatly outnumbered and completely unprepared for our onslaught. William Martel, in particular, fought like a lion before capture. We only realized afterward, of course, that he was acting as a decoy for the king."

"And the king?" Janna asked eagerly.

"Managed to escape." Hugh winced as she began to spread ointment over the ugly gash. "Some of his men ran into the abbey itself seeking sanctuary, but the earl gave the command to follow them in and drag them out." He shuddered. "They were butchered where they stood."

Janna closed her eyes, picturing the scene. It might have been a triumph for the earl's army, and for the empress, but at what a cost. She could not feel glad about the victory; only numb at the thought that the killing would continue until either the king or the empress was dead.

"What of the sisters? And the abbess?" she asked anxiously, quickly opening her eyes to dispel her dark imaginings. "Are they safe?"

Hugh shrugged. "I know not. I saw the great doors of the abbey being smashed in, but after that…"

Janna wondered if he'd followed the earl's troops into the church, if he'd taken part in the killing, or if he'd fled in fear of his life. He wasn't saying, and she didn't want to know.

"The earl has claimed victory. The empress now holds most of the West Country under her control. But it will be a long time before people forget or forgive the damage her army has wrought on the abbey and its surrounds."

Janna remembered how long it had taken the people of Winchestre to recover from that siege, from the damage caused by the bishop's fireballs that had razed much of the town. It is the people who pay the price for the ambitions of those who would rule, she reflected, feeling angry as she thought of the friends she had made in Wiltune who would suffer because of it, like Agnes and her newborn babe. Sudden fear gripped her. At the earliest opportunity she must go back to make sure they were safe.

She took the piece of clean linen that Eleanor had given her and cut it in half. Then, very carefully, she began to bind Hugh's wound. She was conscious of Eleanor standing close by, watching everything she did, but was completely taken by surprise when Eleanor spoke.

"If Godric is to wed Johanna, then we must find him a new place with your aunt, Hugh. She will need a good man now that she has lost her husband."

Janna kept her head bent, wondering if it was concern for Hugh's aunt or Hugh's heart that motivated Eleanor's suggestion.

Hugh himself kept silent, perhaps equally taken by surprise.

"It shall be as my lady wishes," said Godric. Janna hadn't realized that he'd come into the room. Now she burned with anger on his behalf, and shame on her own.

"I need Godric here. I rely on his help," Hugh said firmly. "My aunt has a perfectly capable steward and a good reeve of her own to help her until Hamo is old enough to take charge."

"I think there is not enough room here for two women, Hugh." Eleanor's voice brooked no argument. "If you won't send him to your aunt, then I shall ask my father to find him a position on our estate near Winchestre."

Hugh cast a helpless glance at Janna and rolled his eyes. It was unfortunate that Eleanor noticed. She snatched the bandage from Janna's hands. "You may leave us," she said, and began clumsily to complete what Janna had started.

Janna bobbed a curtsy, keeping her head bent to hide her anger. She walked out of the room, followed closely by Godric.

"It is insupportable that you should be dismissed from your position here on my account," she said, as soon as they were out of Eleanor's hearing.

Godric smiled and took her hand. "If it hadn't happened now, it would have happened soon enough," he said. "The lady is afraid her husband favors you, Janna."

"Stupid – " Janna bit her tongue on the rude word she would have used.

"It matters not." Godric drew her closer and put his arm around her. "So long as I am sure of you and our future together, I am completely happy and content. But you, Janna – have you no regrets for what might have been?"

"None whatsoever!"

"Then I thank God that we are alone at last! I love you, Janna. I always have, I always will. And I promise you that I shall do all in my power to make you happy."

"Shh." Janna leaned into him. She closed her eyes. His lips met hers, tender at first, but deepening into a long and passionate kiss that set Janna's body alight with desire and the determination that nothing, now, could ever set them apart.

*

The messenger Godric had sent at Eleanor's behest soon returned with the assurance that the siege was over and Stephen and his men routed. He also told Janna that her half-sister was alive and safe, and that word had been sent to Dame Blanche in Winchestre. Her father's body was to await burial until their arrival. His news added urgency to Janna's departure, for she wanted to make sure that she had the chance to say goodbye and mourn her father properly before Blanche arrived to shoulder her aside.

Godric, too, was determined to leave the manor as soon as possible following Eleanor's pronouncement. Janna was delighted when he was given permission to accompany her to Wiltune, for she dreaded having to face alone the difficulties that lay before her. Even more delightful was the prospect of being able to spend some time alone with him at last. Hugh argued against their going, and especially against losing his trusted steward, but his wife and Janna united against him, albeit for different reasons: Eleanor, because she knew that Hugh still harbored feelings for Janna; and Janna, because there were far more urgent matters that she needed to see to, with or without Godric by her side. Ignoring Eleanor's prickly demeanor, Janna instructed her regarding the care of Hugh's wound before she left, adding her good wishes for the safe birth of their child.

The journey passed all too quickly as Janna and Godric exchanged loving kisses and told each other about the years that they had spent apart. Godric described his new life with Hugh, and asked about Janna's quest to find her father. In the telling, she was careful to leave out the more poignant particulars of her meeting with Ralph, and his subsequent fate. To her infinite relief, Godric did not press for details, perhaps sensing that some things were better left unsaid. While she knew now that she had never really loved Ralph, she had not known it then, and the memory of their time together and its aftermath still had the power to distress and shame her.

She could not disguise her horror once they entered the abbey's grounds. While the town itself had escaped mostly unscathed, all the earl's might and fury had been unleashed on the king who, while supposedly a guest of the abbey, had turned it into his headquarters once he'd stationed his advance task force there and commenced fortifications. Many of the abbey's outbuildings had been burned or otherwise destroyed; rubble was strewn everywhere, and the scent of charred wood and animal flesh still lingered on the air.

The gatehouse, which once had housed Stephen and his troops, was gone, as was part of the guest quarters where Janna had stayed with her father. She went there first to look for Richildis, but found them deserted, although a party of workers from the abbey's estates was hard at work clearing away the debris and bringing in material to repair and rebuild the damage. The great door of the church had been destroyed in the earl's determination to reach those seeking sanctuary inside, but Janna paused at the portal before venturing into the nave. There she saw the abbess consulting with a carpenter over repairs to the damage within, while several sisters busied themselves sweeping and tidying away the detritus. There was no sign of Richildis, or of Sister Anne, but Sister Ursel was busily wielding a broom in the service of the Lord. Anxious to escape the hawk eyes of the abbess, Janna sidled down the nave to ask her friend if she knew where to find them.

Ursel set aside the broom and looked all set to embrace Janna, until a quick glance over her shoulder suggested caution. "I am so glad to see you safe!" she whispered instead, casting an anxious glance in Godric's direction. "You'll find them in the infirmary. Richildis is in such distress over the death of her father that she has taken to her bed. Perhaps you can comfort her, Janna, for Sister Anne is quite at her wits' end."

"I'll go to her." Janna had no illusions about the comfort she might bring, but knew she should make an effort to see Richildis.

"But your companion must stay here!" Ursel's alarmed hiss attracted the abbess's attention. She frowned as she recognized Janna, and began to walk toward them.

"Ursel, this is Godric, whom I shall wed just as soon as we may. Look after him for me." Janna was warmed by the huge grin of delight that transformed her friend's face. She wished she could hug the nun and share her joy with her. Instead, she thanked Ursel, blew a kiss to Godric, and hurried off before the abbess could reach them.

"Go away." Richildis turned over, presenting her back to Janna when she walked into the infirmary.

Janna shrugged impatiently and looked at Sister Anne. "Where's my father's body?" she asked. "If Richildis won't speak to me, I would like to keep vigil beside him for a while."

Richildis reared up, her face pale and her eyes blazing with hatred. "It's all your fault Papa was killed!" she shrieked. "He only came to Wiltune on your account, because you were so determined to get your hands on his property." Her mouth curved into a spiteful smile. "You won't get anything now," she observed. "Maman will see to that."

Even though Richildis was only saying what Janna herself had already surmised, she wanted to slap the girl. She restrained herself with difficulty. Not deigning to answer her half-sister's charge or give credence to her lies, she said instead, "You should know, Richildis, that our father's last thoughts were for you. He was coming to find you, to keep you safe, when he was struck down."

"It ill befits his memory for you to bear such malice toward your sister," Sister Anne added reprovingly. "You are certainly old enough to know better, even if your upbringing has not taught you how to behave like the lady you would have us believe you are."

Richildis was struck silent. Janna read the mortification on her face, and winced on her behalf as the truth of the infirmarian's reproof hit home.

"You will find your father's body lying in the crypt, awaiting burial," Sister Anne told Janna. "Two of us keep vigil at all times, along with one of the earl's men, so you'll find him well guarded." She paused a moment. "I cannot tell you how sorry I am for your loss," she added softly. She took Janna's hand and pressed it.

Janna returned the pressure, grateful for the infirmarian's gesture. "Have you news of Agnes and her new babe?" she asked quickly. Her friend had once been a lay sister at the abbey; if anyone knew of her fate, it would be Sister Anne. "How did they fare during the siege?"

"Safe and well, both of them. And the bailiff too, God be thanked." Sister Anne released Janna's hand and crossed herself.

"I am relieved to hear it." Janna hesitated, unwilling to leave Richildis without one last attempt to reach the girl through her distress. But Sister Anne gave a small shake of her head, so Janna withdrew.

Although she'd never before been in the crypt, she found it without difficulty; an underground chamber where past abbesses and other church dignitaries had been laid to rest. The air was chill, and already tainted with the stench of decay. She wondered what had happened to those others who had died in the attack, for only her father's body was lying there, with two black-garbed figures on one side and a soldier on the other. She approached her father with trepidation, and sank down on her knees to pray, keeping her eyes closed so that she wouldn't have to look upon his dear, dead face.

She knelt for some time, hardly aware of the tears streaming down her cheeks as she tried to concentrate on her communion with God, on her pleas that her father might rest in peace even though he had died unshriven. But her thoughts strayed first to Eadgyth and the love her mother and father had shared, and her mother's lack of trust in that love and the life they had led because of it. Memory took her onwards to her mother's death and the subsequent search for her father, which had taken her so far and shown her so much of the world. And now she had come to this: facing her father's death, and the heartbreak of losing him just when they had become as close as a father and daughter could be. From there her thoughts jumped to Godric, and her relief that, after all, they could be wed. Which brought Janna to guilt, and further fervent prayer for her father's soul, and the cycle of memory and regret began once more.

She came back to her surroundings at last when she felt a tap on her shoulder, and then Godric's arm came under hers to help her rise, for she was stiff after kneeling for so long. "Your stepmother has arrived and has demanded an audience with the earl," he whispered. "I think you should be there too."

Alarmed, Janna at once nodded her agreement. Taking a moment to cross herself, she withdrew from the crypt and hastened after Godric as he led the way to the abbess's own chamber. Janna knocked and, without waiting for a reply, entered the room. The abbess frowned in reproof, but before she could say anything Earl Robert stood up and bowed to Janna.

"I am delighted to meet you again, Johanna," he announced.

Knocked off-balance by his welcome, Janna glanced from him to her stepmother. Like her daughter, it seemed that Blanche held Janna entirely responsible for what had transpired during the siege. She inclined her head and said in a frigid tone, "So, your father is dead and you think you've got what you wanted, Johanna. But you will pay for the damage your ambition has done to my family. You've cost me a husband, and my children their father."

Aghast, Janna could hardly think how to reply. But Blanche was not finished. She turned on the earl in fury. "And that's not all she's done. That girl wormed her way into my husband's affection and has stolen from us all his property here in England. But you, my lord, will surely not see your half-brother's widow and her unfortunate children condemned to penury now that he is gone."

Janna would have laughed at Blanche's lies if she hadn't been so stunned. Not a word of grief over her husband's death – all she cared about was cutting Janna out of her father's last bequest. It seemed that Blanche's daughter had been truly molded in her mother's image. She turned aside, her lip curling with disgust – and saw that the earl had noticed the gesture, even if he had not understood the reason for it.

"Is there any truth in this?" he asked, reclaiming his seat once more.

"None." Janna answered before Blanche could utter any more poison. "It was my father's intention to leave me his property here in England. His family is to inherit all his lands and fortune in Normandy. I hardly think my father would have wished them to destitution, my lord, no matter what my stepmother might have you believe."

"But the king has not given his agreement to it, Maman."

Janna spun around; she hadn't realized that Richildis was also in the room. She was sitting to one side, half obscured behind her brother, Giles. Rosy was also present; she ventured a smile when she saw Janna looking at her, only to receive a sharp slap from her sister, which immediately wiped it away.

"The king has not yet given his agreement?" Blanche's nose came up, quivering like a bloodhound on the trail. "Where is the testament, then?" Janna was quite sure that, if she could get her hands on it, her stepmother would rip it into shreds.

"The king has it."

"And he won't agree to it. Not now that our father is dead!" Richildis exchanged a look of triumph with her mother.

Godric put his hand on Janna's shoulder, seeking to reassure her of his love and support. Richildis noticed the movement. Her eyes widened. "So she's going to wed the peasant after all," she said. "She has no prospects any more, Maman. She is nothing, now that our father has gone."

Even though she'd already accepted the truth of her position, the words cut through Janna like a sharp blade. The earl held up his hand for silence, his face mirroring his distaste at what he was hearing.

"It would seem that your fears of being left destitute are groundless, my lady," he told Blanche coldly. His scorn was almost palpable. "It seems also that you have no intention of carrying out your late husband's wishes, for all that he apparently made himself quite clear not only to you but also to the king. But don't feel too proud, Dame Blanche. I know that John has substantial property in Normandy, and you can be sure I shall speak to Count Geoffrey at the earliest opportunity as to how it might best be bestowed on someone who supports his cause. Someone who might take you to wife, perhaps, if you have concern for your children's future?"

"No, my lord! No!" Blanche's face reflected both her fear and her fury at this unforeseen threat.

But Robert ignored her. He turned to Janna and his face softened into kindness.

"My sister is well aware of the...services you have rendered her in the past. Indeed, she planned to bestow on you a manor of your own until your father made it clear, when he saw her in Oxeneford, that he intended to make full provision for you as his oldest *legitimate* daughter." The earl's steely gaze caught and held Blanche for a long moment. It was Blanche who looked away first.

"Unfortunately, John's demesne here in England comes within Stephen's gift, and I suspect he will use it to reward one of his own faithful barons rather than honoring your father's wishes, Johanna. So, unless and until my sister succeeds in her bid for the crown, there is little I can do to make sure your father's wishes are carried out. But I, too, am mindful of the debt we owe you. I own a manor and a farm not far from Wiltune. It is not as fine as the property you would have received from your father, but the house itself is spacious and well built, and the surrounding farmland and pasture will bring in an income more than sufficient for your needs."

Speechless, Janna stared at the earl. She was hardly able to comprehend her good fortune, but Godric recognized it immediately. "It was Johanna's father's wish, and the king's too, that she marry William of Marsford," he said soberly.

"*What?*" Janna found her voice at last, but before she could say anything further, Godric continued.

"It would be a good match for Johanna, my lord, begging your pardon for the interruption. I understand Sire William has property and wealth as well as the king's favor. Janna would be well provided for, and I am sure the baron would take her willingly if she can bring your gift to the marriage."

"No! I will not take him!" Furious, Janna faced Godric. "How could you even suggest such a thing?" she shouted. "You promised to marry me! You cannot refuse me now!" Ignoring the earl, the abbess, and her family, all of whom were watching the scene with great interest, Janna grabbed Godric's arm. "You said you loved me." Her voice shook, betraying her agony. "How can you pretend that's not true?"

"Of course it's true," Godric said roughly. "I'm thinking of your happiness, your prospects for the future, that's what I'm doing. William of Marsford can offer you a great deal more than I can."

"But I don't want William, and I won't have him! I want *you!*"

"You love each other, am I correct?" The earl's cool tones interrupted their argument. Godric and Janna swung around to face him. They nodded in unison.

"Then I give you my blessing, for I know only too well the misery of a loveless match. And young man," he continued, before Godric could contradict him, "you'll find that the property I've mentioned will bring in a good income if you manage it well. You'll want for nothing in the future, I shall make sure of it. And I shall send a messenger to my half-sister informing her of my intention, so that no-one here present will dare to gainsay my wishes." He fixed Blanche with his steely stare once more.

"Thank you, my lord." Janna seized the earl's hand and kissed it, knowing at last that her happiness was assured, and her future with it. "My heart is full."

"You are a courageous young woman, Johanna, and I think the debt is all on our side." The earl smiled as he rose to his feet.

"A moment, my lord, if you please." Blanche's sharp voice halted the earl's departure. "I beg your leave to take my husband's body back to Normandy without delay, if you would be so good as to provide me with an escort to the nearest port."

"No!" Janna's cry was instinctive, but thought quickly followed to bolster her opposition to Blanche's request. It was insupportable that Blanche and her family should lie beside her father when their time came, rather than that he should be buried beside his one true love.

The earl turned to her with an enquiring lift of his eyebrow. Janna made a hasty attempt to order her thoughts, to give him an explanation sufficient to override Blanche's wishes.

"My father loved my mother," she said steadily, "and my mother loved him in return. They were separated in life. Please, let them lie together here, at Wiltune Abbey."

Blanche made an angry gesture and opened her mouth to object. But the earl silenced her with an upraised hand, giving Janna a chance to tell him something of her mother and father's relationship and what had transpired to keep them apart. "They loved each other all their lives," she concluded.

A further thought bolstered her argument. "Besides, it's a long journey to Normandy. My father's body will be in an advanced state of decay by the end of it." She remembered once seeing a corpse being pushed in a cart. The smell of it had attracted a large following of hounds that jostled each other as they tried to jump up into the cart. She shuddered with horror, knowing that the alternative was to boil away the flesh from her father's bones before transporting him. She could not bear to think of either course of action.

"Please," she begged, "please save him that indignity and consent to his burial here, so that he and my mother may be united in death as they never were in life."

"It seems like a very good idea to me." The earl looked at the abbess, who nodded slowly. Perhaps her decision was based on a recognition of the truth of Janna's words, or perhaps it was more to do with the thought that the king had been routed, the earl's men were now in control of the abbey, and Blanche and her family would soon return to Normandy. Whatever her reasoning, Janna didn't care. All that mattered was that she'd got her own way in this, the last service she could do for her father.

Epilogue

The manor and its surrounding lands were everything the earl had promised and more, Janna thought with contentment as she looked about her at the comfortable solar. She stood up and moved to the window, seeking signs of Godric. He was out in the fields, for once again it was summer and there was much to do before the harvest could be brought in. Green fields of wheat had turned to gold; there would be a good crop for the picking, sufficient to feed them, the reeve, and all the families in their care, those serfs who tilled these fields as well as their own, and for whose health and livelihood she and Godric were now responsible. In the distance she could see the white woolly dots of sheep that had also come with their new demesne. They'd already received a good income from their first wool clip. She sighed with pleasure as she thought of how far she and Godric had come over the past year.

Her father's funeral had been dreadful, made worse by the histrionics of Richildis and the stinging hatred of all John's family. But the earl had stood by Janna, as had the abbess, to carry out her wishes to have her father buried beside her mother. More than ever had she appreciated the solid strength of Godric through that difficult time.

But then had come her marriage to Godric, the exchange of their vows at the door of the abbey's church, witnessed by Agnes and all the friends she had made both at Wiltune and from her old home. Even Dame Alice had been there, attended by Hugh. Eleanor had not come. Nor had Blanche and her family. Having set a steward in place at the manor house in Winchestre to establish ownership, they'd wasted no time in leaving for Normandy after the funeral, perhaps hoping to catch the sympathetic ear of Count Geoffrey before the Earl of Gloucestre could have his say. All of which worried Janna not a jot, for she would rather have been surrounded only by those who loved her and wished her well. The only one of them she missed was Rosy, but she had secured the girl's promise, in secret, that as soon as she was old enough she would return to England to visit Janna.

"You once asked me to teach you about herbs and healing," Janna had reminded her, and Rosy had nodded eagerly. "I shall teach you all I know, if you've still a mind to learn when you are grown." *And if you need to escape from your mother.* Richildis would soon be wed. Janna wished her new husband all the luck he would need to manage his willful wife. After that, Rosy would be left at Blanche's mercy. But Rosy was strong-willed and knew her own mind. Janna would help her if she could.

"I will come, I promise," Rosy had told her, leaning forward to confide softly, "I don't want to grow up like Richildis, Johanna. I would rather grow up to be just like you."

Janna had been touched by the child's faith in her capacity to bestow happiness, and also encouraged by Rosy's assessment of her sister. It augured well for her future. And she would have much to offer Rosy when she came.

Janna's mouth curved into a smile as she reflected upon what else had been achieved during their first year at the new manor. While Godric had taken all he had learned during his time with Hugh and brought his skills in management to bear on the property now under his control, Janna had set her dream for the future in motion. Her first step had been to plant a large herb garden, with herbs for healing as well as for cooking and for use about the house.

Once that was done, she had asked Aldith to come and stay with her, using that time to teach the midwife all she'd learned from her mother and also from Sister Anne at the abbey. In return, she'd asked Aldith to instruct her in the care of pregnant women and what to do in childbirth, particularly if there were difficulties. She asked for instruction on the care of ailing babies and young children as well, for none of these things had played a part in the daily rounds of the abbey, while her own mother had kept her largely ignorant, preferring to deal with such things herself.

It had been satisfying and beneficial to them both, Janna thought, as she reviewed with satisfaction the newly built hospitium beside the manor which was already in use, being visited by those who were sick and in need of care and treatment. Even more satisfying was the knowledge that she had already helped several children into the world, with another due imminently.

"I have something for you." The counting of her blessings was interrupted as Godric entered the room. He gingerly carried a small sack, which writhed and shifted in shape as if there were a dozen rats inside. He held it out to her, but with her mind full of the vermin it might contain, Janna hesitated to take it.

"You'll like it," Godric reassured her, with a smile. So she took the sack from him and cautiously opened it.

"Oh!" She drew out a small black kitten, which lashed out with sharp claws and bit her finger in fright. "Shh," she soothed, and tucked it into the crook of her arm, keeping it safe and snug while she gently stroked its furry head and tickled its ears. Gradually its frightened mewing quietened into a soft, rumbling purr.

"I shall call it Alfred." Janna smiled her thanks at Godric. He cast his eyes upward in disapproval, and she knew they were both remembering the dreadful fate of the stray cat she'd once taken in and tamed.

"Call it Fluffy," he suggested. "You can name our son Alfred instead, if you wish."

Janna stroked her swollen belly with a contented smile. "What if it's a girl?"

"Then we shall try for a son next time." Godric's hand folded over hers, resting on her stomach in a blessing for the child growing within.

"I shall look forward to it," Janna said demurely, and laughed in delight as she noted a spark of desire ignite in his eyes. She drew him closer, as close as her bulging belly would allow, and sealed her promise with a loving kiss.

Glossary

Alehouse: Ale was a common drink in the middle ages. Housewives brewed their own for domestic use, while alewives brewed the ale served in alehouses and taverns. A bush tied to a pole was the recognized symbol of an alehouse, at a time when most of the population could not read.

Amor vincit omnia: Love conquers all.

Baron: A noble of high rank, a tenant-in-chief who holds his lands from the king.

Besom: A broom made of twigs.

Breeches: Trousers held up by a cord running through the hem at the waist.

Chapman: Peddler.

Cresset: A primitive light made from a wick floating in a bowl of oil or animal fat.

Currency: While large sums of money could be reckoned in pounds or marks, the actual currency for trading was silver pennies. There were twelve to a shilling and twenty shillings to a pound. A penny could also be cut into half, called a "ha'penny," or a quarter, called a "farthing."

Feudal system: A political, social and economic system based on the relationship of lord to vassal, in which land was held on condition of homage and service. Following the Norman conquest, William I distributed land once owned by Saxon "ealdormen" (chief men) to his own barons, who in turn distributed land and manors to sub-tenants in return for fees, knight service and, in the case of the villeins, work in the fields. The Abbess of Wilton held an entire barony from the king and owed the service of five knights in return.

Infirmarian: Takes care of the sick in the infirmary (abbey hospital).

Motte and bailey castle: Earth mound with wooden or stone keep (tower) on top, plus an enclosure or courtyard, all of it surrounded and protected by a ditch and palisade (fence).

Scrip: A small bag.

Scriptorium: A room in a monastery (or abbey) where monks (or nuns) wrote, copied and illuminated manuscripts. In a private home it served as the office of the estate.

Solar: A private room where the lord could retire with his family or entertain his friends.

Steward: Appointed by a baron to manage an estate.

Tiring woman: A female attendant on a lady of high birth and importance.

Villein: Peasant or serf tied to a manor and to an overlord, and given land in return for labor and a fee – either money or produce.

Wortwyf: A herb wife, a wise woman and healer.

Author's Note

1141 AD was a crucial year for the Empress Matilda; it was that year she came closest to winning the crown from her cousin, King Stephen. The king was taken prisoner following the Battle of Lincoln in February. Barons and bishops then swore allegiance to the empress, and she began her progress to London for her coronation. But King Stephen's queen (also called Matilda) had not given up on the king's behalf. She mustered the Londoners and besieged the palace at Westminster, forcing the empress to flee. There is some question as to whether Henry of Blois, Bishop of Winchester and King Stephen's brother, ever switched his support to the empress during this time (even though he officially recognized her claim) or whether he stayed loyal to his brother.

It is certain that, by September, the bishop was actively supporting the king once more. While the queen's troops blockaded Winchester, preventing any supplies from reaching either the empress's army or the townsfolk, the bishop had fortified the old Anglo-Saxon palace in the heart of Winchester. The bishop's firebrands destroyed St Mary's Abbey (the Nunnaminster),

St Hyde's Abbey, and "completely reduced to ashes the greater part of the town." (*Gesta Stephani*)

The empress was forced to flee, while her ever-faithful half-brother Robert, Earl of Gloucester, fought on and was finally captured at Stockbridge. When it became clear that the earl would neither change allegiance nor yield to threats, a complicated arrangement was put in place for the exchange of the prisoners. By the end of 1141, Stephen was back on the throne.

The king was taken ill in the early part of 1142 and for a time was not expected to live. Believing it safe to do so, the Earl of Gloucester went to Anjou to persuade the empress's husband, Geoffrey, to bring troops over to England to help secure her bid for the throne. Instead, Geoffrey kept the earl in Normandy, promising to come to England once he'd brought all Normandy under his aegis. In fact, this proved crucial later on, for many of the barons who supported Stephen in England also had land and possessions in Normandy, and were aghast when these were lost by the king. Stephen, meanwhile, had recovered his health. He began to secure all ports against the earl's return to England, after which he besieged Oxford and surrounded the castle, holding the empress prisoner there.

The earl managed to land at Wareham and recapture the harbor and castle, after which he began to fight his way north to Oxford. But the empress and her entourage were nearing starvation and could wait no longer. It is quite true that the empress and a small escort, dressed in white capes for camouflage, escaped across the ice and walked across fields to safety, although accounts vary as to whether she escaped through a postern gate or was lowered down a rope from the tower. I wouldn't have dared make up such a story, but I did take the liberty of having Janna come to the empress's aid and act as a decoy – for there is some question as to how the empress managed to evade Stephen's troops while she made her escape. It's been suggested that they were so battle weary and keen to go home they might even have turned a blind eye. My version is much more exciting!

In 1143, and with much of the West Country favoring the empress, Stephen made his headquarters in Wilton, fortifying the abbey there with the intention of capturing Sarum (Sarisberie). The earl forestalled him and, on the evening of July 1st, his troops overran and fired Wilton. The king managed to escape the siege, and thereafter the earl secured the loyalty of the West Country. By now, the empress had given up on her own behalf and was claiming the throne for her son, Henry. The civil war (or "Anarchy" as it is sometimes known) continued sporadically for another ten years, until a deal was finally agreed after the death of Stephen's son, Eustace, that the king would officially recognize Henry as his heir.

Henry was duly crowned in 1154, following the death of Stephen. As Henry II he went on to marry Eleanor of Aquitaine and raise several sons, two of whom became kings: Richard and John.

Some of the more important accounts I have used while researching the history on which the Janna Chronicles are based include the *Gesta Stephani*, William of Malmesbury's *Historia Novella*, *The Empress Matilda* by Marjorie Chibnall, *King Stephen* by R.H.C. Davis, and *The Reign of King Stephen* by David Crouch.

While writing medieval England from Australia is a difficult and hazardous enterprise, I have been fortunate in the support and encouragement I've received along the way. So many people have helped make this series possible, and in particular I'd like to thank the following: Nick and Wendy Combes of Burcombe Manor, for taking me into their family, giving me a home away from home and teaching me about life on a farm, both now and in medieval time. Dr Gillian Polack, whose knowledge of medieval life helped shape the series and gave it veracity. Thanks also to my fantastic editor, Kylie Mason, and to all at Momentum for their thought, care and expertise, and for enabling me to introduce the Janna Chronicles to a whole new audience.

www.ingramcontent.com/pod-product-compliance
Lightning Source LLC
Chambersburg PA
CBHW031308280626
47169CB00017B/916